INTERNATION
ERIK

RAW DEAL

AETHON THRILLS

aethonbooks.com

RAW DEAL
©2024 ERIK CARTER

This book is protected under the copyright laws of the United States of America. No part of this publication may be reproduced, stored in a retrieval system, or transmitted, in any form or by any means, without the prior permission in writing of the publisher, nor be otherwise circulated in any form of binding or cover other than that in which it is published and without a similar condition including this condition being imposed on the subsequent purchaser. Any reproduction or unauthorized use of the material or artwork contained herein is prohibited without the express written permission of the authors.

Aethon Books supports the right to free expression and the value of copyright. The purpose of copyright is to encourage writers and artists to produce the creative works that enrich our culture.

The scanning, uploading, and distribution of this book without permission is a theft of the author's intellectual property. If you would like to use material from the book (other than for review purposes), please contact editor@aethonbooks.com. Thank you for your support of the author's rights.

Aethon Books
www.aethonbooks.com

Design, layout, and formatting by Josh Hayes.

Published by Aethon Books LLC.

Aethon Books is not responsible for websites (or their content) that are not owned by the publisher.

This book is a work of fiction. Names, characters, places, and incidents are the product of the author's imagination or are used fictitiously. Any resemblance to actual events, locales, or persons, living or dead is coincidental.

All rights reserved.

ALSO BY ERIK CARTER

From Aethon Books

BURN IT DOWN

RAW DEAL

Want to discuss our books with other readers and even the authors?

JOIN THE AETHON DISCORD!

CHAPTER
ONE

Fifteen years ago
Afghanistan

Ty Draker had just killed a man.
    Well, almost.
    The guy wasn't quite dead yet.
Moments earlier, Draker had bounded up the stairs. Two steps at a time.
Sweat coursing down his back.
Gun firmly in his grip.
He'd kicked in the glass door. Shards peppered the floor.
And there he'd found Frederick Al-Khattab sitting cross-legged before a low table, eating a simple meal of bread and water.
Alone.
Holding a cup, his hand hovering halfway to his open mouth, frozen.
Draker had hesitated.
Then fired.
And now Al-Khattab was slumped on the floor in front of Draker, in a puddle of spilled water, in a puddle of blood.
Staring up at Draker. Blinking.
Still alive.

Al-Khattab coughed. Bloody saliva bubbled in the corner of his mouth.

One hand was up, fingers contorted at unnatural angles, pointing toward Draker, almost reaching for him.

Draker stared down at him.

"It's... it's not..." Al-Khattab tried. His English was perfect. His accent was American. He coughed. "It's not your fault. Just... blind luck." Another cough. "It's not... your fault."

Another gurgle. More blood. A cough. His eyes squinted with pain. Then closed.

Al-Khattab's hand dropped to the floor with a thud.

Draker stared for a moment longer.

Then pivoted.

Back through the shattered glass door, back into the blinding golden glow of the Afghan day. Heat and dust enveloped him as he descended the steps fast, boots pounding. He turned the corner.

And he was gone.

He pushed through the crowd, his mind abuzz. He'd just killed a man—his first. The weight of it pressed down on him, made his limbs feel heavy. But something didn't sit right. Al-Khattab's final words echoed in his ears: "It's not your fault. Just... blind luck."

What did that mean? Blind luck? The mission had been meticulously planned. Burleson's intel had led Draker straight to Al-Khattab. There was nothing lucky about it.

He shook his head. Had to focus on getting out. He'd heard a scream after the gunshot, but thus far, no one seemed to be pursuing him. He was in the clear.

Bagram. He needed to get back to Bagram Airfield, to his CIA contact. Agent Burleson would want a full report.

The narrow alley opened onto a wider street. Midday sun beat down, baking the dusty earth. More sweat trickled down Draker's back—streams of it now—as he navigated through the throng of people. The air was thick with the smell of spices and grilled meat from nearby food stalls.

Suddenly, three men in traditional Afghan shalwar kameez turned a corner ahead. Their eyes locked onto Draker. They pointed, shouting in Arabic, and rushed toward him.

Draker spun on his heel and sprinted in the opposite direction. He darted down a side street, weaving between startled pedestrians. His boots pounded against the hard-packed dirt. The shouts of his pursuers grew louder, closer behind him.

Left turn. Right turn. The town was a maze of alleys and open courtyards. Draker's eyes darted, searching for escape routes.

He dodged a clothesline, bright clothes brushing his face and arms. A burst of saffron and cardamom hit him as he moved past an open door.

A group of children kicking a deflated soccer ball scattered as Draker barreled through. Their shouts of surprise mixed with the angry shouts of the men chasing him.

He looked back. The trio was gaining ground, their faces contorted with determination.

Draker's lungs burned. The heat was a beast, draining his strength. But slowing wasn't an option.

He rounded another corner and found himself in a sprawling marketplace. Stalls crowded both sides of the street, hawking everything from fresh produce to woven carpets. The air rang with haggling voices and bleating goats.

He pushed through the crowd, ignoring the angry shouts that followed in his wake. He knocked over a stack of woven baskets. A woman screamed at him.

Draker risked a glance over his shoulder. The trio of men was still behind him, but now they were struggling to navigate the sea of tumbled baskets, which were spilled in a multicolored mound across the pathway between the stalls, spanning its width—a temporary blockade. It wouldn't hold them for long, but it bought Draker precious seconds.

More people screamed at him. Angry hands grabbed and pushed him, but he shouldered through and turned the corner, out of the crowd and into an open street.

As he ran, his mind raced. The town's layout—which Burleson had given him in the mission briefing—flashed through his memory. He was close. Just a few more turns and he'd reach the extraction point.

Left at the crumbling brick building with the blue door. Right at the small mosque with its single minaret piercing the sky.

The shouts behind him grew fainter. He was putting distance between himself and his pursuers.

One more turn.

And there it was.

The black SUV with blacked-out windows, right where it was supposed to be. Draker exhaled.

He sprinted the final stretch. From behind, he heard the slap of sandals on dirt. The other men had caught up again.

With a final burst of speed, Draker reached for the door handle. He yanked it open and threw himself inside, slamming the door shut just as one of the men reached the SUV.

A meaty thud resonated through the vehicle as a fist struck the side panel.

"Go!" Draker shouted to the driver.

The engine roared to life. Tires squealed against the packed earth as the SUV peeled away. Draker looked through the rear window and saw the men in a cloud of dust, shouting, coughing, swinging fists.

Draker slumped back in his seat. His chest heaved. He gulped down air. His shirt was soaked with sweat.

The SUV took a hard turn onto a dirt road, and suddenly they were beyond the town's limit and racing into the vast Afghan desert, beginning the long return trip to Bagram.

―――

Draker was back.

Back where it all started a few days earlier. Back in the cramped, windowless structure tucked away in a forgotten corner of Bagram Airfield.

Four bare walls, nothing else. An air conditioner clunked and rattled in a cutout on the east wall, struggling to make a dent in the stifling heat. Above, a noisy ceiling fan wobbled, just as useless. Light leaked through the gap tracing the outline of the lone door at the back.

At the desk sat Agent Burleson, his fleshy-cheeked baby face at odds with his protein-shake-and-creatine build. His blond buzz cut glistened in the dusty glow, and that minute freckle on his blue iris caught Draker's eye once more.

To Burleson's left was Simpson—African American, stocky, powerful, calm yet gruff. His neatly trimmed beard showed flecks of gray, and his short sleeve button-up was stretched tight over bulging biceps.

In the back corner, hidden in shadow, sat the third man, the one who'd not been introduced to Draker at the first meeting. Only the man's legs were visible, stretched out into a slash of sunlight—the end of his chinos met polished dress shoes, crossed casually at the ankles.

The man's hands were stacked on a thigh. Though Draker couldn't make out the details, he remembered from the first meeting in this tiny building that the man was missing the last two segments of his pinky finger.

At the first meeting, the nameless man had said nothing. He hadn't even moved out of the shadows. Draker hadn't seen the man's face. He suspected the same would hold true during this second meeting.

Draker was seated before the desk. His muscles were still shaking, and his mind raced.

Killing another human being will do that to you.

Burleson leaned forward, his mechanical smile in place. "Did you eliminate Al-Khattab?"

Draker nodded. "Yes, but—"

"Excellent!" Burelson's smile broadened into something more genuine. Even Simpson's stoic expression softened slightly. "You've done a great service to your country, Sergeant Draker."

Draker rubbed some of the shake out of his hands and leaned closer to the desk. "But there's something else. Al-Khattab said something... weird. Right before he died."

Burleson's smile faltered for a moment. He turned to Simpson, then returned his attention to Draker. "Oh?"

"After I shot him, he said it wasn't my fault. That it was just blind luck." Draker's eyes darted between Burleson and Simpson. "Strange, huh?"

Burleson and Simpson exchanged a quick glance, then Burleson's smile returned, wider than ever.

"Draker, buddy, the CIA appreciates what you've done today," he said, his voice smooth and reassuring. "But you're reading into things. I get it. You've never killed anyone. Your nerves are rattled."

Simpson leaned in toward Draker. "Remember what we told you about this man." His voice was deep and rumbling. "He orchestrated bombings in major European cities. Coordinated attacks on government facilities. Organized a cyberattack that nearly crippled the eastern power grid."

"That's right," Burleson nodded. "And let's not forget Hamburg. Thirteen people burned to death because of him. Two Americans. Four children." He shook his head, his expression grave. "You did the right thing, Sergeant. Whatever Al-Khattab said, it was just the desperate words of a dying terrorist."

Draker shifted in his chair. "But—"

"Look," Burleson cut him off, his tone softening. "You're about to finish your enlistment with the Air Force, right? You've got plans. The GI Bill, maybe a degree?"

Draker nodded.

"Good," Burleson continued. "That's exactly what you should do. Go live your life, Draker. You've earned it. We'll keep you in the background as a sleeper agent, just in case Uncle Sam ever needs you again." He chuckled. "Though I doubt that'll happen. After today, you've already done more than your fair share."

Simpson grunted in agreement. "You stepped up when it mattered."

The man in the shadows remained silent, but Draker could feel his gaze boring into him.

Burleson stood up, signaling the end of the debriefing. "You did well, Draker. A damn good job. Your country thanks you, even if they'll never know about it."

Before Draker could protest further, Burleson was ushering him out.

The door swung open, and Draker found himself blinking in the Afghan sun. The noise of Bagram washed over him—the roar of engines, the shouts of personnel, the constant hum of activity. A massive C-17 lumbered down the runway, its engines drowning out all other sounds as it gained speed and lifted into the cloudless sky.

Draker stood there, watching the plane disappear into the distance. But he only half watched it and only half noticed the heat pressing down on him.

His mind was still in that small town, still staring down at Al-Khattab.

"It's not your fault. Just... blind luck."

CHAPTER TWO

Present day

Draker sprinted toward the massive structure, a sprawling complex of crumbling concrete and rusted metal that had once been Columbus, Ohio's largest shopping mall. Shattered skylights dotted the sagging roof, and nature had begun to reclaim the parking lot, with weeds pushing through cracks and creeping up the walls.

Traffic noise from the nearby interstate faded behind him. Even as he ran as fast as he could, chasing after another man, Draker still felt that strange sense of unwanted nostalgia that had plagued him since he arrived. He was born and raised in Ohio, not seventy-five miles from his current location.

Yes, it was the closest he'd been to his birthplace of Wilmington—a tiny dot on the map that dared call itself a city with fewer than 13,000 souls—in years. And he was there on a grim task: to kill a guy, the one who was now a hundred feet ahead of him, trying to get away, also sprinting for the abandoned Camilla Creek Mall.

At first glance, Marcus Harding didn't fit the image of a ruthless kingpin controlling a criminal empire with an entire city under its thumb. Harding was on the short side, with a soft, slight build. His face was rat-like, as were his eyes—tiny, dark, closely spaced. The guy's milky complexion was amplified by his other rodent qualities—the black, greasy hair and the gross little soul patch on his lower lip.

But everyone, no matter how unassuming, has a few talents. Harding had two: an uncanny knack for running a human trafficking ring and the ability to convince local police and government officials to look the other way.

Harding's misappropriated skills were what had brought Draker to Columbus. To right a few wrongs. Draker had been in the city for three days. He'd confronted everyone complicit in Harding's scheme.

Now, only Harding himself remained.

So far, Draker hadn't had to kill anyone since he returned to his home state. That was about to change.

As Harding slowed slightly at the mall's entrance, he stole another glance over his shoulder. From behind a pair of thick, black-rimmed glasses, his eyes widened as they found Draker barreling toward him. Dressed in all black and dark gray—a tank top, loose cargo pants, and a worn-out beanie—Harding looked ready to blend into the shadows.

And he did.

Harding disappeared into the building, and the rusty door creaked shut behind him.

A few moments later, after crossing the last stretch of crumbling asphalt, Draker approached the entrance.

He stopped and pulled his Glock 19 from its small-of-back holster. Closing his eyes, he took a deep breath as he readied to clear the doorway.

A moment of quiet.

And then explosive action.

Draker grabbed the handle and yanked hard. The steel door

was clearly some sort of postmortem replacement for what must have been a grand glass entryway, and the sudden movement summoned another metallic screech that echoed into the void beyond.

Draker swept through the entry. Moving in, he squinted slightly to adjust to the light—a modest shift. The remnants of massive skylights allowed shafts of dusty light to cut through the gloom, providing adequate illumination.

The change in the air quality, though, was drastic—from everyday city air to dead stagnancy, carrying the scent of decades-old merchandise, bygone eras, and shattered dreams.

Draker brought his hand to his mouth to stifle a cough as the dust tickled the back of his throat. His boots scuffed on the debris-strewn linoleum as he approached a corner, stopped, and listened.

Footsteps in the distance. Echoing. Running away.

Draker adjusted his grip on the Glock, cleared the corner, then entered Camilla Creek's main concourse.

It was a broad sweep of decaying storefronts and scattered kiosks. The merchandise was long gone, leaving only ghostly outlines behind shattered windows. At the center was a massive, empty fountain, its tiles cracked and stained. The ceiling soared, maybe forty feet high, crisscrossed by large steel beams. Motionless escalators climbed to the upper levels.

But no Marcus Harding.

Draker held perfectly still. Listened.

The footsteps had stopped.

Shit!

Maybe Draker had underestimated the guy. Maybe Harding's resourcefulness extended further than simply fooling some rubes with a few clever words and a decent human trafficking operation. Maybe the guy was a true survivor.

Every second that passed vastly increased the chance that Draker had lost him. He pictured Harding slithering out some side door or through a broken-out window.

Draker plastered himself against the wall, eased toward the next hallway, and then—
There!
Footsteps again. Beyond the massive fountain.
Draker took off.
He dashed into the open space toward the sound of the footsteps. Even at a full sprint, the fountain seemed to remain in the distance, never drawing nearer. The place was *that* massive.

When he finally reached the fountain and slowed slightly to clear it, he saw Harding, halfway across the concourse in the other half of the mall, a tiny figure on an expanse of teal and purple tile split by a beam of light. The color scheme and the general look of the place hinted that the mall had shut its doors sometime in the '90s.

Harding was about a hundred feet away, a thirty-three-yard moving target trying desperate evasive tactics, juking left and right. A challenging shot. Harding was slowing rapidly; no matter how much of a survivor he was, he was in poor shape. Adrenaline and the sheer, animalistic will to live could only do so much before impartial limitations set in.

Draker's Glock was fully loaded—fifteen in the mag, one in the chamber—and he gave a moment of consideration to throwing some lead downrange.

But he didn't. For a couple of reasons.

First, while Beau had told Draker he would need to be an assassin in his new position as Beau's Ranger—and Draker had already dispatched several people in just his first couple of weeks—Draker wasn't comfortable shooting a guy in the back as he ran for his life.

Not yet, anyway.

More importantly, there was more critical intel to get out of Harding before eliminating him.

Harding whipped around, chest heaving, footsteps clomping, growing slower. He made eye contact with Draker...

… and pulled a beat-to-shit revolver from his front pocket. A Smith Model 36. A true belly gun. Five chambers of .38 Special. Harding swung the weapon in Draker's direction.

But by now, Draker was close enough to leap at him.

So he leapt.

He launched himself forward, tackling Harding around the waist. They went down hard, skidding across the tile in a tangle of limbs. The Smith & Wesson clattered away, spinning off the tile and into the faded carpet of Bath & Body Works.

Draker quickly rolled Harding onto his back, pinning him down with a knee on his chest. The human trafficker's gangsta-nerdy black glasses were askew, as was his beanie.

"Okay, you got me, all right?" Harding said in a surprisingly high-pitched voice. This was the first time Draker had heard the voice, having finally come face-to-face with Harding after three days of hunting him. "If I tell you everything, you'll let me live, right?" He nodded as he said it, as though answering his own question.

Draker didn't respond.

"There's… there's a container ship. At the port in Cleveland," Harding said. "The *Sea Breeze*. They're in a red container, near the stern. Number *CG2439*. Sailing tomorrow night." His eyes flicked to Draker's Glock again. "All twelve girls will be there."

Draker's mind went to work, already planning the next steps. He'd get this intel to Beau, who would use his tech prowess to contact both the feds and local police in Cleveland—anonymously yet authoritatively. The twelve girls would be saved.

Now, as Draker stood over Harding, there was the next step to attend to—he had to kill this man. As a Ranger, Draker had already executed several people, but never someone lying on his back, unarmed. The thought made him hesitate.

Al-Khattab. Seated, not lying on his back.

But just as unarmed.

"It's not… your fault."

Harding seized the moment. In a move Draker never saw

coming, Harding suddenly produced a small canister from his pocket and sprayed it directly at Draker's eyes.

Pepper spray.

Draker reeled back, shielding his eyes enough to deflect much of the spray. But not all of it. The burning pain was instant and overwhelming.

Memories flashed to him along with the burn. Police training. Years ago. They'd pepper-sprayed him at the academy when he joined the police department in Santa Clarita, California, after his time in the Air Force and earning his criminal justice degree on the GI Bill.

It hurt then.

And it hurt now.

But he couldn't fixate on the pain, couldn't even take a moment to gather himself.

Because Harding was up and on the run again.

Draker gave chase. Through his blurry vision, he followed the hazy form of Harding as it darted down a service corridor.

He burst through a rusted door into the bright sunlight, squinting through watery eyes and scanning the overgrown parking lot.

There.

A blurry flash of movement near a line of dumpsters—Harding.

Draker sprinted after him, and his eyes burned more fiercely with the sunlight.

He followed Harding's silhouette through the maze of broken concrete and encroaching vegetation despite the tears streaming down his face and the constant urge to rub his eyes.

As they reached the edge of the property, Draker's vision began to clear infinitesimally, and he saw Harding getting closer to the chain-link fence.

He thought back to his earlier hesitation about shooting a guy in the back.

On the other side of the fence was a concrete wall belonging to a warehouse just as abandoned as the shopping mall—as good of a backdrop as any in the city to fire a gun.

If he didn't shoot now, his next backdrop might include people.

He raised his Glock, blinking rapidly to clear his vision.

And fired.

A plume of blood erupted from Harding's shoulder. The man spun all the way around and landed face up.

Draker ran up to him, stood over him. They were in the same position they'd been in moments earlier inside the mall: Harding lying down, Draker looming over him.

Just as Draker had overcome his hesitation to shoot someone in the back, he knew he had to overcome this newer reluctance of shooting someone who was lying down, seemingly defenseless.

Without further pause, he fired twice more.

A double tap.

The roar of the gun. The catastrophic damage caused by two 9mm rounds at extremely close range. Plenty of blood.

And Harding was dead.

As the adrenaline faded, the burning in Draker's eyes intensified, overwhelming the other pain in his battered and exhausted body. His vision swam, tears streaming down his cheeks as he blinked furiously against the pain. Through discomfort, a realization crystallized.

He'd almost lost Harding just now.

If the human trafficker had made it over the fence and to a vehicle or a crowded area, he might have escaped entirely. And with him, any chance of saving those girls in Cleveland would have vanished.

Draker's jaw clenched as he stood over Harding's body. He'd relied too heavily on his old police training, on predictable behavior patterns. It had nearly cost him everything.

In this new life he inhabited—the life of a Ranger, an unlicensed investigator, a vigilante assassin—he couldn't afford to be so rigid in his thinking.

He listened for sirens, for the sounds of onlookers' shoes scuffling in the surrounding rubble.

Nothing.

One more look at Harding's corpse.

And he left.

CHAPTER
THREE

Sometimes, a place can stink even worse than it looks. Draker pushed open the motel room door and the smell hit him immediately—a mustiness carrying strong traces of cigarette smoke and cheap all-purpose cleaner. He forced his legs to take him inside.

Willow's Rest Motel.

Peeling wallpaper with faded willow leaf patterns. Above the bed, an askew framed print of a willow tree painting—branches dipping into a pond bathed in a golden dawn.

Willow trees everywhere.

Draker found himself mildly impressed that someone had bothered to tie the decor to the motel's name. It was a level of creativity one wouldn't expect in a place like this, and it hinted that Willow's Rest had seen much happier days sometime in the past.

He was about to drop his backpack on the bed, but he stopped, the bag hovering a few inches over the surface. His eyes took in the threadbare comforter.

A news magazine TV program he'd watched years ago flashed through his mind. The investigative reporter had used blacklight technology to expose the true state of hotel cleanliness, revealing that hospitality industry linens were virtual Petri dishes of dried bodily fluids.

Fluids of a certain type…

Draker sighed, too tired to care about what invisible horrors might be lurking in the fabric beneath him. He dropped the bag.

After unclipping the small-of-back concealed carry holster from his pants, he placed his Glock on the nightstand next to an alarm clock that was every bit as vintage as Camilla Creek Mall. It was one of those old, low-slung models with a brown faux-wood exterior and glowing red numbers. The time showed 10:39 am. With the Harding case closed and no new orders from Beau, Draker had the whole day stretching out before him—perfect for a long nap.

Physical recuperation.

And mental.

A siren wailed in the distance. Shouting erupted from the room next door—perfectly audible through the wall—followed by the muffled thump of a slamming door. Just another day in paradise.

Draker sat on the edge of the bed, ignoring the protesting springs, ignoring the potential dried bodily fluids. He bent down and went to work on his bootlaces. His fingers, clumsy with exhaustion, fumbled against the double knots. Finally, he pried off the boots and let out a groan of relief. He flexed his toes.

Here he was, holed up in a rat's nest motel on the wrong side of Columbus, having just executed another target. He'd lost count of how many people he'd killed in the past two weeks, especially after the carnage of his second mission in Ventura, California, just days ago.

Before this, he'd had a beautiful wife, a beautiful house, and a beautiful career in a beautiful city. He'd left it all behind the moment he got a call from a mysterious stranger warning him that armed men were storming his home. There'd been no time; he'd had to flee.

The stranger who had called was Beau. Since the phone call,

Beau had been helping Draker figure out the mystery of why shadowy forces were hunting down Draker, intent on killing him. In return, Draker had agreed to be Beau's Ranger.

Now, Draker was bouncing from one seedy motel to another, solving problems for a mysterious benefactor.

Beau and Draker had discovered it wasn't the CIA hunting Draker. The mission Draker had taken fifteen years ago in Afghanistan—what he'd believed was an off-the-books mission for the CIA—had actually been unwitting work for a defense contractor named Windbrook.

Fifteen years of relative stability after leaving the Air Force, gone in an instant. His final mission in Afghanistan, the one he thought he'd put behind him, had come back to haunt him with a vengeance.

And Alyssa... God, Alyssa.

His wife of two years, companion for five, the woman he'd built a life with, had turned out to be a stranger named Cassandra Wynne, a Windbrook operative. The betrayal was still fresh, raw, the memory of her trying to kill him just three days ago in Ventura as vivid as if it had happened yesterday.

Ventura. Draker's second mission. Where he'd discovered that his life since the Air Force—the majority of his adult life—had been a lie.

Ventura was also where he'd met Kylie Payton...

Kylie had been his Soul, the term Beau gave to the people Draker was tasked with assisting and protecting. In the chaos of losing Alyssa, he'd grown close to his Soul in Ventura. Too close. This new life—always on the move, always looking over his shoulder, always killing the nation's scum—left no room for the softer side of life.

Draker rubbed his face, trying to push away thoughts of Kylie. But he couldn't. He pictured her now. The bold auburn hair with streaks of blonde. The tattoo sleeve covering her right arm—rose petals and leaves and stems. Her smile.

Suddenly, he wasn't so exhausted.

To refocus his mind away from the unattainable, Draker sat at the desk and grabbed the pen—a simple, plastic Bic number. He pulled his iPhone from his pocket. It was noticeably heavier than a standard iPhone; Beau had customized it—reinforced, bulletproof.

He propped the phone against the wall, opened YouTube, and navigated to one of his saved videos—a tutorial on the Tri-Phase Cascade pen-spinning trick.

Draker enjoyed pen-spinning. One thing he liked most about it was that he could practice anywhere, even in a place like Willow's Rest. All he needed was a pen. While he wasn't as skilled as the experts, he could hold his own in this nerdy hobby.

He'd recently mastered a trick called the Quantum Loop. Last night, he'd begun learning the Tri-Phase Cascade.

Following the video's instructions, Draker positioned the pen's balance slightly toward the tip, letting its weight settle just right. He flicked his middle finger, which sent the pen into a clockwise spin around his index finger. The pen wobbled before settling into a steady rotation.

Draker's eyes narrowed in concentration. He tried again. Each attempt brought a little more control, the forward spin responding better each time.

The appropriately named Tri-Phase Cascade trick had three distinct stages. He was satisfied with his progress on this first stage. He would move onto the second soon.

He stood up and paced the small room. The carpet felt thin and grimy through his socks. Thoughts of embedded bodily fluids returned.

Through the gap between the curtains, he could see Willow's Rest's faded sign. A couple of beat-up cars sat in the parking lot. Someone pushed a shopping cart down the sidewalk.

His old life in Santa Clarita—if the word "old" could actually be assigned to a life only two weeks in the past—flashed before his eyes again, fully formed, like a dream, like the unreality it was.

All of it, gone.

And for what? A mission carried out fifteen years ago in the dusty streets of Afghanistan. He'd thought he was doing the right thing. Now, he knew it had never been about serving his country; he'd been Windbrook's pawn, and he didn't understand why.

There were lots of *whys*.

Why had Windbrook needed to murder someone? Why had they gone to such lengths to monitor Draker—for a decade and a half—even to the point of staging a woman to be his wife? And now, why did they want him dead?

And a big *who*.

Who was the man Draker had killed, the man Windbrook had said was terrorist and radicalized American Frederick Al-Khattab?

Draker's hand went to his pocket, pulled out his heavier-than-standard iPhone. He unlocked the screen. On the front page, among a few common apps, was a series of Beau's proprietary apps: BeauChat, BeauText, BeauSearch Lite, BeauWeb, BeauMail, BeauPics, and BeauCash.

These secure and powerful apps handled the sensitive data Draker used in his position with his handler. They had nearly identical icons—each with an ultra-modern and garish italicized *B*, differing only in their bright colors.

Draker opened the BeauChat app and went to his contact list, which had three people: Beau, Kylie Payton, and Milo Price.

His finger went to Beau. Stopped. He stared at one of the other names.

Kylie Payton.

He blinked.

And tapped Beau's name.

One ring and the call connected.

"Howdy!" Beau said. "Congrats are in order. You killed the bastard!"

Beau's accent was the first thing anyone noticed about him—a Texas drawl so intense it would make a cartoon cowboy blush.

"Mm-hmm," Draker said.

"You did good, son. Real good." Beau paused, his tone shifting. "Listen, I've got some news for ya. I've been digging into your Afghanistan mission, specifically about the men who coerced you into it. I think I'm starting to narrow down some leads on Simpson."

Simpson...

The supposed CIA agent who'd sat at the corner of Agent Burleson's desk in that tiny shack of a building at Bagram. African American. Powerful build with biceps straining his short-sleeve button-up. Neatly trimmed beard with flecks of gray.

Simpson had said less than Burleson but more than the third man in the room, the one hidden in the shadows who'd said nothing.

Of the few times Simpson had spoken, once was when Draker had asked the agents about Al-Khattab's dying words—*"It's not your fault. Just... blind luck."*—and what they could mean.

Simpson had leaned in toward Draker. "Remember what we told you about this man." Deep voice, stern demeanor. *"He orchestrated bombings in major European cities. Coordinated attacks on government facilities. Organized a cyberattack that nearly crippled the eastern power grid."*

During Draker's Ventura mission less than a week ago, he'd been hunted by Burleson who, it turned out, had not only been a CIA agent but also a Windbrook operative. Burleson wasn't his real name; it had been Sean Hunsinger.

At the end of the mission, Draker had killed Sean Hunsinger.

Now, with Hunsinger dead, as Beau and Draker tried to untangle the mess of why Windbrook was chasing him they were left with two of the three men from the Bagram meeting still at large: Simpson and the man in the shadows.

Since the man in the shadows remained a complete unknown, Simpson had been their best lead.

And now, after days of dead ends, there was finally a break on the Simpson front.

Draker's fatigue vanished in an instant. "What have you found?"

"Nothing concrete yet," Beau said, "but I've been combing through old CIA records, cross-referencing data on covert ops and personnel movements from that time. There are some interesting discrepancies that might point to a hidden identity. I'll keep you posted as I uncover more."

"All right."

"Now, don't you get too comfy there in your motel—" at this, Draker looked around the room and smirked, "—because I've got your next mission: Louisville, Kentucky."

Draker's jaw clenched. "Already? I just wrapped up here in Columbus. You promised some downtime between missions, but I've been running nonstop for two-plus weeks since I fled Santa Clarita."

"I get it, Draker. I do," Beau said. "But this can't wait. It's time-sensitive. After this, I promise you'll get that break you need. A real one. Louisville's only a three-hour drive from Columbus. We'll get you in and out as quickly as we can."

Somehow, Draker doubted he'd be "in and out" of Louisville.

After the revelations in Ventura, he needed time, needed to process it all, to figure out what the hell he was doing.

But as he closed his eyes and exhaled, he said, "What's the job?"

"The job," Beau said, "involves a certain homegrown terrorist. You familiar with the Watchdog, Draker?"

"Of course," Draker said.

Like everyone else, Draker had seen the countless news reports over the past year. The Watchdog was infamous, faceless, a specter that law enforcement couldn't pin down.

"An unknown individual with a grudge against modern society," Draker continued. "Thinks the world has gone to shit, and he's the one who's going to fix it. By blowing people up. A latter-day Ted Kaczynski."

"Mm-hmm, that's the fella," Beau said. "FBI's been tracking

him for nearly a year since the New Orleans bombing. They can't find him. He's slipped past every local law enforcement agency he's encountered. Online wannabe-sleuths-slash-wannabe-vigilantes haven't been able to pick up the trail either. The Watchdog is a ghost."

Beau waited a long beat, then added, "And you're the one who's gonna stop him."

CHAPTER
FOUR

He called himself the Watchdog.

It was a self-appointed title, but not a vain one. Society was spiraling into a pit of depravity—values eroding, ignorance flourishing. Social media, smartphones, and what passed for modern culture were breeding grounds for intellectual laziness and ethical bankruptcy. Someone needed to stand guard against this tide, a watchdog to bark warnings and, when necessary, bite.

He was a necessary evil, a brutal check against a world that had lost its way.

The Watchdog eased his van into the shadows beside the abandoned warehouse and tapped an impatient beat on the steering wheel. The supplier should have been here by now. He eyed the surroundings—crumbling bricks, shattered windows, and weeds sprouting through the cracked asphalt. But no other vehicles.

He killed the engine and waited.

Five minutes passed before headlights cut through the darkness. An old pickup rolled to a stop, its engine sputtering before going silent. The headlights stayed on. The Watchdog tensed, hand instinctively moving toward the gun tucked in his waistband.

A figure emerged from the truck. Tall and lanky, clothes hanging loose on his frame. The supplier. He looked like a truck driver, and in a way, he was; the man *did* drive a truck, after all—albeit of the pickup variety—and he transported products for a living.

The Watchdog stepped out of the van. Gravel crunched beneath his boots. He approached the supplier, keeping his movements slow, non-threatening while the other man did the same. They met halfway between the vehicles.

"You're late," the Watchdog said. "You got the stuff?"

The supplier nodded, eyes darting left and right. There was a spasmodic quality to his movements. The Watchdog suspected he was on cocaine. "Yeah. You got the cash?"

The Watchdog pulled an envelope from his jacket's inner pocket and held it out. The supplier snatched it, thumbed through the bills with grimy fingers.

"It's all there," the Watchdog said. "Now show me what you brought."

The supplier jerked his head toward the truck. "In the back. Under the tarp."

The Watchdog moved to the pickup's bed and lifted the corner of the tarp. Ooh, nice. Very nice, indeed. He took in the array of components in the bed—wires, detonators, chemical precursors. The final pieces he needed.

"This'll do," he said, letting the tarp fall back into place.

As the supplier helped him transfer the materials to his van, the Watchdog thought of his associate, the person who shared his vision. Recent conversations played through his head.

His associate was... impressive. The way this individual manipulated others—bending people to an unseen will without anyone realizing it—was pure art. His partner understood, on a fundamental level, how rotten society had become. How the masses had been blinded by their own hedonism and willful ignorance.

Together, the Watchdog and his associate would open eyes. Force people to see the truth.

The Watchdog allowed himself a small smile as he closed the van's rear doors. Soon, his next target would burn. And from its ashes, a small piece of the new, purer world would rise.

"We done here?" the supplier said, interrupting the Watchdog's reverie. He clawed at his neck.

The Watchdog nodded. "We're done."

He climbed back into his van and watched the pickup's tail lights fade into the distance. He sat for a moment and savored the weight of what was to come. His fingers traced idle patterns on the dash.

He considered his associate once more—their aligned purpose, the rarity of finding someone who truly understood. Someone ready to act, to unsettle the corrupt foundations of the world.

A turn of the key and the engine came to life. He rolled out of the warehouse lot and merged onto the empty street. There was no one else out and about in this shithole side of town, but he could hear the faint hum of distant traffic. The scent of the earlier rain shower—misting off the concrete—lingered in the air.

A rattling noise from the back of the van. He flicked his gaze to the rearview mirror, spotted his newly acquired supplies shifting with the van's motions. He grinned. His upcoming attack would be a watershed moment—a decisive line in the sand.

And it would only be the beginning.

CHAPTER
FIVE

As Draker flicked through the mission files on his heavier-than-standard iPhone—keeping Beau on speakerphone—a simple conclusion rang through his mind: the Watchdog was a monster masquerading as mundane.

Over the past year plus, Draker had seen the Watchdog's handiwork plaster every news outlet. The devastation. The survivors with their hollow stares. The officials, fists raised, promising retribution. As a cop in Santa Clarita, Draker hadn't particularly thought the Watchdog would visit his city, but the attacks were so random there was always the possibility.

But now, poring over the mission materials with Beau's narrative threading through the speakerphone, Draker's understanding sharpened—beyond public perception, into the darker depths of the details. It painted a portrait of a man who wielded normalcy and anonymity like weapons. The Watchdog could be anyone—just another face in the crowd.

"Think back to the bombing in New Orleans about a year ago," Beau's voice popped through the speakerphone.

Draker's mind brought forth the memory, augmenting it with the materials on his phone, seeing the same blurred-out photos that had flooded the internet seventeen months earlier. The New

Orleans bombing. Shattered glass, twisted metal, bloodied bodies strewn across polished floors. Over a dozen dead, mass chaos televised in high definition.

"Of course. I remember," Draker said. "Thirty people dead on Bourbon Street."

"And the attack at the tech company in Menlo Park shortly after that?"

Draker scrolled to another set of dark images. The offices of HushMingle, an app startup aiming to be the next Ashley Madison, catering to the adulterous crowd. Building shattered, debris scattered, chaos erupting as people scrambled for safety. Emergency workers in full gear rushing to the scene.

"Yeah, I remember that too," Draker said. "But authorities never concluded it was the Watchdog."

"True, but they're still trying," Beau said. "And then there's the bombing at The Velvet Basement, that nightclub just off campus in Ann Arbor."

Draker frowned. "University of Michigan? No, that one's new to me."

"This club's notorious, not just for the usual revelry but for the substance-trading circles the students themselves run with the club's owners and staff looking the other way, presumably for under-the-counter money. They deal in everything from prescription pills to homemade narcotics. Someone tried to blow it up at the biggest party of the semester. You probably didn't hear about it because the device malfunctioned—failed to detonate. No one was hurt or killed."

"And authorities suspect the Watchdog here as well?"

"That's right."

Debauchery. Infidelity. Illicit drugs. Disturbingly, Draker understood the Watchdog's qualms with modern society. Draker was an old soul, a man born a few decades later than he should've been. For his entire life, Draker had looked around and saw a world steeped in greed, indifference, and a rotting moral core. It was a large part of why he'd become a cop.

But understanding didn't equal agreement, and Draker pushed aside the unsettling thoughts.

"Who's my Soul?" Draker said.

"An FBI agent, Jenna Sullivan, based in the Des Moines Field Office. She believes the Watchdog's next target is an underground fight club in Louisville, Kentucky, called The Pit. Sullivan's superiors aren't buying it, but she's convinced."

Draker's brow furrowed. "If her bosses don't believe her, why should I?"

"Because I do," Beau said. "My research backs her theory."

"Fair enough," Draker said, no hesitation.

Immediate faith in Beau's intel—this was the groove Draker had fallen into with his mysterious new handler. Beau always seemed to have the inside track, tapping into vast resources Draker suspected were mostly digital—probably the work of some ultra-elite-level hacking.

They'd never met, not face to face, not even a video call. Beau was just a voice on the phone—a thick Texas drawl—always dropping exactly what Draker needed right when he needed it.

"Special Agent Sullivan shouted from the rooftops for so long that her bosses let her chase her theory to Louisville," Beau said. "But all they're doing is humoring her, shutting her up; they're giving her no support. She's on her own in Louisville, and from the communiques I've intercepted, she's hit a dead end and is screaming for assistance, but the Agency isn't listening."

"Okay, so what's the plan?" Draker said.

"Go to Louisville, find Sullivan, assist her. Specifically, you're going to be the piece she needs to move past the dead end she's run into."

"And what's this dead end?"

Beau snickered, a genuine laugh but also a bit mischievous. "I'll let her explain that part."

Draker sighed inwardly. Classic Beau—doling out intel in frustratingly precise doses, always holding something back. It was a game Draker was growing weary of, especially since each mission put his life directly on the line.

"Stay safe, Draker," Beau said. "This mission's a big'n."

"Will do."

There was a beep. Beau was gone.

Draker sighed. He pocketed the phone.

And sat there.

His body ached, a patchwork of bruises and strained muscles from his encounter with Marcus Harding, fresh wounds laid down over the still-healing wounds he'd suffered in Ventura, California, where he'd learned his life was a farce, that he was never a CIA sleeper agent, that the man he'd killed in Afghanistan was likely an enemy of Windbrook, not the United States—*"It's not... your fault."*—that Alyssa was never his wife, was never even Alyssa, was a woman named Cassandra Wynne, a Windbrook operative, one of the people hunting him down.

It was a whole damn lot to process at once.

Now Draker was about to embark on another vigilante mission for a man he'd never met in person, never even seen. And this mission involved him taking down a lunatic who'd alluded federal and local law enforcement for a year and a half, one of the most notorious killers in American history.

Another sigh.

As he inhaled, Draker took in more of the Willow's Rest stank—the mustiness, the cigarette smoke, the air freshener.

He eyed the bathroom in the back.

A quick shower.

Then he'd head to Louisville.

CHAPTER
SIX

Jenna Sullivan had a lot of pent-up frustration, and she was taking it out on her poor laptop.

Her fingers hammered the keyboard. Furiously. She was at a booth, huddled in the darkest corner of the dim diner. Not that it mattered. In this forgotten slice of Louisville, no one cared who you were, no one would suspect you were an out-of-town fed.

She glanced up, scanned her surroundings. The diner's 1950s-retro vibe was long gone. Its red vinyl booths sagged. Its checkered floor was scuffed, dull. Time had chewed through the place's attempt at nostalgia. How ironic.

No, no one was looking her way. A few late-night patrons sat in booths, nursing steaming cups of coffee, their faces lit by the pale glow of smartphone screens and the flickering overhead lights.

Ray wasn't among the clientele.

Sullivan's gaze went to the glass entryway.

Ray was not there either.

He was late. He should have stumbled in over twenty minutes ago, the agreed-upon time.

Fucking Ray. Seemed like a solid lead at first, a junkie who babbled about underground fights and shadowy figures. Now he was just another pain in Sullivan's ass—showing up at odd hours, begging for cash or favors.

Jameson would laugh if he saw her now. Hell, Sullivan's Special Agent in Charge had all but laughed her out of his office when she'd presented her theory about the Watchdog targeting the Pit, an underground fight tournament in Louisville, Kentucky.

"It's a waste of resources, Sullivan," SAC Jameson had said, his voice dripping with condescension, his Magnum P.I. mustache twitching with amusement. *"You've based your idea on a supposed 'code' in a dark web forum, and that's just not an angle I'm willing to put much manpower behind. But you go ahead and follow up on it, kiddo. I want to keep you happy."*

Kiddo…

Happy…

What a patronizing way to treat a fellow federal law enforcement agent.

She'd wanted to scream. To grab Jameson by his perfectly pressed collar and shake some sense into him. Didn't he understand? The Pit wasn't just some backwater brawl. It was an institution, drawing fighters and spectators from across the country, an illegal no-holds-barred brawl, savagery at its greediest and most lethal, MMA on steroids—often literally—a projection of society's subliminal bloodlust.

It was a perfect Watchdog target.

No, *the* perfect Watchdog target…

Sullivan shook her head, refocusing on her computer screen. She had to prove Jameson wrong. Had to show them all that her instincts were right. Even if it meant sitting alone in this shithole diner, piecing together scraps of intel like a deranged conspiracy theorist.

The bell on the door rattled and Sullivan glanced up. A figure stepped inside, silhouetted against the faint light from the streetlights outside. About six-foot one. Could be Ray.

But as the man stepped inside, she saw it was definitely *not*

Ray. This guy didn't have Ray's wiry, hunched-over physique. His shoulders were broader, his legs more powerful.

The man came her direction. Sullivan's hand inched toward her hip, fingers brushing against her holstered sidearm.

As the man drew nearer, she took in his appearance. Caucasian, light brown hair, brown eyes, stubble beard. He was around two hundred pounds with an athletic build, wearing a casual short-sleeve shirt, jeans, and black boots.

Not Ray at all.

But since the man was now looking directly at her as he approached, Sullivan had an idea who it was.

Someone she'd been told would make contact with her soon, a notion she'd dismissed, almost forgotten about.

The man stopped at the edge of her booth. Sullivan kept her hand on her weapon.

"Agent Sullivan?" the man said. "Ty Draker. Beau sent me."

"I… didn't think you were real," Sullivan said. "When Beau called me, his whole spiel seemed so absurd I thought it was a practical joke, one of the assholes back in Des Moines giving me more shit about chasing down the Louisville angle."

Draker shrugged. "I'm real."

Sullivan glanced around the diner, then back to Draker. "We should talk outside. We have sensitive information to exchange, and it's best to do it away from prying eyes." She subtly indicated the unsavory lot surrounding them, some of whom were watching.

Draker nodded and turned toward the exit. Sullivan snapped her laptop shut and followed. Truthfully, the conversation could have been held just fine in hushed tones in the diner…

… but she had an alternate reason for taking him outside.

As they headed for the exit, Sullivan studied Draker's physique. A few moments earlier, when he first approached, she'd noted how handsome he was. Now, she couldn't help but notice his nice ass in those jeans.

They stepped into the night. The air was cool. Insects trilled.

Something noxious undercut the greasy scent of the diner, and Sullivan pegged this invading scent on the distant smokestacks. Overhead, the diner's neon sign buzzed, casting its glow across the cracked asphalt.

"This way," Sullivan said as she stepped in front of Draker. "I'm parked over here. Got some materials in my car." Technically this was the truth, but that's not why she was leading him in that direction.

She rounded the corner, and as soon she was momentarily out of his sight, she came at Draker with a leg sweep. The instant he turned the corner, he saw the attack and dodged, barely.

Sullivan followed with a series of jabs. Left. Right. He deflected each. She bolted to the side, managed to grab his wrist, and attempted an arm bar takedown.

But Draker countered, merging his momentum with hers, and hurled her into the brick wall. The pain shot down her body in an electric jolt, and she immediately countered with a front kick to create distance.

But again Draker anticipated, sidestepping, avoiding the strike and never losing his footing.

Sullivan juked to the side, creating space again, and readied for another strike. But stopped. Because Draker just stood there, arms raised, ready but not attacking.

They looked at each other, panting in the darkness.

Between breaths, Sullivan said, "Lift your shirt."

Draker looked confused but complied after a moment's hesitation.

"There," Sullivan said, pointing. "Freckle on the left side of your abdomen. Just where he said it would be."

Another pause from Draker. "Beau?"

"Beau."

Draker lowered his shirt. "Satisfied now?"

"I guess."

"You know, you could have asked me to lift my shirt *first*. You didn't need to attack."

Sullivan shrugged. "Lots of people have a freckle here and there. I needed to see if you could counter my moves. If you couldn't, I knew you weren't the man Beau claims you are and that the two of you aren't to be trusted."

Draker looked at her. Blinked. Then, "Alrighty." He ran a hand along his jaw. "And you think you know what the Watchdog's next target is?"

"I *know* what it is—it's the Pit fighting tournament."

"What makes you so sure?" Draker said.

"I've been digging through dark web searches," Sullivan said. "The Watchdog thinks he's sneaky, but I figured out his alias: *cerberus211212*. Cerberus is the Greek mythological watchdog who guarded the gates of hell."

"And the number's arbitrary, I assume?"

"Not exactly. Twenty-one, twelve, twelve. The 21st of December, 2012, the day the world was supposed to have ended."

"Ah. These scumbags always think they're so clever."

Sullivan nodded her agreement. "The Watchdog searched for information on the underground fighting tournament ten times in the last three months. It's too much to be coincidence. But Jameson—my Special Agent in Charge—he doesn't buy it. Says it's circumstantial." She stepped closer to Draker. "That's where you come in. Beau's got it all worked out. He's arranged for you to go in undercover as a fighter in the tournament."

Draker's eyebrows shot up. *"He what?"*

"I know, it's crazy," Sullivan said. "But Beau's good. Like, scary good. He's already got a fighter to drop out, created a whole new identity for you. It's bulletproof."

She watched Draker's face, noting the tightness in his jaw, the flash of irritation in his eyes. And a bit of concern. She couldn't say that she blamed him, suddenly being propositioned to fight in an underground tournament among some of the nastiest dudes on the planet.

After what felt like an eternity, Draker gave a resigned smile and said, "All right. I'm in. I played *Mortal Kombat* a few times as a kid. I think I got the gist of it." He gave her a grin.

Sullivan's laugh came out at the same time as an exhale of relief.

For the first time since arriving in Louisville, she didn't feel like the Bureau's odd one out, like some fool on a wild goose chase. Now she had Draker. With him on her side, maybe she could make this work.

And wouldn't that be something to rub in Jameson's smug face?

CHAPTER
SEVEN

Draker hadn't driven many trucks. But this one was growing on him.

He stood beside his rented dark-blue Ford Maverick pickup truck in the parking lot. The neon sign above the diner painted the surrounding vehicles in a wash of unnatural light while its soft buzzing sound competed with the occasional swoosh of a car passing by in the background. Draker watched through the diner's window as Sullivan waited to square her tab at the counter.

Sullivan was second in line, and she stood tapping her foot behind the man who was paying. She wore a navy skirt suit that accentuated her trim figure—athletic but not bulky, a runner's physique. Asian American. Pale skin. Dark hair pulled back into a no-nonsense ponytail. A mole on her right cheek was her most distinctive feature—prominent but aesthetic, of the Marilyn Monroe variety—even more defining than her set of razor-sharp cheekbones.

The man in front of Sullivan smiled at the waitress behind the cash register and walked away, then Sullivan stepped forward to pay. Draker noted the swift precision of her movements, and he thought of her attack a few moments earlier.

Though Draker had countered every strike, it hadn't been easy. Sullivan had executed her moves in textbook-perfect style which, along with her evidently dogged investigative skills, led him to believe she was a by-the-books sort of cop.

Draker took his iPhone from his pocket, opened BeauChat, placed a call. He leaned his weight against the Maverick.

He'd picked up the rental truck a few days ago upon arrival in Columbus, Ohio. With Louisville being only a three-hour drive from Columbus—and with no concern toward the exorbitant fee for retuning the rental vehicle at a different location than the one from which it was rented—Beau had instructed Draker to drive the Maverick between the two missions.

Beau had arranged the entire rental process, of course, as he did all of Draker's travel needs. This was part of their agreement. Between missions, Draker used whatever modes of transportation were available, often unglamorous options—anything from Greyhound buses to freight trains, even hitchhiking. Often he used the Hitcheroo app, an innovative ride-sharing platform for long-distance travel that Beau had designed but allowed Silicon Valley whiz-kid Glen Ainsworth to take credit for.

But for the missions themselves, Beau promised rental cars.

During Draker's previous mission in Ventura, California, he'd had a brand-new BMW 3 Series coupe. A few days before that, on his first mission—in Kingman, Arizona—he'd driven a tiny Nissan Versa. Now he had this pickup.

Variety was the spice of life.

Inside the diner, Sullivan was digging into her laptop bag. She retrieved a wallet. But Draker was staring only absentmindedly in her direction. His focus was on the telephone conversation. He had a death grip on his iPhone.

Beau's thick Texas accent came through. "Howdy, Draker."

"You didn't say you were signing me up for a fight tournament!" Draker growled.

"You're not always gonna get advance notice with this new gig of yours, son," Beau countered, his tone maddeningly calm. "Be ready for anything. Survival hinges on the ability to adapt."

Draker fumed. "Adapt? I was in the military. I was a cop for years. I can handle myself in a scuffle, but I'm not a damn cage fighter!"

"I know you're not. That's why I'm sending you to Grady Larkin. He'll help you out," Beau replied. Then his tone shifted, becoming more serious. "But before we get to that, I've got some news about Simpson."

Draker's anger subsided; suddenly, it didn't matter. "What kind of news?"

"Using facial recognition tech and cross-referencing with operational data from the time period you were in Afghanistan, I've narrowed down our list of suspects to five men who might be the fella you knew as 'Simpson.' I'm sending you the photos now. Take a look and let me know if you recognize anyone."

Draker's phone buzzed. He opened BeauChat to find five photos of different men. All black, all in their late fifties to early seventies. His eyes scanned each face carefully until he reached the third photo—a bland pic of a muscular older man posed against a bland wall, some sort of inventory photo. Draker didn't need to look at the final two images.

His breath caught in his throat. He swallowed.

"That's him," Draker said. "That's Simpson. The third pic."

"In the white polo shirt? You're sure?"

"Positive."

Draker stared at the image, memories flooding back. He saw Simpson in that building in Afghanistan, sitting at the corner of Agent Burleson's desk, muscular build, sour disposition. The man in the photo was older now, with a bit more weight and gray hair at his temples, but there was no mistaking those eyes, the set of his jaw.

"Alrighty," Beau replied. "The man in that photo is Daniel Harper. I'll dig deeper into his background and see what I can find out."

"Okay," Draker said, still staring at the image.

"Now, back to the matter at hand: Grady Larkin."

Draker's phone buzzed again. Another text from Beau—Larkin's address. Draker shook his head, amazed. Beau's lightning-fast responses and Johnny-on-the-spot dispersal of information was stunning.

"Who's Grady Larkin?"

"You'll see," Beau said with a mischievous flair. "Adios, Draker."

Again, Draker's fist tightened. Why the hell was Beau being so coy?

"Bye."

A disconnect sound. Beau was gone.

Draker opened the text message, read the address, and pocketed the phone. Frustration simmered.

The bell on the diner's door rattled and Sullivan stepped out, her laptop bag slung over one shoulder. Her heels clacked on the blacktop.

"I guess we're going to 1845 Sycamore Street," Draker said, lifting his phone as Sullivan stepped up to him.

Sullivan raised an eyebrow. "Beau?"

"Beau."

Sullivan shrugged. "All right. I'll follow you."

They walked to their respective vehicles, Sullivan heading for her black Mercedes on the other side of the lot while Draker opened the Maverick's driver-side door and climbed in. He input Larkin's address into the navigation system.

As soon as he started the engine, his phone rang. A video call. Milo.

Shit.

Draker had forgotten about their scheduled video chat.

Just as Draker was assigned Souls, he was also assigned Pals—people Beau instructed Draker to befriend and continuously support, primarily through video chat.

Unlike the Souls assigned for each mission—people Draker

was meant to extricate from dire straits—his work with Pals was ongoing. Beau had mentioned that, in time, Draker would be assigned multiple Pals, but for now Milo was his one and only.

He and Milo had been in touch for over two weeks now, from the very first day when Draker and Beau connected on the phone, the day Draker had to flee his home and his old life back in Santa Clarita.

Milo, a young man grappling with social anxiety in Chandler, Arizona, relied on Draker for regular check-ins and emotional support. It was an unconventional setup, but one Draker had grown to value deeply, aware of how much Milo depended on their interactions.

Draker answered the video call as he flicked on his turn signal and pulled out of the parking lot, checking his rearview mirror to make sure Sullivan was following in her Mercedes.

Milo appeared on the screen, light-brown eyes wide with anxiety. "M-Mr. Ty," Milo stammered, his thick Southern drawl and heavy stutter more pronounced than usual. "I... I n-n-need to talk to you."

His freckled face filled the screen. It was a wide, round face to begin with, even if Milo didn't always hold the phone too close. Milo was in his early twenties and of mixed-race heritage. His fair skin stretched over big jowls, and his wild, reddish hair seemed almost electrified by his current anxiety. Despite his struggles, he was usually prone to guileless, naïve smiles—not now, though.

"What's wrong, Milo?" Draker said, checking to the left before turning out of the parking lot.

"I... I h-haven't left my apartment in days, Mr. Ty. It's... it's like a p-p-prison now."

The Maverick's navigation system said, *In one mile, turn right.*

Draker glanced at his side mirror. There were the Mercedes's headlights, following. "Have you tried stepping outside? Even for a minute?"

Milo shook his head violently. "I c-c-can't. Just thinking about it... I can't b-b-breathe."

"Listen, Milo," Draker said. "We'll figure this out. Small steps, okay? Maybe start by just opening your front door."

Milo nodded, but his expression remained fraught with fear. "I'll... I'll try, Mr. Ty. Th-thank you."

"Remember," Draker added, turning onto the main road, "you need to feel the change and accept it. It's part of moving forward."

Whoa...

Draker felt a chill. He'd just told Milo to *feel the change and accept it*. Wasn't that exactly what Beau had told him? To be adaptable, to embrace change rather than resist it?

Here he was, only minutes later, passing on that wisdom to Milo.

The student had become the teacher in record time.

Someone call Mr. Miyagi. Quick.

Milo's brow furrowed. "F-feel the change?"

Draker nodded. "Sometimes, to get over something, you gotta face it a little bit at a time."

"I... I'll try to remember that, Mr. Ty."

The navigation system chimed in, *Turn left, and then your destination will be on your right, 1845 Sycamore Street.*

Draker glanced at the screen, then back at the road. "Milo, I gotta go. I'll talk to you soon, buddy."

"Okay, M-Mr. Ty." His voice was unabashedly disappointed. He never wanted to hang up. "Bye."

Draker tapped to end the call just as he pulled up to the address, surprised to find himself facing what looked like an old factory. The only giveaway that it was something else was the plain sign marked "GYM" hanging above a metal door.

The building was nearly derelict, its facade a patchwork of rust and peeling paint, windows boarded up. If it weren't for the smattering of vehicles in the pothole-riddled parking lot, Draker would have thought the place was completely abandoned.

He half-expected to see tumbleweeds rolling past.

He stepped out of the truck.

Sullivan parked her Mercedes beside the Maverick, cutting the engine. A moment later, the door opened and she came up beside him, stiffening as she looked across the parking lot, her eyes scanning the run-down facade before them. She glanced over at Draker.

"Um... *this* is where Beau sent us?" she said.

Draker considered double-checking the address. Didn't. First, because he knew he hadn't incorrectly entered it into the GPS.

Second, because he was starting to think he understood why Beau had been so coy...

"Yeah," Draker sighed. "This is the place."

With a resigned shrug, Sullivan grabbed her bag from the Mercedes's backseat. "Alrighty then."

They navigated the vehicles—many of which were older, many of which were battered—and approached the heavy steel door, its surface pockmarked with age. Draker rapped a knuckle against it.

For a moment, nothing.

Then the door groaned open, and inside was a scene that belied the exterior. Punching bags, worn but tough, dangled from exposed rafters. A boxing ring staked out the center of the floor. Around the periphery, weight benches and assorted gear clung to the walls.

It was straight out of an old boxing movie—*Rocky* or *Raging Bull*.

A mountain of a man stepped into view, filling the doorway. He was black, tall, and built like a brick shithouse, with biceps that strained against his t-shirt. A jagged scar dominated the left side of his face, and the eye above was milky white.

"You Draker?" the man said. His voice was volcanic.

Draker nodded. "That's me. You must be Grady Larkin."

Larkin's good eye narrowed as he looked Draker up and down. "So you're the guy I'm to train, huh?" Larkin snorted, a massive breath from a massive nose, like a bull. "You got muscles, kid, but you don't look like a fighter."

Kid. Draker nearly laughed. He was pushing forty years old.

But this momentary amusement quickly evaporated in the face of tarnished pride. Because not only had Larkin called him a kid, but he'd also said he didn't look like a fighter.

Draker bristled.

"I was a cop until two weeks ago, for over ten years. I can hold my own."

Draker immediately felt the irony, the moment the words left his lips. Just a few minutes ago, he'd protested to Beau about his lack of fighting experience, saying he couldn't possibly keep up with seasoned cage fighters.

Now here he was with a bruised ego, puffing out his chest like a belligerent drunk at the local Applebee's bar, staring down a beast of a man who was surely a veteran pugilist, a man with a scar on his face and a dead eye.

Larkin scowled and moved toward Draker—it was only then that Draker fully noticed how tall the guy was, easily six-four, a good three inches taller than Draker—but Sullivan stepped between them to diffuse the tension. "Mr. Larkin, we appreciate your help. This mission is crucial. We need Draker ready as quickly as possible."

Larkin stopped. Looked at Draker. Then turned to Sullivan, his expression softening slightly. "Beau vouched for you two. Said you're good people in a tight spot. And Beau helped me out of a tight spot years ago." He jerked his head toward the interior. "Come in. We've got work to do."

CHAPTER
EIGHT

Grady Larkin sized up the man standing before him.

The man's name was Ty Draker.

Ex-cop… or maybe a current one. Beau had been confusingly ambiguous about that point. Nonetheless, Draker had a military background as well. Decent build, not huge, but quite muscular and clearly in shape. Larkin had seen his type before—guys who thought their badge and/or military basic training made them invincible.

Well, this Draker dude was in for a rude awakening.

They were in the ring, he and Draker, both donning seven-ounce sparring gloves, facing each other amidst worn ropes and faded canvas. Around them, the gym regulars leaned against the walls and equipment, watching—some of them smirking, other sneering—clearly entertained by the prospect of Larkin dining on some fresh meat.

Jenna Sullivan stood just outside the ring, her business suit and computer bag standing out against the gritty surroundings. Some of the men's gazes lingered on her, clearly viewing her as fresh meat as well… but in a totally different sort of way.

She was a fine-looking woman, for sure, but Larkin, the overseer of this rusty domain, kept a watchful eye. His presence alone was enough to keep the circling sharks at bay. They knew what would happen if they did anything more than stare at Agent Sullivan. Anyone who got too close would receive a beatdown before a permanent eviction.

"All right, hotshot," Larkin said to Draker. "Show me what you've got. Try to stop me."

He didn't wait for a response, just lunged forward. He swung a right hook, half power, keeping it nice and slow, wanting to see what Draker would do but knowing full well how the kid would react.

Sure enough, the ex-cop took the bait. Draker stepped in, going for a textbook arm-bar takedown. Larkin almost laughed. It was like watching a training video in slow motion.

Larkin twisted, feeling the breeze created in Draker's path as he glided past. After ducking under the attempted hold, Larkin swept Draker's legs out from under him.

The guy went down hard. The impact echoed through the gym.

People laughed.

"Pathetic," Larkin growled, watching as Draker clambered back to his feet. "What the fuck was that? My granny could've seen that leg sweep coming, and she's been in the dirt for thirty years."

Draker's face flushed red—both embarrassment and anger. Good. Anger was useful if channeled properly.

"That was a basic sweep," Larkin continued. "Day-one stuff in any decent gym. And that arm bar you tried? You telegraph your moves like you're sending a damn Western Union. Same tired old police training. I've had plenty of ex-cops come through here before." He waved a hand toward the animals watching them.

He paced around Draker, whose eyes darted to the deep scar running from Larkin's temple to his jawline, then to Larkin's dead eye. Larkin caught the glance and let out a chuckle.

"Wondering about these beauty marks, huh?" Larkin said. "Got 'em in my last fight, decades ago. Some son of a bitch caught me with a spinning kick I never saw coming. Found out later the bastard had glued bits of glass to his boots, hiding 'em under the laces. Took my eye—one of the reasons I haven't stepped in the ring as a fighter since. Now I just train other poor bastards like you."

Larkin's good eye narrowed, fixing Draker with an intense stare while he tapped a finger under the other eye, the milky white one.

"In a place like the Pit, rules are afterthoughts. And there aren't many rules to begin with. You gotta be ready for anything, or you'll end up looking like me... or worse. The Pit ain't some controlled sparring match. It's not the same type of fighting you're used to as a cop, where your backup's a radio call away. It's a fucking *meat grinder*, and if you go in there thinking like a policeman, you'll come out in pieces."

Draker's jaw clenched. "I can handle myself."

Pride. Goddam foolish pride. Larkin had seen it in the kid's eyes the moment he opened the door.

Larkin snorted. "Yeah, you just proved that real well, didn't you?" He stopped pacing and squared up to Draker. "The key to survival in the Pit is adaptability. You gotta be water, just like Bruce Lee said; you gotta flow with the fight, flow with the unexpected. Right now, you're about as fluid as a brick."

Larkin could see the wheels turning in Draker's mind as he scowled back, moving in a circle, hands up but not far enough. Larkin would have to fix that too.

"Again!" Larkin barked. "This time, forget everything you think you know. Forget the damn police academy. React, don't think."

He didn't give Draker time to prepare. Larkin charged, feinting left before dropping low for a tackle. Draker hesitated for a split second—old habits dying hard—before improvising. He sprawled, using his weight to counter Larkin's momentum.

It wasn't pretty, but it was better. Larkin disengaged, nodding grudgingly. "Not completely hopeless," he said. "But you've got a long way to go, and not much time to get there."

Larkin glanced out of the ring to check on Sullivan. She stood off to the side, watching intently. There was a sharpness to her gaze that Larkin respected. She, at least, seemed to grasp the gravity of the situation. Now none of the men were looking in her direction. They had clearly picked up on Larkin's unspoken threat.

Good.

Beau had told Larkin about Agent Sullivan's theory—that the Watchdog's next target was the Pit. To get inside, to stop a tragedy, Sullivan needed a fighter.

In record time…

Draker was going into the Pit tomorrow under a fake name, taking the place of a fighter who had suddenly dropped out—which was Beau's doing, of course.

Larkin had his work cut out for him.

He turned his gaze back to Draker. The guy's breathing had steadied, back to even. He stood upright, eyes narrowed, focused. Larkin had to admit—the kid had something. Maybe there was hope after all.

But hope wasn't enough, not with what this slapdash, motley trio of Larkin, Sullivan, and Draker was trying to accomplish…

They needed a miracle.

And Larkin had stopped believing in those a long time ago.

"Come on, hotshot," Larkin growled. "Show me what you've really got."

He lunged at Draker.

CHAPTER
NINE

The Watchdog had always liked working with his hands. He twisted wires and soldered circuits. The van was parked in a secluded corner of an abandoned lot, and it rocked gently with the movement. A light clipped to the shelf above him cast long shadows across his workbench.

His coffee-stained mug sat within reach, half-full, the contents long cold. The mini-fridge hummed; inside were energy drinks and meal-replacement bars, all stacked up on each other Tetris-style. He sat on the sofa which doubled as his bed. Every inch of space had a purpose—from the milk crate of technical manuals to the tackle box repurposed for electronic components.

He grabbed a pair of wire strippers, then peeled back the plastic coating, revealing shiny copper wires in perfect coils. It was a pleasing action. Visceral. Hands-on. Small, seemingly benign, but ultimately powerful. Much like how each part of his van setup was purposeful, each wire was a component in his overarching plan. The world outside this van was rotting. The Watchdog could smell it, the stench of moral decay seeping through the walls. No escaping it.

Social media. OnlyFans. TikTok. A litany of platforms designed to exploit the basest human instincts. The Watchdog's lip curled in disgust. How far they'd fallen. Once, humanity had dreamed of the stars. Now, they were content to wallow in digital cesspools—peddling flesh, chasing fleeting fame.

Using a clamp to hold his work steady, he soldered the freshly stripped wire to a detonator.

And it was done.

The Watchdog smiled.

The Watchdog's phone buzzed. A text from the contact he'd labeled "Friend"—his associate. Two words: *All set.*

He didn't reply. No need. They both knew their roles in this production.

Returning to his work, the Watchdog took a pair of tweezers and carefully placed a blasting cap into a brick of C-4—plastic explosives, pliable under his touch, like modeling clay, even had the same gray color as modeling clay. In a way, that's exactly what the C-4 was: clay, a raw material from which the Watchdog would sculpt a new world.

His gaze drifted to his cellphone a few inches away on the workbench, propped up by a pile of wire scraps. He had it muted and a news broadcast played silently, closed captions flashing across the bottom. Another story about an online influencer's latest scandal. Another nail in society's coffin.

He turned back to his work. Let them get lost in their distractions, in the spectacle of it all. They were fools, all of them. Soon, they'd have no choice but to face true reality.

It was a liberation, really.

A liberation the Watchdog was providing.

Even with his generosity, the gift came from a place of alienation. He was never truly one of them. He remembered his past life, the corporate drone he once was, watching them all—blindly, willingly—participate in the very system devouring them.

Fucking idiots.

The Watchdog put the tweezers down, leaned back, and studied his latest creation.

… and imagined what it would look like when it exploded.

CHAPTER
TEN

"The Pit" didn't seem like an appropriate name—"Pile of Shit" would have been more fitting, as this place wasn't a hole in the ground but a sprawling warehouse, obviously long out of commission, barely holding itself aloft.

Draker stared at it, an old giant of rust and shadows. Floodlights from a nearby lot cut through the darkness, drawing Draker's attention to the jagged roofline—a staggered saw blade pattern, teeth biting into the night sky. He tried to determine the architectural reasoning behind such a design. Couldn't.

Its brick walls were pitted and scarred from decades of neglect, while all the oversized window openings were boarded up. The steel doors were chained shut, save for the one a few yards ahead. The ground was uneven—sparse gravel overtaken by weeds. A smell both earthy and mechanical filled the air.

But Draker's focus was on that bizarre roofline, an aggressive stair-step outline climbing into the sky.

Standing beside him was Sullivan. They were about twenty feet from the non-chained-up door. Waiting. They'd been like this for a few minutes.

Draker's muscles ached, a dull throb that fell in rhythm with his elevated heartbeat. Battered, bruised. Larkin's "training" had been more like a beating.

And there was more training yet to come that night...

The rusty steel door finally opened with a screech that split the quiet. A woman stepped into the dim light. She was maybe five-three, built slight. Her brown hair was pulled back in a ponytail. T-shirt, jeans. She approached with urgency, arms wrapped around herself against the slight chill in the air.

Nina Hollis was nothing like Draker had imagined. He'd pictured some burly, scarred-up brawler of a woman. Instead, he found himself face to face with a petite lady whose eyes held a razor-sharp intelligence. Those eyes fixed their gaze on him, full of skepticism.

A moment of this staring, then Nina switched her attention to Sullivan. "So, you're the woman who's been trying to contact me?"

Sullivan nodded. "Yes, and this is the fighter who's taking the empty slot in your tournament."

Nina's eyes narrowed as she brought them back in Draker's direction, looked him up and down. "Well, you're handsome, bub, I'll give you that. And you got some muscle. But how do I know you're a fighter?"

Draker bristled at the dismissal—much as he had with Larkin's dismissal, more foolish pride—but kept his mouth shut. This was Sullivan's show, and he'd follow her lead. So he focused on his role as Sullivan's taciturn associate—projecting confidence, squaring his shoulders, and meeting Nina's gaze head-on. He said nothing.

Nina returned her attention to Sullivan.

"He's never been to any of the other tournaments," she continued, crossing her arms. "No one's heard of him. And you expect the monsters in there to take him seriously?" She hooked her thumb over her shoulder toward the building behind them.

"We're prepared for that," Sullivan said. "Draker's got the skills, and we've got a backstory to support his entry."

Draker watched the back-and-forth.

"Skills or not, it's a close circle," Nina said. "They won't just open up to an outsider."

Sullivan took a step closer. "That's why we need your support. You vouch for him, and the others will follow."

Nina sighed, eyes dropping to the ground. A moment later, she turned to face the warehouse. She stared. Under the harsh glare of the floodlights from the next building, Draker saw dark circles under her eyes. Whatever was unfolding behind those weathered brick walls was wearing her down.

"It's not just about the trust," Nina said as she continued to stare at the building. "It's the fights. One slip and he's a goner. This tournament is... brutal."

"I know the risks," Draker said.

His mind flashed to Larkin's gym, to the punishing training session he'd just endured. As if reliving the nightmare, his ribs ached worse, a fresh wave of pain coursing through them. But Larkin had driven home one point above all others, something that resonated louder than the pain: adapt or die.

He was prepared to put that lesson to the test.

Nina shifted back and forth between Sullivan and Draker. She said nothing for a moment, then, "I haven't told anyone else in the Pit about your undercover status, Draker, and I won't. Not even my assistant, Leon Alden."

Sullivan nodded her approval. "Good. The fewer people who know, the safer you'll be. And Draker too. This needs to stay between us."

"Of course," Nina said to Sullivan. She faced Draker. "But if they somehow figure out you're not who you say you are, I can't guarantee your safety. These fighters... they don't take kindly to deception."

"I'll be careful," Draker said.

Nina fell silent, her eyes moving between Sullivan, Draker, and the looming warehouse. Draker could almost see the gears turning in her head, weighing pros and cons, risks and rewards.

Finally, she nodded, looked at Draker again, and said, "I'll make the arrangements. Be back here in two hours."

Nina turned and marched toward the warehouse. Draker watched.

"Two more hours," Sullivan said. "That's more time than I thought we'd have, more time for last-minute training. Larkin will be pleased."

Draker sighed.

He was going to get his ass beaten *twice* in a matter of hours.

"Yippee," he said.

CHAPTER
ELEVEN

The guy had left for a little while, but now the fresh meat was back in Larkin's gym.

And the clock was ticking.

So Larkin swung at Draker. Hard.

Larkin's fist connected with Draker's jaw, sending the younger man staggering.

"Too slow!" Larkin barked. "You're telegraphing again, every damn time. Might as well send up a fucking flare."

Draker shook his head. His face was painted with bruises, slick with sweat, yet there was a new blaze in the eyes, kindled in just the last few hours. Good. He was going to need every spark of that fire for what lay ahead.

"Again," Larkin said, falling into a fighting stance.

Larkin and Draker had been at it for an hour, time ticking away while Larkin drilled lesson after lesson into Draker's thick skull. Overhead, the fluorescent lights buzzed, throwing long shadows across the empty gym.

For a while, a few observers remained outside the ring—snickering less and less as respect for Draker grew—but the last one had left a long time ago. Now, the only observer was Sullivan, who'd returned to her earlier position a few yards away from the ropes, arms crossed over her chest.

Draker lunged, feinting left before throwing a right hook. Larkin saw it coming a mile away. But this time, there was something different. A slight hesitation, a change in rhythm. Larkin moved to counter, but Draker had already shifted, his leg sweeping out in a low kick.

Larkin grunted as the kick connected. Pain shot up his tibia, electric. He hopped on one leg for a moment.

Not bad. The kid was learning.

"You're getting there, Draker. But remember, in the Pit, it ain't just about what you can see." He pointed toward his dead eye. "Sometimes the worst hits are the ones you never saw coming, the ones you could never had dreamed up, not in your worst nightmares. Again!" He fell back into his fighting stance.

As they circled each other, he wondered how much Draker was puzzling over the origin of his scars and dead eyes. These exteriors marks were nothing compared to the one he carried inside, the other reason he'd stepped away from fighting, the true force driving him to push Draker so hard.

But that wasn't something he was ready to share—if ever. Right now, his job was to make sure this kid survived long enough to maybe tell his own story someday.

He took a step to the left, and his leg partly buckled with the pain Draker had inflicted moments earlier. He lifted it, taking the pressure off for a moment, and pointed at it.

"That was a good move. You're getting better," Larkin said, bringing his leg back to the mat with a grimace.

Draker nodded. His shoulders were drooping. "Appreciate it."

Larkin began circling again. "But 'better' ain't good enough. You need to bring your best. In the Pit, 'better' gets you killed. You gotta be unpredictable."

He demonstrated, closing the distance in a blur. Before Draker could react, Larkin had him in a chokehold. "See? Unpredictable."

Draker nodded. "All right, all right," he said between breaths. "I get it. Unpredictable."

"You get it, huh? Show me."

They reset and began circling again. The mat beneath them was slick with sweat. The air was hot, moist, thick.

Draker made the first move, closing the gap with a flurry of quick jabs. Larkin responded, juking left, but Draker was already one step ahead, ducking low and rising with an uppercut that landed with a solid crack to the underside of Larkin's chin.

Larkin's head snapped back. Spots exploded in his vision. For a moment, he was back in his prime, facing down opponents twice his size in smoky backroom brawls. The taste of copper filled his mouth— familiar, almost comforting.

Larkin stumbled backward, planted his left foot, stabilized. He sucked blood through grinning teeth, "Now that's more like it."

But just so the kid didn't get too satisfied, Larkin shot forward, catching Draker with a spear strike to the chest, sending him reeling backward like Larkin himself had done a moment earlier.

Wheezing. Feet wobbly. Arms windmilling

Boom.

Draker landed on his ass.

Larkin snickered. He brought a hand to his lips, wiped away some of the blood.

"You're ready," Larkin said with a sigh. "At least, as ready as you're gonna be."

Draker looked up, chest heaving, gloves planted in the mat, surprised. And grinning. Too confident. "Yeah?"

Larkin nodded. "But don't get cocky. You're still gonna get your ass handed to you at the Pit. But you just might survive long enough to do what you came here to do."

He extended a hand. Draker took it. Larkin pulled the other man to his feet, and for a moment, they just stood there.

"Remember what I taught you," Larkin said. "Be water. Adapt."

"I'll do my best."

Larkin watched from his corner as Draker limped off, moving like a guy who'd been taken to the edge and pushed over. He came to the ropes, grimaced, and squeezed himself through. His feet thudded onto the concrete. He stumbled, caught himself on the turnbuckle.

Sullivan rushed over. She said something to Draker, but it was beyond Larkin's earshot. Draker nodded, his jaw clenched in a grimace. They made their way across the gym floor. Every now and then, Sullivan's hand brushed Draker's arm, her touch tentative, retracting almost before it landed, as if she questioned her own place at his side.

The careful way Sullivan aided Draker made sense—they'd only recently met, after all. There was an awkwardness to their dynamic, a newness evident in every hesitant touch and concerned glance. As they reached the door, Larkin called out.

"Hey, hotshot."

Draker turned.

"You did good," Larkin said. "For fuck's sake, don't get yourself killed."

Draker nodded.

As the door closed behind Draker and Sullivan, Larkin let out a long breath. He shook his head.

He'd played his part; the rest was up to Draker.

He stepped out of the ring, followed the path Draker and Sullivan had just taken, and flicked off the lights. The gym fell into darkness, silence.

Draker... there was something different about the kid. A resilience that went beyond physical toughness. Larkin had seen it in the way the guy had taken every punch, every takedown, and came back asking for more.

Maybe this one would make it out alive.

CHAPTER
TWELVE

Draker was back at the Pit.

And this time he was going in.

He stood beside Sullivan's black Mercedes, staring at the decrepit building. 11:37 pm found this forgotten side of Louisville in a quiet state. Distant traffic. Insects singing to each other. The Mercedes's engine idled.

"Remember," Sullivan said, leaning over the center console to speak to Draker through the open passenger-side window, "trust your instincts. You've got the skills. Use them."

Draker nodded. "Will do."

"Good luck," Sullivan said, her voice softening. They looked at each other for a moment, and when Sullivan turned away, the window rolled up. There was a *thunk* as the transmission found its gear, then the Mercedes rolled past Draker in a quiet loop, going for the street.

Draker caught Sullivan's eye again as she swept past. She gave him a subtle nod. He returned it.

He watched the tail lights disappear past some trees. Then he was alone.

He checked his watch. Seven minutes early. As planned. He had the time he needed. He began to circle the building, his eyes scanning every detail. As he walked, he put the tip of his finger into his right ear and did a double-tap.

A moment later, Beau's voice was in his ear canal. "Howdy, Draker."

"Testing, one, two, three. Can you hear me?" Draker whispered.

"Loud 'n clear."

Draker was using an in-ear communication device Beau had shipped to him—a marvel of technology, well ahead of the curve. Beau, ever the tech wizard, had outdone himself.

The device was completely invisible from the outside, nestled deep within the ear canal, well past the outer ear. It utilized bone conduction technology for audio transmission, coupled with a subvocal microphone that could pick up the faintest whisper. The device employed advanced encryption protocols and operated on a frequency that was virtually undetectable by standard scanning equipment. It was a two-way device between him and Beau, but Beau also had the ability to patch in other calls if necessary.

"This will be our only means of communication since cellphones are prohibited in the tournament," Beau's voice crackled in his ear. "And I trust you left the Glock behind, since weapons are prohibited too?"

"That's right," Draker said. "Sullivan has both my iPhone and gun."

As they spoke, Draker continued his circuit of the building. Bricks crumbled at the corners. Sheets of corrugated metal patched gaping holes. The air smelled of rust and stagnant water.

Draker looked up. "I'm looking at the roofline now, Beau. Any idea what's with that saw-tooth pattern?"

"Could be left over from its industrial days," Beau said. "But focus on what matters. You see the cameras?"

Draker's attention shifted to the numerous security cameras dotting the exterior—sleek, modern, jarringly out of place on the crumbling facade. "Yeah, they're everywhere."

"Okay. Now, about that window I mentioned..."

"I see it," Draker said, spotting the transom window ahead, seven feet up on the wall. "It's covered with particleboard, just like you said it would be."

"If you stick to the shadows, away from the cameras—both interior and exterior—then that window will be your portal in and out of the place," Beau said. "I want you to continue training with Larkin and meeting with Sullivan. The window will also be your escape hatch should…" a slight pause. "Things go south. My recon suggested it's less fortified than the others. How's it look in person?"

Draker studied the window, noting the two lazy nails holding up the board, as well as the window's position relative to the cameras. "Yeah, the board should be easy enough to take down and put back up. And the window's in a perfect blind spot. Clear path to the woods too, also out of view. Your intel was spot-on."

"Always is, son. Think you can manage it?"

Draker sized up the window. Two feet by three. Not much room to work with. Draker was a muscular six-one.

"It'll be tight," Draker said. "But doable. The board's just particle wood, held up with a pair of rusty nails."

"Good," Beau said.

Satisfied with his reconnaissance, Draker turned and retraced his steps to the front of the building. He checked his watch again. Right on time.

"I'm heading back to the front now," he said. "Nina Hollis should be coming out soon to meet me."

"All right, son. Be safe."

"Thanks, Beau. Over and out." Draker placed his fingertip to his ear and tapped twice, ending the call.

He rounded the corner, stepped into the floodlights spilling over from the building next door. The steel door grated open, metal on metal, loud in the night. Nina Hollis stepped out, a dark shape against the dull glow bleeding from the warehouse behind her.

As the door swung open, Draker caught sight of another figure behind Nina. He was a stocky man in his fifties, not tall, maybe five-nine, but he filled the doorway with his presence. His face was lined, weather-beaten. Dark hair. Trim beard. Draker's gaze was drawn to the man's eyes—sharp, assessing.

Nina approached—with her companion following right by her side—and Draker noticed her demeanor had softened since their last encounter.

"So, 'Mav' is what you're gonna call yourself, huh?" Nina said with a small smile.

Draker nodded.

"Not a bad name," Nina mused. "Any significance to it, or is it just a flight of fancy?"

There was an unnecessarily complicated answer to that question.

Though Draker had been driving a rented Ford Maverick for this mission—and the previous one in Columbus, Ohio—Beau hadn't specifically requested a pickup truck—just a car, as usual.

But when Draker had gotten to the rental office in Columbus, they were out of every single passenger car. The only options were SUVs and pickups, and in that wonderfully frustrating way rental companies do, they claimed they were giving Draker an "upgrade" when they handed him the keys to a truck.

Since he was driving a Maverick, when the time came to choose his one-word alias for the Pit—something Nina had implemented for the contestants' anonymity and safety—the name "Maverick" was already lodged in Draker's head, especially since the Pit's naming conventions were akin to fighter pilots' wonderfully over-the-top call signs.

And since Draker was a film buff whose tastes went almost exclusively to the older stuff, the connection to *Top Gun* was automatic, especially with the recent sequel, *Top Gun: Maverick*, still fresh in his memory.

So he went with the name Mav.

But all he said to Nina was, "It just has a nice ring to it."

Nina smiled again. She looked him up and down. "Well, you

don't look a thing like Tom Cruise, but you're damn cute." She gestured to the man beside her. "This is Leon Alden, my personal assistant."

Interesting. In Draker's experience, personal assistants were usually younger than their employers, and certainly not this rough. But then, Draker's frame of reference was shaped by his time as a police detective in Santa Clarita, California, where the business owners he interacted with had assistants who greeted him with smiles and cappuccinos.

Those assistants hadn't looked like they could tear his head off his neck.

Alden extended his hand. Draker shook it. Mechanically strong grip. Callused palm. "Nice to meet ya," Alden said, his voice as tough as his appearance.

As the handshake separated, Draker noticed Alden's other hand moving subtly and he caught a glimpse of what looked like small stones being rolled between his fingers.

"Ready to enter the lion's den, Mav?" Nina said with a small smile.

Draker nodded again. "Now or never."

"You know the rules now. I can't let you have a phone in there. No weapons either, of course."

"Of course."

"Arms up, please," Nina said.

Draker complied, lifting his arms and spreading his legs slightly. Nina stepped up to him and began patting him down.

Alden took a step back, giving her space. He watched the proceedings with a keen eye, arms crossed over his chest.

Nina checked Draker all over, her touch professional but... thorough. When her hands reached his crotch—patting him thoroughly there too—Draker tensed.

Satisfied, Nina stood up. "All right, you're clean. Let's go."

She turned and stepped away with Alden beside her. Draker followed.

Their footsteps crunched in the gravel/grass mixture, and in a few steps they were at the building. The door groaned again as Nina pulled it open—a harsh, metallic sound that Draker was beginning to grow accustomed to.

Draker squinted as light spilled out. He squared his shoulders.

He'd adapted to military life, to being a cop. He would adapt to the Pit too. Had to.

For his ultimate goal of uncovering Windbrook and clearing his name.

For his old life.

For a chance to make things right.

Draker blinked, his surroundings clarifying. A long hallway. Concrete. Flickering amber lighting.

As Draker followed Nina inside, Alden fell into step behind them. Draker's hand instinctively moved to his lower back, seeking the reassuring weight of his Glock. But there was nothing there.

In the military, he'd been taught to always have an exit strategy. As a cop, he'd learned to trust his gut, no matter what. But here—in the world of illegal brawling—none of that meant a damn thing.

The door clanged behind them—a prison cell slamming shut.

CHAPTER
THIRTEEN

Draker followed the other two, stepping into the repurposed warehouse.

A stench hit him hard: sweat, blood, desperation. The building creaked and groaned. Voices in the distance—shouts, laughter. Peeling paint, exposed wiring, makeshift partitions.

The Pit.

Their footsteps echoed off the bare concrete walls as Nina led him down a corridor, dimly lit by bare bulbs dangling from wires stapled along the ceiling. The lights flickered, revealing flecks of dust.

Alden stayed at Nina's side. One hand was held in a light fist, fingers moving. Draker caught the faint sound of stones clicking together.

Nina glanced back.

"So, Mav," she said. "Here's how it works."

"I'm listening."

"I've got a look-the-other-way deal with a few crooked cops. That's how, for the last few years, we've been able to use this place. Two days. Out of three sixty-five. That's it. But for those two days, inside these old walls, the fighters transform. Out there, they're nobodies—construction workers, landscapers, office drones. In here, they're titans. Me? I'm just a humble waitress." She snickered.

They turned a corner.

"Fighters are divided into Cells," Nina continued. "Groups of six. You bunk together."

"Why the small groups?"

Nina shrugged. "It creates a sort of... self-regulating environment. These guys are maniacs. I can't control them myself."

At this, Alden gave a slight nod, his first communication of any sort since he'd shaken hands with Draker.

They turned another corner.

"No leader in the Cells," Nina continued. "It's about mutual respect and..." she hesitated.

"And?" Draker prompted.

"And fear of collective punishment," Nina said, meeting his eyes. "One fighter steps out of line, the whole group pays. Keeps everyone in check."

Draker raised an eyebrow. "Intense."

"It is," Nina said. "But it works. They keep each other in line better than any guards could."

She glanced back at him with a look that said, *You're not gonna be a troublemaker, are you?*

"Fighting begins tomorrow. I open the door for fifteen minutes, let the wives and girlfriends in to watch from the stands. Few show up. Most don't want to see their men get their faces smashed in."

They walked on. The Pit's oppressive atmosphere pressed down. Nina paused, pointing to their left. "It's not all work here though. We have three communal spaces spread throughout the building."

Alden positioned himself to the side, watching Draker take in the new environment.

Draker followed Nina's gesturing hand to a crude rec area of sorts. Mismatched, battered sofas and chairs sat around a few scarred coffee tables. Dog-eared magazines were strewn about, many of them pornographic.

A small, outdated TV hung on the wall, the screen flickering with static. Stacks of DVDs and—delving even deeper into anachronistic nostalgia—VHS tapes were on the wall beside it.

In one corner stood a pool table with a few bent cues leaning against it. Orange extension cords twisted on the floor. Draker heard the rumble of generators from somewhere on the other side of the exterior wall.

Despite the room's rough appearance, a handful fighters were lounging—muscle-bound arms and legs splayed over vintage furniture— engaged in hushed conversations. Two of them looked Draker's direction, scowled.

"Helps keep the tension down," Nina explained. "At least a little."

She took off again. Draker and Alden followed.

Nina said, "I keep it pretty simple around here. No phones. No weapons. No leaving the Pit."

"Any other rules?" Draker said.

Nina smirked. "Just one: survive."

As they continued down the corridor, Draker noticed a short, empty hallway branching off to their left—dark, no visible security cameras. His internal compass kicked in, and he realized they were in the area of the building where the transom window should be.

He surreptitiously glanced down the hallway. There was the window—at the far end of the hallway, hidden in the shadows.

Alden's eyes narrowed slightly, as if he'd noticed Draker's interest in the hallway.

Nina stopped at an intersection. "You're in Cell 3. The room is down there, on the left. Good luck, Mav. You're gonna need it."

With that, she turned and vanished into the shadows.

Alden, however, lingered. His gaze fixed on Draker. A moment later, he followed Nina into the darkness.

And Draker was alone in the Pit.

CHAPTER
FOURTEEN

Draker moved through the corridor, following Nina's instructions. More echoing footsteps. The air grew thicker.

Ahead was the door to his cell—another rusty job, not unlike the main door at the front of the building. "3" was spray painted on it.

The smell of too many bodies seeped out. He heard rumbling voices, a belt of dark laughter.

He paused. Hand on the doorknob—the metal was scratched, uneven, too warm. He took a breath, exhaled, pushed the door open. Hinges screeched.

Inside was a concrete box. Air thick with unclean humanity. Lights flickered, casting sharp shadows. Five men looked up. They wore tank tops, tees, jeans, boots. Hard eyes, sizing Draker up. Hostility hung heavy.

Draker scanned the room. Rusted bunk beds against peeling walls. Thin, stained mattresses.

This was a cage, not a room.

The fighters lounged on beds and leaned against walls. They were battle-worn. Scars, crooked noses, cauliflower ears. Eyes wary and aggressive as they stared at the newcomer.

A big man stepped forward. Caucasian. Thirties. Looked like a biker. Wild beard, tattoos up his arms. A mountain of muscle.

"Well, well," the man rumbled. "You lost, pretty boy?"

Draker met his gaze, kept his face neutral. "Nope. Not lost. I'm where I'm supposed to be."

The man puffed out his chest. He smelled of stale cigarettes and cheap booze. "That so?"

"Mm-hmm. I'm here to fight," Draker said. "Same as you."

The man's eyes narrowed. "They call you Mav, huh? Funny, never heard of you."

Draker stayed silent, jaw clenched.

Tension thickened. The others watched. Draker surreptitiously took in more of his surroundings—noting the exits and potential weapons. Out of habit.

Just as the situation seemed ready to explode, a smaller man pushed his way between them—a young, wiry guy, with twitchy movements, wearing a stained tank top and baggy pants.

"Whoa, whoa, guys! Let's not do this, all right?" the newcomer said, his voice high-pitched with anxiety. He turned to face the biker, hands raised in a placating gesture. "Come on, Crusher. You know Mav, right? From that club in Detroit?"

Detroit? That wasn't part of "Mav's" backstory. Draker had barely developed any backstory at all for his character; Beau hadn't given him time.

The guy was lying on the spot.

So Draker kept his face blank, went along with it, whatever this stranger was doing.

The smaller man turned to him. Offered a tentative smile. He was young, maybe twenty, with an old-fashioned face, like he just stepped out of the celluloid of a 1950s movie. Deep-set eyes. Shaggy hair.

"Good to see you again, Mav. Remember me? I'm Tank, man!" He emphasized the name, as if trying to jog Draker's memory.

Despite the deadly situation, Draker had to suppress a grin.

No matter how good of a fighter this kid might be, he was no "Tank"—he was about five-seven, sub-150 pounds.

The big guy—"Crusher," Draker now knew his name to be—looked between them. Scowled. For a moment, it seemed like he might call the younger man's bluff. But then he shrugged. "Whatever," he said and shot Draker a glare. "Watch yourself, Mav. This ain't Detroit."

He turned away.

Tank exhaled. Tension drained from his shoulders. "Close one," he whispered.

"Why'd you do that?" Draker said.

Tank scanned the room, making sure they were off the radar, then leaned in close. "Last year was my first Pit tournament. Look at me—don't exactly inspire immediate fear, do I?" He snickered, a wry twist to his mouth as he motioned to his slight frame. "I heard there was going to be an unknown newcomer joining our Cell, figured I'd lend a hand."

Draker nodded. "Thanks."

"I'm Ricky, by the way," he said, whispering even quieter. "I go by Tank here, but my real name's Ricky." He looked at Draker expectantly.

"I'm just gonna stick with 'Mav,' sorry," Draker said.

A flash of disappointment on Ricky's face. Then that youthful grin returned just as quickly.

"Okay, sure. Sure thing, Mav. Come on."

As Ricky led him away to the opposite side of the space, Draker's attention snagged on a lean, muscular black man resting against the far wall, watching Draker. Cold eyes. A predator's stare.

"That's Blitz," Ricky said. "Mean dude. I'd steer clear if I were you."

Draker nodded, filed away the information. He'd encountered men like Blitz before—the quiet ones who exploded into violence without warning. They were often the most dangerous.

"And Crusher you met," Ricky continued, jerking his thumb

toward the tattooed biker. "Always looking for a fight, so watch your back." He gestured to two others. "Viper and Jackal. They keep to themselves mostly."

Draker absorbed it all, his mind working on how to navigate this volatile environment. Each fighter was a potential threat.

"Tournament starts tomorrow." Ricky said as he sat on the lower bunk. "Brutal stuff. No holds barred. People die."

Draker felt the weight settle. He was deep in now, surrounded by killers and desperate men. But somewhere here were the answers he and Beau needed...

...to catch the Watchdog.

Up to this point, Draker had been hyper focused on becoming Mav, on hardening himself to survive the tournament. So much so, he'd nearly lost sight of the bigger picture: halting a terrorist attack.

This fight wasn't just about making it out of the ring—it was about tracking down a predator hidden among wolves.

"Thanks for your help," Draker said to Ricky as he climbed into the bunk above the younger man.

Springs dug into Draker's back the moment he lay down and clasped his hands behind his neck. He smelled mold.

The room grew quieter, but Draker could still feel eyes upon him. He ignored it, stared at the cracked ceiling. Water stains formed abstract patterns in the dim light—Rorschach tests waiting to be interpreted.

And though he'd moments earlier reminded himself of the need to refocus on the Watchdog, his mind went to a different person.

Alyssa.

Alyssa—Cassandra—the wife he'd had, lost, the woman he'd loved for five years, was married to for two, the woman who'd tried to kill him less than a week earlier in Ventura, California.

Even now—after the revelations, after she'd tried to kill him—Draker's mind sometimes couldn't separate the fake Alyssa from the true Cassandra.

There had been many dark and deadly moments already in his short career as Beau's Ranger, and despite knowing who Cassandra truly was, he still found himself yearning for his wife, Alyssa.

In the dark moments.

Moments like right now.

Lying in a bed, surrounded by the roughest men in the world. Ruthless fighters. Killers.

Cassandra Wynne was a killer. She'd tried to kill Draker.

But still, he felt Alyssa's warmth by his side, yearned for it, something soft and beautiful to push away this hell he'd found himself in.

Draker closed his eyes.

CHAPTER
FIFTEEN

The next morning

I t had been a long time since Ricky Braddock had been optimistic.
 But today was different.
He sat on the edge of his bunk. The tournament was about to begin—less than an hour till Nina Hollis's opening speech. This year was Ricky's chance to change everything. He didn't dwell on the details. Didn't want to jinx it. But the possibility of winning buzzed inside him. Because someone new had arrived last night—Mav—and with his arrival, Ricky felt a change in fortune, something like… hope.
He glanced around the dump that was his two-day home: Cell 3. Blitz, Crusher, and most of the other fighters were still asleep, at least two of them snoring. The rusty bunk beds that groaned.
Ricky's eyes settled on Mav. The new guy. Already awake, looking groggy yet prepared. Something about him inspired confidence. Tough as nails, no doubt. Ricky would get his ass beat if he had to face him in the ring, no doubt. But if not—having someone like that on his side would be a boon.

He decided to break the ice, walked over to Mav's bunk. "How'd you sleep?"

Mav looked down at him, stretched, grimaced. "Like shit."

Ricky chuckled. "This ain't exactly a luxury suite here."

Mav swung his legs over the edge of his bed, stretched again, arms going over his head. He hopped down.

"You ready for the Pit?" Ricky said.

"As ready as I'll ever be."

"You'd better be! You already dropped a thousand bucks on this."

"Huh?"

Ricky just stared at him for a moment. "The thousand-dollar entry fee."

"Oh, yeah. Right. Remind about the prize money?"

Again, Ricky just stared.

Why the hell would Mav need a reminder about the prize money? That was the only reason anyone came to the Pit!

Ricky remembered last night's discussion among Cell 3 before Mav arrived. Everyone was confused about this newcomer, someone no one had ever heard of before.

Blitz had said that Mav might be a cop...

Ricky considered this now.

No! No, Mav wasn't a cop. No way. Ricky had such an optimistic feeling about the guy; he wouldn't let that be soiled by Blitz's perpetual skepticism.

He disregarded it all.

"Everyone puts in a thousand buck to enter," he told Mav. "Winner takes fourteen grand. Second place gets six. Third takes home four. Everyone else gets zip."

Mav raised an eyebrow. "That's some serious incentive."

"Tell me about it," Ricky said. "A grand's no pocket change for guys like us. Some here are unemployed. Some are addicts. It's a big risk." He paused. Thought about his own situation. "For many of us, that entry fee was everything..."

Mav turned to face him. He seemed to understand the subtext of what Ricky had just said.

"I was here last year," Ricky continued. He'd tried to say it as a statement, but it came out as an admission—which, really, it was. "I lost my thousand dollars when I didn't place. But this year..." he let the sentence hang for a second, visualizing his outcome. "This year's gonna be different."

Before Mav could respond, a loud bang on the door made them both jump.

"Time to gather, ladies!" a gruff voice shouted. Leon Alden.

Ricky stood up. Heart pounding. "This is it," he muttered.

They joined the others in the hallway. Familiar faces mixed with new ones. Ricky glanced at Mav again. Yeah, this year was definitely going to be different.

They turned a corner and entered the central area of the warehouse—thirty-foot ceiling with trusses spanning its width, steel columns, concrete floor. A fighting cage dominated the center, chain link in an octagon pattern. Flattened cardboard boxes were spread haphazardly over the concreted floor as rudimentary padding. Rows of bleachers surrounded the cage.

The setup looked like something out of a dystopian movie. Rusted metal. Dim lights to the side; blaring spotlights in the center. The air thick with anticipation, sweat, testosterone, cortisol.

Ricky spotted Nina Hollis and her assistant, Leon Alden, near the cage. Nina was deep in conversation, her face serious. Leon nodded, scribbling notes.

Alden, a burly figure and an old salt within the Pit's hierarchy, wore his usual impassive expression. The man was ostensibly Nina's assistant, but he was just as much—if not more so—her bodyguard. He stayed at her side like a well-trained dog, barking and biting at anyone who got too close.

Ricky had always wondered about Alden. The man seemed wired into every corner of the Pit. If Nina was the queen here, then Leon was her steward. Nina was the first of the Pit's leaders to have such an assistant, and many of the fighters viewed Alden as almost a second in command, not just an assistant, which pissed off a lot of them.

"Everyone, listen up!" Nina's voice cut through the murmurs. "Take a seat on the bleachers. Now!"

The fighters scrambled to comply. Boots clanged on metal as massive bodies dropped heavily onto the bleachers. Ricky found himself wedged between Mav and a burly guy he didn't recognize. There were metallic creaking sounds as the benches warped under the weight of muscular figures; Ricky hoped the seating wouldn't give way entirely.

Nina stepped into the center of the room. Her gaze swept over the fighters. Sharp. Calculating. Ricky felt electrified as her eyes passed over him, a split-second acknowledgment.

"Welcome to the tournament," Nina said, her voice booming through the vast space. "Welcome to the Pit."

CHAPTER
SIXTEEN

Draker felt like he was back in high school. Well, a nightmarish, macabre form of high school, anyway.

Because he was sitting on cold metal bleachers, the kind you'd find in any American school, wedged between Ricky and a burly fighter he didn't know. Nina Hollis's words still hung in the air. Behind her, dwarfing her, lit up brilliantly in the middle of the abandoned warehouse floor, was the octagon.

There was that smell again—a mix of old sweat, dried blood, and raw desperation. It seeped from the very walls, more apparent now than ever.

If the Pit hadn't felt real before, it did now.

Draker's eyes locked onto Nina Hollis. Even dwarfed by the cage, even surrounded by throngs of massive human beings—all of those brutes masquerading as men—her presence was commanding.

"Some of you have been here before," Nina said. Her voice carried through the space. "For others, this is your first time. Listen up."

Nina paced in front of them, eyes scanning the crowd.

Alden was positioned a few yards away at the corner of the

cage—the farthest Draker had seen him from Nina. His arms were crossed, bulging his biceps over his barrel chest, straining his gray t-shirt. His eyes scanned the crowd.

"In the Pit, it's simple," Nina said. "No eyes, no dick punches. Tap out if you must, but know that the other fighters are gonna shit all over you for doing so. Everything else?" She paused, gave a slight, dark smile. "Everything else is fair game. Show us what you're made of!"

The crowd gave an enthusiastic response of shouts and guttural noises and whistles.

"This is a double-elimination tournament," she continued. "Lose once, you're in the losers' bracket. Lose again, you're out. Winner takes home fourteen grand. Second place gets six. Third gets four. Fourth and below, you get jack shit."

A murmur rippled through the crowd.

Nina raised a hand. Silence fell. "The Pit wasn't always like this. It wasn't always held in this warehouse, and it wasn't always a tournament. It started as a regular fight club. Two guys, Jay McGarry and Tommy Burrows, started it."

A few older fighters nodded. They knew the history.

Alden was one of those who nodded.

"Things went south," Nina said. "McGarry and Burrows had a falling out. Turned into a bloodbath. That's when I stepped in. For the past five years, I've been running this tournament. Made it what it is today."

She let the words sink in. Her control over the crowd was impressive. Every fighter hung on her words. Draker included.

"Now, let's talk about our former champs," Nina said. "If you've won before, like Leon here—" She motioned toward Alden "—you can't compete for prize money again. But you're required to come back for exhibition fights when I call. Speaking of which..."

She turned toward the cage, gestured dramatically. "Let's kick things off with two of our former number ones. Gentlemen, if you please."

The crowd erupted as two men stepped forward. Draker was nearly thrown to the floor as the large man beside him jumped to his feet, hollering, waving a fist. Ricky got to his feet as well, like the rest of them. Draker followed suit.

His eyes widened as he studied the pair of men causing the commotion. They were massive. Bodies bulging with muscles. Faces like tree bark. Hands like bricks.

Not just fighters. Gladiators.

The first was black and fifty-something. As solid as one of the nearby steel columns. His beard was streaked with gray. His gaze was steady.

He reminded Draker a bit of Simpson...

On the opposite side was a white man in his forties—fiery red hair and a thick beard matching his intense presence. He moved with raw, aggressive energy, his pale skin marred by scars from past brawls.

The men entered the cage. No ceremony. No bell. No referee. Just immediate action, two behemoths sprinting from opposite sides of the octagon and colliding in an explosion of fists and elbows.

Draker felt something in his stomach—a sinking sense of dread. He'd been in more than his fair share of fights, both as a cop and now as Beau's Ranger. But this was different. Raw. Primal.

Knuckles met flesh. Sickening thuds. Grunts of pain and exertion filled the warehouse. Draker remembered the rules—or lack thereof. No eye gouging. No low blows. You could tap out, but it earned you nothing but scorn.

Everything else was fair game.

The fight was fast and ugly. The older guy swung a wild haymaker. The other man ducked under it and fired back with an uppercut. Blood flew in a spray, catching the light before it peppered the cardboard.

The older man spat blood but didn't fall. Charged again, slamming his opponent into the cage. Metal rattled and groaned under the impact.

Beside Draker, Ricky whooped and hollered. Draker stood motionless. This wasn't a fight. It was barely controlled savagery.

The younger fighter broke free, only to take a knee to the gut. He folded in half, gasping for air. The other man hammered down fists. Each blow echoed over the crowd.

More blood spattering the cardboard. And a tooth.

Just when it seemed to be over, the younger man wrapped his legs around the other one's torso. He flipped their positions. Now on top, he unleashed a barrage of elbows.

The brutality dragged on, neither man willing to surrender. Time blurred. The thuds became rhythmic, predictable. Draker's palms were slick with sweat. Heart pounding.

Finally, the older fighter landed a spinning back fist. Connected perfectly, right across the jaw. The other man's eyes rolled back. He crumpled.

The victor stood unsteadily. Chest heaving. Face masked with blood. He raised a trembling arm as the crowd roared.

Arms, shoulders, hands bashed into Draker from all sides. He stumbled.

And stared.

At the octagon.

The motionless man. The other one, staggering, barely staying on his feet.

Reality hit Draker hard. He would soon have to fight like that, endure that punishment.

As the cheers continued and Nina stepped forward to face the clamoring crowd, Draker faced his first true sense of doubt since he'd arrived. He had faced danger before. Plenty of times. But this was something else. A different game. No rules, no mercy, just raw, relentless combat.

He would have to adapt.

Fast.

The Pit was about to open. And Draker was going in.

CHAPTER
SEVENTEEN

Three more hours of brutal savagery.

And now it was time for a break.

The octagon had seen a relentless parade of violence since the initial exhibition bout between the two former champions. Fight after fight, leaving the cardboard on the floor stained dark with blood and sweat.

Draker's own bout was still to come, but he'd watched—dread percolating—as more than one man was carried out unconscious.

Finally, Nina had called for a midday intermission—a "lunch break," she'd called it with a smirk. Draker felt the weight of what was to come—an anticipatory dread—as the fighters around him dispersed from the bleachers, seeking food and a chance to take a shit.

Now, Draker was in one of the Pit's so-called "communal spaces," leaning back on a sagging couch, the kind where the stuffing was half gone and the springs dug into your spine. Cigarette smoke curled in lazy tendrils under the overhead lights, mixing with the smells of sweat and beer. A half-dozen guys, including Ricky, were in the space with him.

On the table in front of Draker was a smattering of bent-up magazines—a copy of *Hustler* on top. For a moment, Draker wondered why the magazines were so well used in this day of digital distractions, then he quickly remembered: no cell phones in the Pit.

When Draker had first arrived, fighters had filled the room, but now, thirty minutes later, only a half dozen lingered, most of them huddled near a pool table with a ragged felt top at the center of the room. Two of the guys were hunched over it, eyes narrowed, chalk dust on their knuckles, waiting for their turn to break. Behind them was a dartboard, lopsided, its face a cratered mess from years of missed shots.

In the chair next to Draker, Ricky fidgeted. Eyes darting around. Fear slathered all over his young face, nothing like the bravado he'd shown earlier. The three hours of brutality they'd witnessed had left a mark.

Draker felt his own nerves jangling. Training with Larkin, years on the force, and two weeks of experience as a vigilante fixer—it all seemed inadequate now. The cage fights loomed large, unlike anything he'd faced before. He'd been in scuffles, sure. But not this. Not raw, unrestrained violence.

"You okay?" Draker said.

Ricky jolted, as if he'd forgotten Draker was there. "Yeah, I'm... I'm fine," he said, voice shaky.

Draker raised an eyebrow. "You sure about that?"

Ricky's shoulders slumped. "No," he said. A beat passed, then, "I'm nervous as hell. I don't know if I can do this."

"It's normal to feel that way," Draker said. "This isn't a walk in the park. And besides, you did it before at last year's tournament."

"I know, but it's more than just nerves. I'm... I'm a fraud, man. I don't belong here."

Draker recognized the signs. He'd seen it in rookie cops fresh out of the academy. Even felt it himself once upon a time. A sense of being out of one's element, of being out-classed, overpowered.

"Why do you say that?" he said.

Ricky hesitated. "You guys are bigger than me. All of you. It's no secret; I obviously can't hide that fact. But there's this move I've been practicing. A flying knee strike. Could be devastating if I pull it off, but..."

"But what?"

"What if I mess up? Get hurt? Or embarrass myself in front of everyone?"

Draker turned to face him. "Listen, you have every right to be here. I'm sure every fighter here has had his doubts. The difference is in how you handle them."

Ricky looked up. A glimmer of hope in his eyes.

"That flying knee?" Draker continued. "It's your move. Own it. Don't let anyone, especially yourself, tell you otherwise."

That glimmer of hope on Ricky's face turned into a slight smile. There he went again, looking like so young, so old-fashioned, almost naive. If Draker didn't know better, if he wasn't fully aware that Ricky was a seasoned fighter who'd been in this brutal tournament once before, he would have sworn the kid was innocent.

"You think so?" Ricky said.

"I know so."

For a few moments, Draker had forgotten his own trepidation, but his encouragement for the other man brought the magnifying glass in his direction.

He'd offered Ricky his confidence... but was Ricky confident in himself?

His jaw tightened, hands twitched. The echoes of the day's fights still thudded in his ears—every brutal impact, every slap of flesh against flesh.

Draker had trained hard. And fast. Larkin had done a damn good job on him. But the blood, the fury—nothing could have prepared him for that.

Doubt came slicing through the edge of his confidence.

A soft beep sounded in Draker's ear. The communication device. Since he couldn't respond, he cleared his throat—the agreed-upon non-verbal. A moment later, Beau's voice came through, urgent. "I need you to meet with Sullivan and Larkin. Use the predetermined exit."

Draker cleared his throat again. He straightened. "I need to take a walk," he told Ricky. "Clear my head."

Ricky nodded. "Sure. Okay. Thanks, man. For everything."

Draker gave a quick nod and turned away. He kept his pace measured as he moved down the hallway. Didn't want to draw attention. The few fighters loitering around paid him no mind.

He headed for the escape route Beau had laid out, finding his way back to the corridor he'd first entered with Nina the previous night. Left turn, then right. Another left. The warehouse was a maze, but he'd memorized the path.

Finally, he reached the short, dark hallway that branched off to the side. There it was—the transom window in the shadows.

He double-checked that no one was looking, then he eased to the side, out of view of the nearest camera. Sticking to the shadows, he did a loop and circled back, going down the side hallway.

The transom window was at the very top of the wall, so he had to stretch to reach it. There was a small latch that he unclasped, then he eased the window open, wincing at the slight creak. He listened. No alarm.

He carefully pressed against the window's particleboard cover until it worked itself free of the two nails—falling with a soft thud onto the grass outside—then used his arms and core strength to pull himself up and into the opening, his face thrusting out into the cool night air. It was a tight fit, but he struggled for only a few moments before he slipped outside, falling into a controlled roll beside the piece of particleboard.

Outside, the crisp breeze was a jolt after the stuffy interior. He scanned the area. The warehouse loomed behind—a hulking shadow. Ahead, a line of trees. Leaves rustled softly.

"Okay, I'm outside, Beau," Draker whispered as he got onto his tiptoes, reached back through the opening, and pulled the window shut.

"Good," Beau's voice crackled in his ear. "Anything to report before we proceed?"

"Actually, yes. A person of interest within the Pit: Leon Alden. He's ostensibly Nina Hollis's bodyguard and assistant, but he gave me a... strange feeling. He seemed to be watching me more carefully than others."

"Interesting."

"Nina assured me she told no one else in the tournament about my undercover status, but I'm wondering if, for her own security, she might have informed Alden without telling me. Because he seemed very interested in my presence."

"Wait..." Beau said, his Texas drawl taking on a note of excitement. "You think you got a lead on the Watchdog already?"

Draker shook his head, even though Beau couldn't see him. "Not necessarily. But Alden is definitely worth looking into. Something about him just doesn't sit right with me."

"Understood," Beau said. "I'll dig into his background. Now, before you meet Sullivan and Larkin, I've got some news of my own to share. Remember that lead on Simpson? Well, I've found out more about Daniel Harper."

Draker was kneeling to pick up the particleboard. He froze. "Go on."

"He's a former CIA operative who used various aliases during his career, including some that resemble 'Simpson.' Harper's records show involvement in covert activities around the same time and places as your supposed Agency mission in Afghanistan."

As Draker grabbed the particleboard and stood up to cover the window again, his mind whirled with the revelation. If Daniel Harper had used multiple aliases, what did that mean for the depths of Windbrooks's operations in Afghanistan?

Beau continued. "I've uncovered a series of addresses, financial records, and travel logs connected to Harper. I'm working on tracking down a current location for him. I'll keep you posted."

Draker placed the board back onto the window, giving it a soft push. "Thanks, Beau."

"You betcha. Your friends are waiting for you. Talk soon."

Another soft beep in Draker's ear and Beau was gone.

A flash of light—a cell phone screen—signaled from the tree line.

Draker scouted the nearby cameras, then moved toward the light. Twigs snapped underfoot. Each sound amplified. Two figures emerged from the shadows. Sullivan and Larkin.

"How's it going in there?" Sullivan said, keeping her voice low.

"It's been... interesting," Draker said. The word didn't cover half of it. "I'm alive."

Larkin smirked. "Alive, he says. That's why I'm here. To make sure you stay that way. We're taking your ass back to the gym."

Sullivan glanced between him and the warehouse. Tense. "We don't have much time. You need to get back before anyone notices."

Draker looked at Larkin, who had a sparkle in his eye, seemingly eager.

"Well..." Draker said. "What the hell are we waiting for?"

CHAPTER
EIGHTEEN

Larkin would make a fighter out of Draker, whether the guy liked it or not.

His right hook was well placed, but Draker twisted and it missed his chin by a hair.

Not bad.

The gym was silent except for their heavy breathing and the dull thud of blows.

A single overhead lamp. Plenty of shadows.

"What did you learn watching the fights today?" Larkin said. He threw another hook.

Draker ducked. His reflexes were sharp, despite the fatigue written all over him. He parried the next punch. "That this is going to be brutal. That I'm in over my head."

Well, that was a hell of a disappointing response after how well he was performing...

The kid had potential, but he wasn't digging deep enough. Larkin had seen it before—the surface-level stuff, the easy answers. He wanted more from Draker, needed more.

The kid wasn't there yet. Nowhere close.

"Gloves off!" Larkin barked.

He stripped off his gloves. Draker did the same.

They circled each other, each searching for an opening. Draker moved first. Lunged for a takedown. Larkin sidestepped, letting Draker sail right past. In a heartbeat, Draker was on the mat, arm pinned.

"It's about adaptability," Larkin said, releasing him.

Larkin got up, stepped away, allowing Draker to climb to his feet.

They reset.

Draker was more cautious now. He feinted left, went for a single-leg takedown. Larkin countered, swept Draker's other leg...

... and sent him sprawling again.

"Adaptability, damn you!" Larkin repeated, shouting this time as he moved in, dropping to the mat, pinning Draker with a heavy forearm.

As they continued to grapple, Larkin found himself impressed by Draker's raw strength and determination. The kid had heart, no doubt about that. But he was still too rigid, too stuck in his ways. Every move was textbook perfect, and that was the problem —real fights weren't won by the book.

Draker managed to get Larkin in a headlock, but his grip was too loose. Larkin slipped out easily, transitioned into a rear naked choke. "*Adaptability*," he hissed into Draker's ear.

Draker broke free, scrambled back to his feet, fists up but too low, panting. There was fire in his eyes now.

Good. Maybe he was getting it.

But "maybe" wasn't enough. Larkin needed to drive the point home. He set Draker up, feinting a shot for the legs.

As Draker moved to defend, Larkin changed direction, sweeping Draker's legs out from under him. In a blink, Larkin had him pinned.

"*Adaptability!*" Larkin said, practically screaming now. It was the fourth time he'd had to say it. Draker deserved to be screamed at.

He stood, looking down at Draker, this quasi-student of his

who had been forced upon him. Frustration mingled with concern. Draker had potential. But he wasn't there yet.

"That's your problem," Larkin said sharply. "You're too rigid. Stuck in your cop training."

Draker sat up but didn't get to his feet this time. He wrapped his arms around his knees, panting. Exhausted, confused.

"You know, kid," Larkin said, "you remind me of someone. Octavius. He's... the real reason I stopped fighting, not this." He pointed to his milky white eyeball. "Hell, I could've kept going with one eye. Depth perception be damned. But Octavius... that's a whole other story."

Larkin shook his head. For a brief moment, he felt it again, the whole of it, the brunt of it—the old pain. But as quickly as it had appeared, he pushed it away again.

Draker's eyes were on him, possibly searching for clarification, for details about who Octavius was.

He wasn't going to get them.

Larkin had seen fighters like Draker before. Talented but trapped by their own mindset. Some learned to adapt. Others broke.

Which would Draker be?

CHAPTER
NINETEEN

The woods seemed to close in around the Watchdog, breathless with anticipation, as if they knew something big was about to happen.

He crouched in a patch of open ground, eyes fixed on the gadget he'd placed on the dirt ahead. Sunlight sliced through the trees in streaks. He had the entire area to himself. No prying eyes anywhere.

He glanced at his watch—12:37 PM. Right on schedule.

A deep inhale, exhale, steadying his hands. Then he made the final adjustments to the miniature bomb—only a fraction of the size of what he had planned for the actual attack. Slowly, sloooowly, he pulled his hands away from the device.

One backward step. And another, his eyes remaining on the device.

It looked stable.

Satisfied, he turned around, crunched through the undergrowth to a safe distance, then crouched again, this time behind a massive oak. He peered out from his cover as he took out the detonator.

... which also happened to be his cellphone.

Gotta love modern technology.

The Watchdog took a deep breath. Held it. Then he tapped the button.

For a split second, nothing happened.

Then the world opened up.

The blast reverberated through the forest. Visceral. So loud the Watchdog felt it in his bones. A smoky funnel of dirt rocketed into the sky. The shockwave crashed into him a moment later, a force that rippled his shirt, his pants. He grabbed the oak, nearly toppled over.

All around were the sounds of debris settling in the undergrowth. Coughing in the dust cloud, the Watchdog removed his right arm from where he'd placed it over his head to shield himself; he pulled his other arm from the tree trunk. He stood, blinking as he wiped dirt from his face. Then he approached the blast site.

There was a crater—three feet wide, two feet deep. The surrounding earth was scorched black.

He smiled. It had worked perfectly.

After making his way back to the van—which he'd parked just past the tree line—he threw open the rear doors and plopped his ass on the floor with his legs dangling outside. For a moment, he listened to the trees, to the hollow emptiness that was even quieter than when he'd first set up his experiment—the blast had scared the forest into quietude.

Then he pulled out his phone and typed a message.

It's done. The test was successful.

The response came almost immediately: *Good. Any complications?*

None. Everything went according to plan.

His associate replied: *Fantastic.*

The Watchdog deleted the conversation, dropped the phone into his pocket, shut the doors. He circled around the van, climbed into the driver's seat, and turned the key.

Gravel crunched under the tires as he pulled away, leaving the clearing behind. With the experiment complete, he immediately moved on, planning his next moves in the bigger scheme. Specifically, he thought about how he would put his explosives to use.

The people he was going to kill were the epitome of the intellectual decay he despised. It was a thrill indeed to know he would soon strike a blow against this decadence.

But it was just the beginning. The entire system was broken, starting with compulsory education, which pumped out waves of people who couldn't think for themselves.

Universities took the lead from there, more focused on coddling soft minds than sharpening them. The end result was a society where ignorance thrived and wisdom took a backseat.

The Watchdog's own education had been the beginning of his revelations. Growing up in suburban Houston, he'd always felt out of step with his peers. He'd excelled in school, driven by a thirst for knowledge the other kids lacked. Even then, even so young, he'd seen the cracks in the system—teachers more concerned with test scores than actual learning, students who viewed education as a chore rather than an opportunity.

He went to the University of Illinois looking for kindred spirits. Found none. Just the same old scene—a lazy pursuit of degrees for future paychecks. He graduated with a business administration degree, more disillusioned than ever.

The corporate world was the last straw. As a project manager at a mid-sized firm, he saw it firsthand. Mindless consumption. Mediocrity on a pedestal. The lowest common denominator celebrated daily.

With years of exposure behind him, he saw the results of a broken system everywhere he looked. People glued to their smartphones, devouring mindless content. "News" that was nothing more than thinly veiled propaganda. A populace so distracted by trivialities that they couldn't see the decay eating away at the foundations of society.

That's when the idea formed. Humanity needed a wake-up call—a violent shake from its slumber. So he quit. Sacrificed everything—his home, his ties to the "normal" world. All to pursue his mission: enlightenment through destruction.

His next attack would be a wake-up call. Loud and violent. A reminder that actions had consequences. When the dust cleared and the bodies were counted, people would have to face the hard truths they'd been avoiding.

The Watchdog smiled at the thought. Everything was falling into place. His associate's obsession with revenge afforded the Watchdog the perfect accomplice, too blinded by personal goals to see the bigger picture. Truly, his accomplice wasn't a partner but a pawn the Watchdog was moving around the board.

Driving through the trees, his mind ticked through the details. The test bomb had gone off without a hitch, which meant the bigger devices would be even better…

… or worse for those who would absorb the brunt of it.

Everything was a matter of perspective.

A few adjustments were necessary, but everything was shaping up as the Watchdog had mapped it out, right on target.

He thought about the components stacked in his storage unit —wires, detonators, explosives. All handpicked and gathered over months. Taken individually, the pieces were not intimidating. Some of them were entirely benign.

But together, they'd be something else entirely.

Together, they'd change the world.

CHAPTER
TWENTY

Of course Draker looks beaten, Sullivan thought. *He's been literally beaten for the last hour.*

Sullivan stood in the dimly lit gym, eyes fixed on Draker. He sat hunched over a battered folding chair outside the boxing ring. Shirtless. Dripping sweat. Larkin's training session showed itself in Draker's flushed skin, the contusions, the nicks and cuts.

The latest round of training with Larkin had concluded three minutes earlier. Draker had limped out of the ring to the chair, and Larkin had disappeared in the opposite direction. Sullivan hadn't moved. Draker seemed to need a moment or two alone.

Her gaze lingered on Draker's muscular torso. She'd noticed his physique before. But seeing him like this—raw, exposed—was different. Impressive. She pushed the thought aside. Focused. She walked over to him.

"Beau mentioned your tip on Leon Alden," she said, her voice breaking the silence so abruptly it even startled herself. "He and I have been investigating Alden, and I've discovered something."

Draker looked up. Eyes sharp despite his exhaustion. "What is it?"

Sullivan pulled over the other chair. Its feet scraped loudly against the concrete. "There's a connection between Alden and one of the fighters from the Pit's original schism."

Draker winced as he shifted positions, a quick spasm as one of his bruised ribs protested. "Wait, you've mentioned this schism before, and so did Nina Hollis. Something about two guys named McGarry and Burrows. I need the whole story."

Sullivan nodded, realizing she'd skipped over vital context before plunging Draker into the thick of things. There had been so little time though. One minute she was meeting Draker, the next she was watching him get his ass beat by Grady Larkin, and then she was driving away from him, leaving him alone at the Pit.

"Right, sorry," she said. "Let me back up a bit."

Draker began to nod his thanks, but it was quickly truncated by another grimace as he dabbed at a cut above his eye.

"The Pit started as a small fight club in Louisville, Kentucky," Sullivan began. "Two laid-off factory workers, Jay McGarry and Tommy Burrows, founded it after the 2008 financial crisis. It was their way of coping, I guess."

"A fight club, huh?" Draker said. "Like the movie?"

Sullivan nodded. "Exactly."

"You know, in almost every shot of *Fight Club*, there's a Starbucks cup. It's a fun little Easter egg to search for when you watch the film," Draker threw in casually.

Sullivan blinked, taken aback by the randomness. "Um…"

"I like older movies," Draker said, answering her non-question.

"*Fight Club* isn't *that* old."

Draker shrugged. "October '99. That's more than a quarter-century."

Sullivan opened her mouth. Then closed it. Damn. She didn't realize how old she was getting.

She shook it off. "Anyway, at first the Pit was just chaotic brawls in any number of locations, wherever they could find. It wasn't a contest. No money traded hands. It was more of a male-bonding experience. Therapy, if you will. Like the movie. The fights were tough, of course, but not so savage."

Draker hissed as he stretched out his leg, turning it to find a nasty bruise on his calf. "How'd it turn into... this?"

"As it grew, they started implementing rules, structure. And a money structure. It spread beyond Louisville, attracting fighters from all over. That's when the problems began."

"Let me guess," Draker said, rolling his shoulder experimentally. "McGarry and Burrows didn't see eye to eye?"

"Exactly. McGarry wanted to keep it raw, underground, and free. Burrows saw dollar signs. Wanted to expand, commercialize."

"And the other fighters took sides."

"That's right. It all came to a head in a massive brawl in a parking lot. We're talking an all-out war here, Draker. Dozens of fighters, maybe even a hundred, tearing into each other with bare fists, improvised weapons, anything they could get their hands on. By the end, the parking lot looked like a war zone. McGarry, Burrows, and several others died in the chaos, including Nina Hollis's boyfriend, Ryan Hayes. It was a bloodbath that changed everything."

"Shit," Draker said.

"After that, Nina took over," Sullivan said. "The fighters were sympathetic to her grief over losing her boyfriend, Ryan, in the brawl. It also helped that she had a reputation as a natural mediator from her volunteer work with a local conflict-resolution center—something she did on the side of her regular job as a waitress. The men saw her as a neutral party who could potentially heal the divide.

"Most of the fighters rallied behind Nina to unify the organization, though some remained bitter about a woman taking over their men's club. Despite the initial resistance, Nina managed to expand the Pit into what it is today." Sullivan paused, watching

Draker absorb the information. "Which brings us back to Leon Alden."

Draker leaned forward, wincing slightly. "What's his connection to all this?"

"That's what I'm trying to figure out," Sullivan said. "He seems to have had a strong tie to one of the original factions."

"Which side? Jay McGarry's or Tommy Burrows's?"

"Don't know. I've found evidence of continuous, encrypted communications between Alden and an email address I've traced back to a close associate of either McGarry or Burrows, someone with ties to the original schism, lost to time. The encryption is tough to crack, so I can't tell which of the two men it's linked to yet, but it's definitely one of them. These communications have been ongoing since before Nina took over, suggesting Alden has deeper ties to the Pit's original leadership than we thought.

"And here's where things get really interesting. Ostensibly, Alden is there to support Nina, to protect her from the whole no-tiny-woman-is-going-to-run-my-men's-fight-tournament thing. But what I've found suggests he's more than just Nina's assistant and bodyguard. I'm not sure about his exact role yet, but there're records of Alden attending meetings with fight promoters and venue owners in other cities, often without Nina present. He also seems to handle a lot of the financial aspects of the Pit, beyond what you'd expect from a typical assistant and bodyguard."

Draker's gaze drifted. Wheels turning. She admired that about him. The way he pieced together fragments. When Beau had first called and made his offer of help by dispatching a field agent named Ty Draker, he'd told her Draker was a high-level investigator. She could see why.

"You've done your research," Draker said as he turned back to her. "And you said your boss was just humoring you by sending you out here? Jameson, was it?"

Sullivan scoffed. "Yeah. SAC Jameson basically laughed me out of his office."

Draker's eyes widened. "Seriously?"

"He said it was a waste of resources, that my leads were flimsy since I dredged them up from the dark web. He told me to go ahead and follow up on things if I wanted, but only because he wanted to 'keep me happy.'" She clenched her fists. "It cut deep. Not gonna lie. Jameson's always had my back, even if he can dismissive sometimes. But this time... it felt different. Like he didn't respect me or my work at all."

"Then we're just gonna have to prove him wrong, aren't we?" Draker said. He gave her a grin.

Sullivan chuckled. "Damn right we are."

A particularly dark bruise on Draker's side caught Sullivan's eye. Without thinking, she reached out and touched it. Draker winced but didn't pull away.

Her hand lingered on his warm skin, fingers resting in the valleys of his side—obliques and the contours of his rib cage. A jolt ran through her. She felt a flush rise to her cheeks.

Their eyes met. Held. Realizing how long her hand had been there, she pulled back.

And turned away.

"Want me to get you something for that?" she said, motioning toward the bruise without looking back at him.

Draker smirked. Glanced around the rundown gym. "What exactly are you going to get me?"

She returned her attention to him, grinned. "Fair point."

"But thanks," he said softly.

She cleared her throat. "How are you feeling about the tournament?"

"Oh, I'm as optimistic as can be hoped," Draker said, his tone bordering on sarcastic. "There's this guy in my cell, Blitz. He took an immediate disliking to me. Don't know if it's related to our investigation, but I don't like the look of him."

Sullivan nodded. Made a mental note. "Anyone else?"

"Yeah. A young guy. Ricky. Seems innocent enough, but..." Draker trailed off, shaking his head. "Who's *really* innocent in the Pit?"

She studied his face, saw something else in his eyes. Worry.

"Is that it?" she said. "Seems like something else is bothering you."

Draker hesitated. Then sighed. "There's this guy I look out for. Milo. I take care of him from afar through video calls—part of my work for Beau—but I can't do that here without my phone. Milo's my Pal." He laughed suddenly. "That's 'Pal' with a capital P, another Beau-ism." His mood became more serious again. "And Milo's been suffering from agoraphobia. I'm just... worried about the kid, I guess."

A warmth spread in Sullivan's chest. This protective side of Draker that had just presented itself made him even more attractive.

"I'm sure he'll be okay," she said. "You can check on him soon." She paused. "I wish I'd brought your phone with me so you could call him. Sorry."

Draker waved it off, but the worry remained on his face. Sullivan fought the urge to reach out again. To offer more than words. But she held back. Aware of the line between them.

"What led to Milo being a shut-in?" Sullivan asked.

Draker looked off for a moment. "Rough childhood. A lot of trauma."

Sullivan didn't respond.

When Draker turned back to her, he tilted his head slightly and said quietly, "Can you relate?"

He'd picked up on the consternation on her face. He was perceptive.

Of course he was.

Sullivan nodded. Hesitated. Then said, "When I was a kid, I went through some... trauma myself, yeah." She stopped, swallowed. "My stepmother, Linda. She was... cruel. She liked having control, and I was just an easy target for that. There was this incident when I was ten. I accidentally broke something of hers."

Draker leaned in closer, crossing his arms on his knees. "What did she do?"

Sullivan hesitated, then continued. "One night, I knocked over a vase. Some old family heirloom of hers. Broke it into pieces. She went ballistic. And the more scared I got, the angrier she became. She grabbed me by the arm, dragged me to the basement door. I was crying, begging her to stop, but she wasn't hearing it. She just shoved me down into the basement. It was pitch black down there. And then she locked the door."

"Shit."

"I was down there for four days. Four *days*, Draker. Dad was out of town on business. Linda only opened the door to toss me some bread and water and to yell at me every few hours. The basement was unfinished and in the middle of renovations. No electricity. So... no light, no idea when it would end. Just me, alone, in the dark. All I could hear was the creaking of the floorboards when Linda would walk overhead... it was terrifying. I was huddled in a corner the whole time, too scared to move. I kept thinking... this is it. She's never going to let me out."

Draker said, "And when she did?"

"She released me with this cold look on her face. Just said, 'Next time, you'll stay down there longer.' Like it was nothing. But it wasn't nothing. It was everything to me. I was weak; I was broken."

Draker didn't say anything for a moment, just watched her carefully. Then he placed a hand on her shoulder. "No one should go through that. Not as a kid, not ever. But you're stronger than Linda ever was. Remember that."

Sullivan gave a weak smile. "I try. The incident had a huge impact on my life though, even now as an adult. It's given me certain phobias that have affected my career as an FBI agent. And sometimes I find myself struggling in situations that most normal people wouldn't think twice about."

Draker nodded slowly.

There was silence between them then.

After a moment, sensing a shift, Draker stood, wincing slightly. Sullivan winced too, as though she could feel it herself.

She'd gotten Draker into this predicament when she'd accepted the offer of a man named Beau, a perfect stranger who'd called her out of the blue.

Now, Ty Draker was pushing himself to the limit. Risking everything. Risking his life.

And all Sullivan wanted to do was touch the guy one more time.

CHAPTER
TWENTY-ONE

Back into the void. Draker eased through the window—with the particleboard pinched under his arm—wincing as his bruised ribs protested. He suppressed a grunt as he dropped into the hallway, which was dark and quiet. After waiting to listen, he was satisfied that he was alone and no one was approaching from the perpendicular main corridor. He replaced the board and continued on.

Back in the main hallway, he navigated the maze. Overhead lights, flickering. Shadows stretched long. Echoing footsteps. Passing by gruff faces, bulging arms, deadly eyes. Every turn looked the same. He was beginning to truly loathe this place.

Rounding a corner, two more fighters appeared. Hulking figures. They barely glanced his way. Faces hard. The hostility was immediate. Every man an island here at the Pit.

He returned to the communal space he'd left an hour earlier. It was now empty.

Finally, some luck.

He paused. Seeing the empty sofa somehow made his exhaustion even more apparent, his body subconsciously pulling him in that direction. He considered it. A few minutes alone wouldn't hurt. He slipped into the space and dropped onto the battered sofa with a soft groan.

He closed his eyes.

And he thought about Sullivan. A few minutes earlier. At the gym. The way her hand had lingered on his side. The electricity of her touch. He could still feel it. Unexpected. Something had shifted. She'd driven him back here to the Pit. They'd spoken for the first few minutes—comparing ideas about her intel on Leon Alden—but they'd been quiet for the final few minutes.

When Draker had stepped out of her Mercedes, he'd held the door open for a moment and turned back to find her leaning over the center console just like she had the previous time she dropped him off. She'd blinked. Large brown eyes. Soft Asian American features. She'd smiled tentatively. There'd been an awkward goodbye.

The thoughts of Sullivan led to Kylie Payton, a jarring shift, like an unintentional jump cut in an old silent film.

Kylie.

The woman he'd left behind in Ventura. They'd grown close quickly. Bonded under pressure. They'd spent a night together…

Well, only a few hours.

There'd been an urgent phone call from Beau, and they'd had to jump out of Kylie's bed, flee her house in the middle of the night.

But before that…

… they'd been together.

He shook his head. Tried to clear the memory. Part of him wanted to go back to California—not to his old life in Santa Clarita but to Ventura—to flee this hellhole, to heal his body during the cross-country trip, to go back to that city he'd grown to know during his second mission for Beau, to show up at Kylie's door…

But that wasn't an option.

This was his life now. A fixer for Beau. Jumping from crisis to crisis. Never staying long enough to form genuine connections. Larkin's voice echoed in his mind: *adaptability*.

Let go of the past.

Embrace the new reality.

But an entirely new reality wasn't an easy thing to adapt to. Just weeks ago, he'd thought he was happily married. Then, the truth about Alyssa had shattered that illusion. Five years together—a lie. She'd been spying on him for Windbrook. His world was upended.

For five years, Alyssa had been all he'd wanted, the only person he thought about in the ways that really mattered.

Now, he was thinking about Kylie. And he was thinking about Sullivan. All the while preparing for an underground fight.

If that wasn't a crash course in adaptability, Draker didn't know what was.

He sat up. Ran a hand through his hair. His gaze fell on magazines scattered across the table, a splash of color in the drab room.

Next to the stack was a pen.

Nice!

Draker grabbed it. Though he didn't have his iPhone, he'd memorized the details of the tutorial he'd been studying the last couple of days.

He'd mastered one step of the Tri-Phase Cascade pen-spinning trick; it was time to tackle the second step—the vertical flip transition.

He shifted his ring finger into position. As the pen completed its forward spin, it flew off his finger, clattered on the concrete.

Four more attempts sent the pen back to the concrete twice and to the table the other two times.

Draker picked up the pen. On his fifth try, he applied gentler pressure, lifting the pen smoothly. This transition needed just the right amount of force to flip the pen without disrupting its momentum.

His fingers adjusted, and he found the perfect balance between control and fluidity. The pen arched gracefully, flipping vertically into a new plane.

Draker grinned.

Second phase accomplished.

He set the pen back down beside the magazines, one of which caught his eye. Peeking out from beneath one of the porn offerings was a glossy general interest magazine, its cover adorned with celebrity photos and sensational headlines about the latest Hollywood gossip.

Amid the celebrity news and fashion tips, a smaller headline read, "Overcoming Agoraphobia: One Woman's Journey."

Milo immediately came to mind.

Draker picked up the magazine, flipped through the pages. This wasn't exactly a peer-reviewed journal, but without his phone and the invaluable BeauSearch Lite app, it was the best resource he had at the moment for Milo's struggles.

He found the article, started reading. The piece detailed Sarah Thompson, thirty-four, an accountant battling severe agoraphobia for over a decade. Before he got too deep into the article, Draker looked up, scanned the room, spotted a crumpled receipt. He retrieved it, flattened it out, and picked up the pen again.

"Exposure therapy," he said, writing the term down on the back of the receipt. The article described how Sarah's therapist had guided her through a series of gradually increasing challenges. It started with simply standing in her open doorway for thirty seconds a day, progressing to short walks to her mailbox and eventually to brief trips to nearby stores.

Draker read about cognitive-behavioral techniques Sarah had used to manage her anxiety. He scribbled down "breathing exercises" and "positive self-talk." Knowing Milo so well already, either of these techniques seemed well suited.

The article also touched on the importance of a support system. Sarah credited her recovery partly to a friend who had patiently accompanied her on her first outings, providing encouragement without pressure. Draker felt a pang of guilt, wishing he could be there for Milo in person.

But that was one of Beau's rules—Draker was never to meet his Pals in person.

Though Draker had broken that rule once already.

As he neared the end of the article, Draker found himself nodding along with Sarah's concluding thoughts: "Recovery isn't linear. There were days I felt I'd taken two steps back for every step forward. Persistence is key. Every small victory, no matter how tiny, is progress."

He set down the magazine, looked at his hastily scrawled notes. It wasn't a comprehensive treatment plan by any means, but it was a start. A sense of purpose settled over him. He might be stuck here in the Pit, surrounded by violence and danger, but he could still help Milo. His mind churned, formulating a plan, adapting Sarah's journey to fit Milo's needs.

Draker drew a line through the middle of the receipt beneath his notes and used the blank half to draft a clear, step-by-step guide for Milo. He knew he'd have to convey this information quickly the next time he had phone access.

As he wrote, he felt a tiny spark of hope.

Even in this hellish shithole, he could make a difference in someone's life.

CHAPTER
TWENTY-TWO

Draker had finished his notes, had taken a walk through dank hallways, and still had a few minutes to kill.

He wasn't sure why he'd come back here.

But he had.

He pulled open the pitted steel door with "3" spray painted on it. The rusty hinges bellowed, and the heavy door thudded shut behind him. Ricky and Blitz were there. Two other fighters from a different Cell were there too, napping. Why they were here, Draker assumed, was anyone's guess.

As Draker approached his bunk, Blitz stood up, approached, and stopped between Draker and his bed.

Blitz's eyes flicked to the clock on the wall. "You've been gone for an hour, *Mav*."

He'd put a particular emphasis on the last word, Mav—something like distrust or skepticism.

Draker shrugged. "Went for a walk."

It wasn't technically a lie, only a partial truth.

Blitz smirked. "Something's felt off about you since you got here. And I'm gonna figure it out."

They stared each other down. Draker's muscles tensed, ready to spring into action if needed.

Blitz's eyes narrowed. "You a cop?"

Draker almost snorted at the irony. He had been a cop only a couple of weeks ago in Santa Clarita. Blitz was either an incredibly good guesser or very intuitive; Draker suspected the latter.

But he stuck to his cover and said, "You're way off base."

Movement caught Draker's eye—Ricky was approaching them. Blitz's smirk widened. "Ah yes, you've been here less than a day, and you've already gotten yourself a little lapdog. Here, puppy, puppy!"

Ricky ignored the jab and positioned himself between Draker and Blitz. His eyes darted nervously. He hesitated once, twice before he spoke. "Come on, guys. We don't need this right now. The tournament's about to start up again."

Blitz's narrowed his eyes. "Stay out of this, shithead. Doesn't concern you."

"It concerns all of us," Ricky said. He'd said it confidently, but his voice had a tremor. "We're all in this Cell together. We should be watching each other's backs, not starting fights."

For a moment, Blitz looked like he might push past Ricky. His fists clenched at his sides, muscles tensing. But then…

… he snickered, body relaxing, shoulders lowering.

"Fine," Blitz said. His eyes flicked back to Draker. "But this isn't over. I'm watching you… 'Mav.'" He jabbed a finger in Draker's direction. "And when I find out what you're really doing here, you're fucked."

With that, Blitz stalked away, shouldering past Ricky roughly. Ricky grunted, grabbed his chest.

The tension in the room slowly dissipated, but Draker could feel Blitz's eyes boring into him from across the room. He didn't turn to look.

Draker turned to Ricky. "Thanks for stepping up. That right there proves you're not an impostor like you said earlier. You belong here as much as anyone else."

Ricky nodded, and a small, almost bashful smile formed.

Draker climbed into his bunk, and Ricky slid into the one beneath him.

As Draker stared up at the stained ceiling, he considered how Ricky's imposter syndrome was, strangely enough, somewhat similar to the agoraphobia Milo was suffering from.

It struck him that he was trying to help the similar issues of two very dissimilar young men.

Good to be needed...

A blaring alarm shattered his train of thought. It was blaring from the hallway beyond the steel door.

Intermission was over.

Time to return to the octagon.

The two non-Cell-3 fighters snapped awake in their bunks and rolled out of bed. Everyone—Draker, the two sleepers, Ricky, and Blitz—filed toward the exit.

As they neared the door, Blitz cut in front of Draker. He shot Draker a wicked stare as he passed.

This shit with Blitz was only going to get worse before it got better.

CHAPTER
TWENTY-THREE

An hour after the fighting recommenced, it was finally his turn. Draker stepped into the octagon.

His first fight.

He stood in the middle of the octagon, right there on the bloodstained cardboard.

The smell hit him again, this time up close and personal—sweat, old blood, anticipation. The warehouse echoed with voices. Fighters. The handful of other spectators. Packed into metal bleachers around the cage.

He took a deep breath. Scanned the crowd. So many eyes upon him. Bloodthirsty. Some of the faces were screaming. Some laughed wickedly. Fists pumped.

Then he found Ricky, who nodded encouragement. Draker nodded back. A moment later, he spotted Nina Hollis at the corner of the cage by the only door, chained shut. Her gaze was calculating.

Draker brought his attention back to the interior of the fence walls and faced his opponent.

The opponent was Crusher...

…the biker guy who'd confronted Draker the previous night, a man who already had it in for Draker, almost as much as Blitz. The wild beard. The tattoos circling up tree-branch arms. The crazy, beady eyes. The mounds of muscle.

This was Draker's first opponent. It couldn't have been any of the other fighters. The *dozens* of other fighters.

No, of course it couldn't.

Fate, it seemed, had a sense of humor.

Fuck my luck, Draker thought.

The bell rang. Sharp and sudden. Draker went on the defensive, assuming a modified version of a stance he'd been taught at the police academy. This modification was something Larkin had taught him moments after their training had begun.

Crusher charged. A massive fist swung at Draker's head. He ducked, felt the air rush past. He countered with a jab to the ribs. It barely fazed the big man.

Crusher changed tactics, using legs now, sending an oversized boot in Draker's direction via a surprisingly limber front kick. It caught Draker off guard, landing half on his chest, half on his stomach. Draker went flying into the cage. Pain shot through him.

The fence rattled. But he regained his footing.

The crowd roared. Deafening. Draker's senses sharpened. Every movement amplified. A glance to the crowd, and he saw Ricky's worried eyes. Nina watched too, expression unreadable.

Crusher surged forward, forcing Draker back into the fence again. A barrage of punches descended upon Draker. He raised his arms, deflecting most of the blows, muscles straining. It wasn't enough. A few powerful hits found their mark, sending sharp pain blooming across Draker's ribs, his shoulder, his jaw.

Desperation kicked in. Draker twisted free, every muscle straining. He spotted an opening and didn't hesitate. A solid punch connected with Crusher's jaw, snapping the big man's head back.

Seizing the chance, Draker unleashed a flurry of strikes. Crusher staggered, teeth clenched, but refused to fall. He shook his head clear and a guttural roar escaped his throat as he lunged forward again.

Draker was ready. He juked left, letting Crusher crash into the fence. The metal groaned under the impact and Crusher bounced off, momentarily dazed.

Energy was fading. Fast. Draker shook his head and bolted toward Crusher in this split-second moment of opportunity. As Crusher regained his balance and stood to his full height, Draker saw something he hadn't yet noticed—a slight limp in Crusher's gait, a telltale sign of an old injury. A weakness Draker could exploit.

Without hesitation, Draker targeted the leg. A swift kick, going low. It connected. Crusher howled, dropped to one knee. The crowd's roaring swelled. Draker bolted forward, standing over his fallen opponent.

Fury twisted Crusher's face. He rose and charged…

… limping badly where Draker had just struck him.

Draker dodged, felt the wind of Crusher's massive fist. He countered with a spinning kick. It connected with Crusher's temple. Crusher stumbled, his balance now obliterated.

Draker didn't hesitate. He rushed forward, and with everything he had left, he unleashed a final punch that landed squarely on Crusher's jaw.

The sound was disproportionately loud, projecting itself over the crowd's roar.

Crusher's eyes rolled back.

A stumbling step forward. Another.

His knees buckled. The gimpy leg gave way first, followed quickly by the second.

Draker stepped to the side just as Crusher crashed to the floor, his frame thwacking on the wet cardboard. The impact vibrated through the soles of Draker's boots.

Silence hung in the air. There was a long moment of nothing.

Then the crowd erupted.

The bell rang. It was all over. Draker stood over his fallen opponent. Chest heaving. Muscles screaming.

He'd won his first fight.

He'd *survived* his first fight.

Barely.

As reality sank in, he looked around. Faces showed admiration. Envy. Some nodded in respect. Others glared. Ricky was beaming, whooping, pumping his fists in the air—left, right, left, right.

Draker couldn't deny it—luck had played a part. He hadn't noticed Crusher's slight limp until well into the fight.

He was quite certain he wouldn't be able to rely on luck the next time.

He went to the octagon's door. Nina smiled at him from outside the cage as she uncoiled the chain. Once it was free, she swung open the door, smiled again, and made room for him to pass.

Adrenaline faded. Pain surged with each step. Draker saw Ricky again—relief on his face.

Draker's mind pivoted to future fights…

… the competition was only going to get fiercer.

CHAPTER
TWENTY-FOUR

One moment, he was a fighter; the next, he was a spectator.

Draker was back in the bleachers in the same spot next to Ricky as he had been the night before. He was slumped over. Every muscle ached from his fight with Crusher.

The crowd was roaring again. Two new fighters were going at it in the octagon. Next to Draker, Ricky leaned in, enthralled.

Chaotic noise washed over Draker. But his mind was elsewhere. He'd barely won against Crusher. If not for that last-second opening, things might have gone very differently. He could practically hear Larkin scream, *Adaptability is key!*

Indeed it was. It had saved his ass in there.

The fighters circled each other. One was tall, shredded, Hispanic. The other was a short black guy with shockingly fast fists. Sweat glistened on muscled bodies under the harsh lights. One feinted left, then lunged right with a powerful hook. The other barely dodged, the fist whistling past his ear.

The crowd's roar swelled with the near miss. Draker winced, remembering the sting of similar blows from his fight with Crusher.

His ribs throbbed in sympathy.

For a few moments, the fighters had kept each other at bay. But suddenly, explosively, they were tangled up.

Another burst of noise from the crowd.

Arms clambered over each other. Legs thrashed. The men crashed as one against the fence, rattling it. Grunts of exertion pierced through the shouts and jeers from the bleachers.

Ricky was on his feet now, hollering. He seemed to have a favorite among the two fighters. He shouted encouragement. Draker remained seated, his eyes unfocused, gazing not at the fight but through it. He was still caught in the fog of his own recent battle.

A resonant crack pulled Draker's attention back to the octagon. One of the guys had landed a devastating punch. The other one went windmilling backward into the fence.

But before he could drop, the first man was on him again, keeping the guy on his feet long enough to send a knee into his stomach, barely north of the belt.

It connected with a sickening thud. The recipient's mouth opened in a silent scream.

Draker winced again.

The crowd's collective breath held in anticipation.

Then, the defeated man went limp and crumpled to the concrete, missing the cardboard entirely.

The crowd screamed its approval.

Arms raised, the winning fighter screamed along with the crowd, blood and sweat mingling in rivulets on his skin, dripping onto the cardboard below.

The frenzy reached new heights—a wall of sound that seemed to make the air vibrate.

Beside Draker, Ricky was jumping up and down.

Draker just looked away.

And something caught his eye.

An irregularity in the throng.

A crowd member who wasn't watching the fight but watching his hands, which were on his lap, doing something. His movements were furtive, almost anxious. He seemed to be fumbling with an object.

... and perhaps trying to keep it concealed.

Draker focused on the man's gestures—all those twitches, subtle turns. The man was up to something.

Another moment of watching. Then Draker stood up.

Ricky gave him a curious glance. "What are you doing?"

Draker waved him off, not taking his eyes off the suspicious individual. He began making his way along the side of the bleachers, pushing through the mass of sweaty bodies.

Draker's tensed. The noise of the crowd faded into the background. He tried not to draw attention to himself, but the bleachers creaked beneath his feet. He brushed past a large man who growled an obscenity and shoved Draker. He barely noticed, his eyes locked on his target.

The noise surrounding him grew even louder—a new fight beginning in the cage—becoming something physical, something Draker could feel all the way through his flesh and into his bones. Cheers and jeers fused into a vibratory roar. The air was stale, hot, moist—smelled like bodies and breath.

He moved closer to the other man, who was still looking down, still fidgeting. Closer now, Draker could see more of what the man was doing. There was... something in his hands. A box. Small enough to fit between his palms.

Darker sucked in a sudden breath.

A detonator.

The Watchdog.

The crowd's fervor escalated. Bodies crowded Draker from every side, pushed at him. Everything was turning chaotic.

In the cage, the fight was just as chaotic. One man was being beat to hell. Covered with blood. Draker wouldn't have been surprised if the guy died.

Finally, Draker reached the man with the device. He was about to make his move...

... when he stopped.

Because now that he was only a few feet behind the man, he had a clear view of what the man was holding. It wasn't a detonator. It was a stopwatch—an old-fashioned mechanical stopwatch. Beside it, on the man's thigh, was a small notebook.

The guy was timing the fights, jotting down notes. Probably for betting purposes.

Relief washed over Draker, quickly followed by embarrassment. He'd let his imagination run wild.

He took a deep breath, trying to slow his racing heart.

As Draker turned to head back to his seat, he sensed something—an instinct honed by years of being a cop told him he was being watched.

He stopped, looked across the crowd, past the heaving mass of screaming brutes, all focused intently on the savagery in the octagon...

... and discovered not one but *two* sets of eyes staring at him.

The first belonged to Nina Hollis, standing by the cage door. She was watching him with a look that was both skeptical and disapproving. Clearly, she'd just seen Draker's aborted attempt to confront the man with the stopwatch.

Draker's mind flashed back to the start of their arrangement just yesterday. Nina had her doubts about letting an outsider into her tournament. She'd made it clear the other fighters would be suspicious, that Draker would have to work hard to show he was the real deal, just as much a fighter as any of them. It was a straightforward challenge, the kind Draker liked.

And now he'd nearly blown his cover.

No wonder Nina looked pissed.

They locked eyes, and Nina let the stare linger for a long beat as she narrowed her eyes at him. There was something in that glower that hit harder than Draker would have thought possible; it was like a disapproving glare given from a parent to a child, a teacher to a student. Chastisement. Then, as if dismissing him entirely, Nina turned her attention back to the cage.

But Nina wasn't the only one watching. There was that other pair of eyes too.

Draker turned his head an inch. And found the other eyes. At the far end of the bleachers, a solitary figure stood out from the rest.

Blitz.

Unlike the rest of the crowd, Blitz wasn't watching the fight. He was watching Draker. Focused like a laser. Or a tractor beam. Surrounded by the swirling mass of arms and screaming faces, Blitz looked eerily still. Just staring away at Draker, arms crossed over his chest.

Draker locked eyes with Blitz, just like he had with Nina a moment before. Nina's glare had made him feel like a scolded kid, but there was no chance in hell he was backing down from Blitz. The roar of the crowd dulled to a hum. Everything around him slowed to a crawl.

The two of them existed alone now, separate from the rest of the Pit.

Blitz's head dropped a fraction of an inch, jaw muscles flexing. The change was subtle. Almost imperceptible. But to Draker it spoke volumes. It looked like a theat.

Blitz seemed to be communicating—wordlessly, telepathically. *I saw what you just did. I saw you approach the guy with the stopwatch.*

Earlier, Blitz had accused Draker of being a cop. The guy was already suspicious.

Now Draker knew with absolute certainty that Blitz had seen through his cover.

The game had changed.

As the crowd erupted in a deafening cheer, signaling the end of the fight, Blitz broke eye contact, sat down.

Draker turned and continued to his seat, pushing through the throng. Ricky gave him a puzzled look as he returned. Draker just shook his head.

When he sat, Draker glanced over to where he'd seen Blitz. Waited for him to look over again.

Blitz never glanced back at Draker.

CHAPTER
TWENTY-FIVE

A few minutes earlier in the bleachers, under Nina Hollis's withering stare, Draker had felt like a kid being chastised by a teacher.

But now, as he stood in Nina's office, waiting for her to speak, his earlier analogy became modified slightly. Now he felt like an elementary school student being summoned to the principal's office for bad behavior.

The office was as stark as the rest of the Pit, a reminder that this was a once-a-year affair, nothing permanent. Bare walls. Simple desk—a big, battered steel number that reminded Draker of old-school setups he had seen in many small local police departments back in California. Minimal paperwork scattered about. The air smelled of dust and metal and a hint of Nina's perfume. The rumble of the crowd filled the room, shook the walls —the latest fight had started a few moments earlier.

For once, Leon Alden wasn't at Nina's side. It was just the two of them in the office.

"What the hell did you think you were doing?" Nina said, voice sharp, eyes blazing. "You're supposed to be undercover, and you just caused a scene over a guy with a damn stopwatch!"

Yes, Draker was indeed in the principal's office…

He felt the weight of her gaze.

"I apologize," he said. "It was a mistake. A lapse in judgment."

Nina's eyes narrowed, scrutinizing him. Draker held her gaze. He could sense her evaluating his worth, questioning his abilities. There was a long moment where they said nothing.

When it was clear she wasn't going to respond, Draker said, "I'm still going to find out if the Watchdog is planning to attack here. And if he is, I'll stop him. I swear to you."

Nina exhaled heavily, her eyes briefly drifting off. When they returned to him, there was a change—something softer, almost vulnerable, flickered across her expression.

"Look," she said, much quieter than she'd been, "I need to tell you something." She paused a beat. "I've known about the potential Watchdog attack the whole time, even before you and Agent Sullivan first contacted me."

The words hit Draker like a physical blow. "*What?*"

Nina nodded, turned away from his stare—now she was the one assuming the role of a browbeaten child. She circled around the metal desk, pulled out a screeching door, and retrieved a sheet of paper, handed it to Draker.

It was a sheet of standard computer paper with two lines of text printed in the center:

You're next.
-the Watchdog

"Why did you play dumb before?" Draker said.

Nina took the paper back, looked at it, shook her head. "I... I didn't believe this was genuine. I thought it was some sort of prank from one of the fighters. They're a bunch of assholes, you know."

"But why didn't you even *mention* this to Sullivan?" Draker had to fight not to shout.

"I... I... I didn't want him to... I didn't want..." she trailed off.

"You didn't want what?"

Nina just shook her head. Her eyes were now glazed over, lips parted. She stared over his shoulder, into the void.

Draker's mind raced, synapses firing at breakneck speed as he tried to process it all. The rumble of the crowd faded away. He thought back to what Sullivan had told him about Nina's assistant/bodyguard Leon Alden and his connection to a fighter from the Pit's years-earlier schism.

Nina had just said the word "him." Draker had assumed she meant the Watchdog…

"Wait," Draker said. "Alden. Leon Alden."

This brought Nina's attention back to Draker. Her eyes were still glazed over, now glistening. Her lips remained parted. She tried to speak. Couldn't. Tried again.

"Yeah. Leon. I knew that if I told Sullivan how I received the note—that I came in here one day last week and found it in the drawer—she would start investigating people within the Pit."

"Current intel suggests the Watchdog is from somewhere out west," Draker said. "Montana, Colorado, Idaho. And you wanted Sullivan to continue with that assumption."

Nina nodded. Her lip quivered.

"Because you were trying to protect Leon Alden," Draker continued. "You thought that if Sullivan knew the note originated from within the Pit, she'd very soon suspect Alden, the second in command, a former champion who sided with one of the two club founders."

Nina nodded again. A tear escaped, raced down her cheek. "That's right. And now…" she took in a shuddering breath. "And now you're going to focus on Leon, aren't you? *Aren't you?*"

"You're damn right I am."

"*No!*"

"Why are you so protective of Alden?"

No response, only a shake of the head and more tears.

"Which side of the schism did Alden side with?" Draker said.

"What does that matt—"

"It matters! *Which side?*"

Nina jumped. "He... sided with Jay McGarry."

"Uh-huh. The guy who wanted to keep the Pit simple, to tone down the savagery and erase any monetary element. Now the Pit has turned into this—a bloodthirsty tournament where everyone's fighting for the possibility of prize money."

Nina stepped toward him, pointing. "See? *This* is why I didn't tell Sullivan about the note. I knew she'd think Leon is the Watchdog. And now you do too, don't you?"

She stopped right in front of him, panting, jaw jutting out, chin lifted.

Draker stared down at her. "Yes, I do. You received a note from inside the Pit—in your *office*—and Alden is constantly in your orbit. He aligned himself with those who wanted to preserve the Pit's purity, seeing it as a form of martial arts therapy, not a venue for profit-driven brutality. The Watchdog detests greed, debauchery, and savagery. It makes sense that Alden could be the Watchdog. He's now my top suspect."

"Fuck!" Nina said and spun around, back now turned to Draker.

"I'll ask again," Draker said. "Why the hell are you so protective of Leon Alden?"

Nina didn't turn around. For a long moment, she said nothing, and Draker assumed she was going to leave another of his questions unanswered. But then she spoke.

"My boyfriend, Ryan, is dead. Murdered." She wrapped her arms around herself. Draker watched from behind as she ran her fingers up and down her arms. "That title, 'boyfriend,' sounds kind of silly, doesn't it? Like something for teenagers. But he was... everything to me. And he was killed in the brawl between the two schisms.

"I was there. At the battle. I saw them kick his face in. He was screaming, but they didn't stop. Two of Burrows's guys. Not that it mattered whose side they were on. Ryan hadn't chosen a side, neither Jay McGarry's nor Tommy Burrows's. He just loved the Pit, loved the brotherhood. And those two guys kicked his face until there was nothing left, long after he stopped screaming, until there was just a big bloody fucking hole where my man's eyes and lips used to be."

She turned around now. Looked shellshocked. Stepped toward Draker, right into his space.

"I loved Ryan," she said. "*Loved* that man. But love means different things to different people. And it isn't always tied to lust. We had an open relationship. I like fighters. I like their hard bodies; I like their rough hands. I like taming their savagery, feeling it inside me." She looked up at him. "Leon has always been one of my favorites, and that doesn't change a damn thing about how much I'm *still* mourning Ryan."

Ah. Now it made sense why she was protecting Leon Alden. Crystal-clear.

"Ryan let me fuck whoever I wanted, whichever one of his big, strong fighter friends turned me on," Nina continued. "In return, I let him have whatever pussy he managed to chase down. Some people call it 'polyamory,' but to me, it's trust, Draker. Love is nothing without trust.

"That's how I got to this point—in charge of the Pit. Though I'm sure my volunteering at a conflict-resolution center played a part, the real reason the fighters let a woman lead their men's club was because I was so... um, 'friendly' with several of them."

She gave a small laugh, no shame. She moved closer. Her hand brushed Draker's arm. Light but deliberate.

Draker said, "But you have something special with Leon Alden, don't you?"

Nina shrugged. "Of course. I have my favorites. Some of them are just fucks, but others... are special. I told you, Ryan was my man, but that doesn't mean I've never bonded with anyone else. Oh, yes. Leon Alden, Andrew Cavanaugh—those two... they took care of me when Ryan passed, supported me when some of the jerks didn't want me in charge of the Pit. We almost became like a... a little family, the three of us. Andrew abandoned me." She stopped to scoff. "But Leon is still there. *Still* there. By my side. Every day."

Draker smirked. "Always nice to have a support team."

Nina stepped even closer, right up beside him. "I like fighters," she said again. "And I like you. You've proven yourself. 'Mav.' Earlier, when you fought Crusher.... Mmm." She bit her lip.

Her hand came back to him, this time overtly; she placed it on his shoulder.

Draker tensed. He removed her hand.

Disappointment showed in Nina's eyes. Draker suspected she wasn't trying too hard to conceal it. She withdrew slightly.

"I... should leave," he said. "We can discuss the Watchdog later."

He turned for the door. Mind swirling.

"Wait!" Nina said.

Draker's hand was on the doorknob. He stopped, looked back.

"Leon's a good man," Nina said. "A former champion. He is *not* the Watchdog."

In his mind, Draker replied, *Like hell he's not, lady.*

They looked at each other for a moment longer.

Then Draker left.

CHAPTER
TWENTY-SIX

For a moment, all the chaos blended together, canceling itself out.

The crowd roared, deafening. Draker felt the ache of his wounds and the turmoil from Nina's revelations. All of it congealing into a gray, undefinable haze. He was numb to everything, locked in a trance.

A literal trance.

He stared forward—intently—but he wasn't looking in the same direction as the crowd surrounding him on the bleachers, wasn't watching the two latest fighters in the octagon, locked in brutal combat, bodies glistening with sweat under the harsh lights.

No. Draker's eyes were locked on Leon Alden, who stood next to Nina at the corner of the cage.

Alden was an imposing figure despite his average height. His barrel chest strained a gray t-shirt, while faded jeans clung to his muscular legs. A weathered face marked with scars. Dark hair and a lumberjack beard. As Alden leaned in to shout to Nina over the roaring crowd, Draker noticed Alden's left hand was moving, small undulations of his fingers—fiddling with the polished stones again.

Draker's mind had been racing since he left Nina's office and rejoined Ricky in the bleachers. Connecting the pieces. Leon Alden had backed McGarry during the schism years ago, and McGarry's mission to keep the Pit pure and free from commercialization aligned with the Watchdog's modus operandi.

The note Nina had received from inside the Pit only solidified Draker's suspicions—Alden was determined to finish what McGarry had started, to dismantle this corrupted version of the Pit that had strayed so far from its true purpose.

Somewhere along the line, Alden had expanded his vision and become the Watchdog, deciding to target multiple forms of societal decay, doing so in the months between last year's tournament and this year's—appetizers to the main dish.

Suddenly, Alden and Nina broke apart from their hushed conversation. Alden's head snapped up, eyes scanning the crowd until they locked onto Draker. His gaze was intense, even from a distance.

Nina had just told him what happened in the office.

Yeah, I see you too, asshole, Draker thought, meeting Alden's stare.

They held each other's gaze for a long moment before Alden turned away, returning his attention to Nina.

Without taking his eyes off Alden, Draker leaned over to Ricky and yelled over the crowd, "Why does he do that?"

Ricky was caught up in the fight and barely registered the question. "Huh?"

"Alden."

Ricky turned his attention to Draker, cocked his head.

Draker pointed in Alden's direction, toward the man's moving fingers and the polished stones beneath. "What's he doing with those stones?"

"It's Alden's thing. He's always got them rocks with him— three of 'em, black, white, and gray. Been doing it for years, way before I started fighting here. Some guys say it's a meditation thing, like a yoga practice or something, helps him stay calm. Others think they're related to some kind of martial arts shit.'"

"Which version do you believe?"

Ricky shrugged. "Beats me. But I'll tell you this—when those stones stop moving, that's when you gotta watch out. It means something big is about to go down. Fighters get nervous when they see Alden's hands go still." Ricky lowered his voice even further. "There's a rumor that one of the times Alden stopped rolling those stones was right before the big fight that tore the Pit apart years ago. You know, when the two founders and a bunch of others got killed."

Draker nodded, shifting in his seat to get a slightly closer look at Alden, who was watching the fight intently by Nina's side. He moved the stones in his hand.

Ricky continued. "But hey, that's probably just talk, right? Still, it's freaky how he never puts those things down. It's like they're a part of him or something."

Draker thought of something he hadn't considered. He finally took his eyes off Alden, brought them to Ricky. "Both of the founders were killed in the battle—McGarry and Burrows. Who killed Burrows?"

Ricky just stared at him, blinked. "I... don't know. McGarry was trampled in the crowd, but Burrows was stabbed in the back. *Literally* stabbed in the back. No one ever found out who did it."

Hmm...

A soft chirp in Draker's ear broke his concentration—an incoming call from Beau. He placed a finger to his ear, double-tapping the device to accept but said nothing, not yet.

He gave Ricky a nod and said, "Be back."

He stood and pushed his way through the crowd, descended the steps, and slipped out the double doors.

The sounds of the fight echoed through the hallway, but otherwise it was quiet. Draker was alone. Still, he remained cautious, keeping his voice low and trying to move his lips as little as possible as he responded to Beau.

"Yes?" Draker whispered.

"Need you to leave again," Beau's voice crackled in his ear. "Time for more training with Larkin."

Draker groaned. "More? Come on, Beau. I should be investigating, not—"

"What have you found?" Beau cut him off.

"My hunch was right," Draker said, maintaining his whisper as he moved cautiously through the empty hallway. "That gut feeling I had—I now think Leon Alden is the Watchdog."

"Okay, we're getting somewhere."

"Alden is Nina Hollis's right-hand man—her bodyguard/assistant. And her lover. Nina received a note from the Watchdog note—*before* Sullivan reached out to her and from *within* the Pit. Also, back when the club tore apart, this Alden guy sided with McGarry, one of the Pit's original founders, the one who *didn't* want the club to get commercial, the one who saw it as almost a men's spiritual retreat. It all lines up." He came to a stop. Thought he'd heard something. Listened. Nothing. Continued on. "Which is why I need to be doing more investigation, not prizefighting."

"Damn good work, boy," Beau said, "but you need to keep up your skill set if you're going to survive the Pit. So stop bitchin' and get your ass back to Larkin."

Draker rounded another corner, nearly colliding with a lone fighter who eyed him suspiciously. He nodded casually and continued on, waiting until he was out of earshot before responding. "Beau, I need to focus on what's important here! We're running out of—"

"Stop bitching," Beau repeated.

The line went dead.

Cursing under his breath, Draker made his way to the short, dark hallway. There, he worked the particleboard loose and squeezed through the transom window.

As he dropped to the ground outside, he caught a quick flash of headlights in the darkness beyond.

Sullivan's Mercedes...

… Draker's ride to another grueling session with Grady Larkin.

CHAPTER
TWENTY-SEVEN

The clock in SAC Arnold Jameson's office had always ticked too loudly.

Exactly how high did someone have to climb up the totem pole before such annoyances were absent?

The loud-ticking clock showed the time as several minutes past 10 PM. Another long day.

The seconds *ticked, ticked* by, and Jameson punctuated them with the thud of his finger tapping against the polished mahogany of his desk.

The Special Agent in Charge of the Des Moines Field Office scowled at the stack of reports before him. Specifically, the folder on top. He scratched at his salt-and-pepper mustache, another idle habit of his.

And he thought about Special Agent Jenna Sullivan. Yet again.

Damn her.

His eyes went to a framed photo behind his desk—himself, a decade younger, receiving a commendation. The memory usually brought a smile to his face; tonight, it just made him feel old.

Jameson leaned forward in his chair. The leather wheezed. He reached for his coffee mug, which had left yet another ring on a case file, joining a constellation of similar stains.

He tasted the coffee—room-temperature, several hours old, *bleh!*—pushed the mug to the side, and picked up Sullivan's report, skimming it for the umpteenth time.

The Watchdog. The Pit fighting tournament. Louisville. It all seemed so far-fetched, the kind of wild goose chase that could derail a promising career.

And, now *his* career, if he wasn't careful.

Because he'd turned Sullivan's theoretical wild goose chase into a tangible one—he'd sent her to Louisville to sate her investigative itch. She'd given him little choice; she wouldn't *shut up* about what she saw as a sure bet: that the Watchdog's next target was the Pit.

Jameson stood, pacing the length of his office, his oxfords sinking into plush carpeting, FBI blue. Five steps, turn. Five steps, turn. Yet another habit of his. Jameson was a creature of habit, many useful but many idle.

He paused at the window, staring out at the Des Moines skyline. Jameson was from Chicago, so of course the buildings here didn't compare. But he liked it here. Loved it, as a matter of fact. He'd carved out his own piece of the world in this corner of Iowa, and he was the king.

But it came with a price: the consequences of a leader's choices.

Which further led to a lot of second-guessing.

What if Sullivan had been right?

The thought, unbidden and unwelcome, stopped Jameson cold. He ran a hand over his mustache again.

Sullivan had good instincts, he had to admit. Unorthodox methods, sure, but results were results.

And Jameson had always been protective of her. Fatherly, even. Sullivan was undeniably attractive—an Asian American beauty with a tone physique, an avid runner and a gym rat. She was smart, typically pleasant, and highly motivated. Naturally, the male agents had taken a shine to her since she arrived in Des

Moines three years earlier, and Jameson had done his best to keep them at bay.

But when it came to her investigations—all those unorthodox methods and wild leads—Jameson had a tendency to be... slightly dismissive.

Hell, if he was being honest with himself, he'd have to admit that he'd even been condescending with Sullivan from time to time...

... including recently when she was adamant that she'd found the next target of the most-wanted terrorist in the nation.

Jameson had protected Sullivan for three years.

And now he'd shipped her off alone.

Because she'd annoyed him.

Shit.

He ran a hand over his mustache yet again.

His phone buzzed, rattling against the desk. Jameson snatched it up, hoping to see Sullivan's name. Instead, "SA Weaver" flashed on the screen.

Special Agent Weaver was one of Jameson's most trusted guys. A real bloodhound.

... like Sullivan.

"Jameson."

Static crackled, then Weaver's voice came through. "The Pit isn't what we were thinking. There's a long history there. I emailed you. Sullivan's onto something big."

Jameson exhaled. "Fine."

He ended the call, dropped the phone onto the corner of his desk.

Shit.

He returned to the desk and slumped back into his chair. Reached for the laptop. Hesitated.

Had he screwed up? Sent Sullivan into something bigger, more dangerous than either of them realized?

Eschewing the laptop, he pulled Sullivan's coffee-mug-stained file closer, this time reading every word with laser focus. The dark web chatter she'd picked up, the patterns she'd identified—it was thin, sure…

… but maybe not as crazy as he'd first thought.

Jameson reached for his phone, dialed Sullivan's number. Straight to voicemail. He hung up without leaving a message.

The clock *ticked, ticked, ticked*. Jameson pounded a finger on the desktop.

Okay…

Okay, he knew what he had to do

He had calls to make, favors to call in. If Sullivan was right—and the knot in Jameson's gut told him she might be—they were going to need all the help they could get.

The SAC in him knew it was a long shot. But the agent—the part of him that had joined the Bureau all those years ago to make a difference, the part that wasn't so different from Jenna Sullivan—knew he had to try.

Jameson picked up his phone.

CHAPTER
TWENTY-EIGHT

Draker was back in Larkin's ring.

It was almost midnight.

He moved. Mechanical. Lifeless. The gym's dim light cast long shadows over battered equipment. No intensity left. Just emptiness.

A few yards away was Sullivan, watching from the other side of the ropes as she had before. This time her arms were crossed over her chest. She wore a concerned expression.

Draker moved on autopilot—punches, kicks, blocks. His mind was elsewhere. His body felt numb. Larkin scowled, circling him, striking harder with each angry frown.

"Pull it together, shithead," Larkin barked. "You're not even in this room."

Draker grunted. Barely heard him.

Frustration brewed in Draker, threatened to boil over. The intel from Nina's office burned in his mind—crucial information that could blow this whole thing wide open.

When Beau had called, Draker had urged Beau to let him take immediate action, but his handler had shut him down. Instead of taking action, Draker was ordered back to Larkin for further training.

And this pissed Draker off.

Here he was, on his fourth mission as Beau's Ranger—Kingman, Ventura, Columbus, and now Louisville.

Louisville, where he was getting his ass beaten—*literally*—again and again and again.

Louisville, where he was made to hide under an alias only weeks after coming face to face with a brand-new identity, one he hadn't fully adjusted to yet. Not even close.

Louisville, where he was being told to *not* investigate his leads, to *not* follow his investigative instincts.

The weight of inaction pressed down on Draker, landing as hard as Larkin's strikes.

Sweat dripped. Muscles ached. Draker went through drill after drill, his body moving without conscious thought while his mind raced. He was learning, sure—marginally. But mostly he was just getting his ass kicked... *yet again!*

Larkin decided to push. He'd had enough of Draker, evidently. His eyes narrowed, jaw set. He came at Draker with renewed intensity. A flurry of jabs, each one faster than the last. Draker's arms moved sluggishly, too slow to block.

Impacts jarred Draker's body. He stumbled.

But Larkin didn't let up.

A kick swept Draker's legs out from under him. He crashed to the mat, back slamming hard, breath expelled from his lungs. Larkin's silhouette loomed over him, shouting.

Draker glanced to the side, across a plane of canvas, and locked eyes with Sullivan. The concerned expression was still on her face, hadn't changed.

He stumbled to his feet...

... for only a moment.

This time, a shoulder throw from Larkin sent him flying.

The world spun.

And he was back down again. On his stomach. Cheek pressed to the mat, lips wet. The copper taste of blood filled his mouth.

"Where's your fight, huh?" Larkin's voice echoed through the empty space. "Where's your damn spirit?"

Draker got back to his feet and put up his gloves, but his defenses crumbled with each impact. Arms dangled limply in front of him, barely providing cover, no will left to raise them. He simply endured, taking the punishment. Again and again Larkin sent him down, and again and again Draker rose.

"You're still playing by your old rules," Larkin said, circling him. "Everything you learned as cop. How many times have I told you. *You gotta adapt!*—in the ring and in life."

Draker scowled. What the hell had Larkin meant by "in life"?

"Beau told me about you," Larkin continued. "Not the details, of course. But he told me enough. Said you were a cop, and now you're hunted, on the run, pining for a life you'll never get back. That's your problem: your rigid thinking, holding onto the past. It's dragging you down, kid. You think fists and guns solve everything. Life's not that simple."

Draker stopped moving. Body tense. His muscles spasmed—biceps, pecs, quads—and knew that it had nothing to do with his exhaustion.

It was a fresh wave of adrenaline, this time fueled by rage.

"You're stuck in your head, dumbass," Larkin pressed. "You're not the first of Beau's Rangers I've met, but you're the most blinded. You can't see what's right in front of you. Wake *up*, Draker. If you don't, you're gonna get yourself killed… or you're gonna get someone else killed."

Something snapped in Draker then.

He stepped back, tore at his gloves until he had the strings loosened, then he threw them to the mat. "You know what? I'm sick of this bullshit. Who the hell do you think you are lecturing me? You haven't been a fighter in years. *Decades.* You gave up because of some mysterious reason you refuse to share, because of this Octavius person you mentioned."

Larkin's face hardened, then softened. Both eyes glistened—

the brown one and the milky white one. "You want to know about Octavius, huh? Fine."

There was long pause. Larkin lowered his fists. Took a step toward Draker. Swallowed.

"Octavius was my little brother. Twelve years younger. Our old man split when Octavius was just a baby, so I practically raised the kid. I was his big brother *and* his daddy."

Larkin's voice cracked as he continued. "Octavius idolized me, wanted to be just like me. When he turned eighteen, he begged me to train him. I should've said no, should've protected him. Instead, I let him follow me into the ring."

He paused again. "I was in a club at the time, a lot like the Pit. This was in the '70s, mind you." He gave a dark snicker, shook his head. "The club wasn't *exactly* like the Pit—not nearly as savage—but it was bad enough, man. Octavius's last fight... God, I can still see it. It was brutal. His opponent was juiced up—back in those early days of 'roids before people knew all the dangers—way out of Octavius's league. I tried to throw in the towel, but Octavius wouldn't let me. He was too proud, too stubborn. Just like me... at the time."

Larkin's fists clenched at his sides. "That bastard beat Octavius to a pulp. Cracked skull, ruptured kidney. By the time the ref finally stopped it, it was too late. Octavius died in my arms, right there in the ring."

He looked at Draker, hard, and Draker felt it more from the man's dead eye than he did the living one.

"That's why I quit fighting. Not because of this." He pointed at the milky eye. "Octavius is the reason I'm so hard on all my fighters, including you. I want them to avoid any real fights, especially in the Pit. But most of them are too stubborn, too bullheaded."

There was another pause here, longer, and Draker felt like saying something. No words came.

Larkin continued, his voice softer. "In your case, Draker, I know you *have* to fight in the Pit. There's no way for me to talk you out of it, because it's your mission. Unlike those other kids, you got no choice. That's why I've been especially tough on you, mentally and physically. I need you to be ready."

For a moment, Draker's opinion of Larkin softened. But only for a moment. Because a word Larkin had just said was ringing in his head: *mission*. Draker was there in Louisville to stop the Watchdog, not to participate in a fighting tournament, not to train endlessly.

"Yeah? Well, I'll make it easier on you," Draker said. "You don't have to train me anymore. Our sessions are over. I don't give a damn what Beau says."

He turned, stepped through the ropes, and hopped down onto the concrete. Sullivan uncrossed her arms and took a tentative step toward him, lips parting. Draker looked her way, made eye contact for a brief moment, but didn't stop walking toward the exit. He heard her heels clacking on the concrete behind him, following.

"Is this how you adapt, Draker?" Larkin called out. "By running away?"

Draker didn't turn, kept on walking. He threw open the heavy steel door. A gust of cool nighttime air swept over him, tingling his wounds. He held the door open for Sullivan. As she passed, Draker looked back into the gym.

There was Larkin. Still in the ring. Illuminated by the gym's only light—like a dust-particle-polluted spotlight. Forearms crossed on the top rope. Staring at Draker, the dead eye visible against his dark skin even from a distance.

Draker stared back at him.

Once Sullivan was outside, Draker let the door slam shut behind them.

CHAPTER
TWENTY-NINE

The bang of the door echoed into the night.

Sullivan hurried after Draker as he cut across the parking lot. She stumbled in her heels as she navigated the crumbling asphalt.

"Draker!" she called out. "What the hell are you doing?"

Draker didn't slow down, didn't turn back to look at her as he said, "Focusing on the mission."

Sullivan caught up to him, slightly out of breath. She fell into step beside him. "What do you mean?"

Draker stopped abruptly, turned to face her. "I'm gonna look into Nina Hollis's former lover, Andrew Cavanaugh, the guy she mentioned in passing when she told me about Leon Alden. He's the only tangible lead we got, and I can't waste any more time locked up in either the Pit or that damn gym back there."

Sullivan frowned. "But... that means you're quitting. Quitting the tournament, at least."

Draker shook his head. "No. I'll come back." He took off again. Sullivan followed. "I'll keep going undercover for you in the tournament, don't worry. It's after midnight; I'll be back in time for tomorrow's fights."

They reached Sullivan's Mercedes. She reached for the door

handle, hesitated, and rested her hand above the door. She looked across the roof to the opposite side, where Draker stood, waiting to be let in.

"Won't the other fighters notice you're gone?" she said.

Draker shrugged. "I don't care."

"Won't Beau be pissed?"

"I *really* don't care."

Sullivan sighed and pulled on the door handle, activating the keyless entry. They both got in.

"This is insane, Draker," Sullivan said, quieter, as she settled into the driver's seat. "You can't just run off without a plan."

"I got this." He paused, then added, "Did you bring my phone this time? I need it."

Sullivan hesitated again. Sighed again. And nodded. She opened the glove compartment.

"I need my gun too," Draker added.

Sullivan froze—hand inside the glove compartment, fingers wrapped around Draker's phone. She stiffened. Then shook her head, handed him the phone, and reached under her seat.

"Whatever," she said. Arguing was pointless—Draker was determined to follow his own path. He was a good guy but stubborn to a fault. If Beau's objections didn't shake him, Sullivan's certainly wouldn't make a difference.

From beneath the driver's seat, she pulled out the portable gun safe where she'd stored Draker's Glock 19. A quick press of her fingertip on the biometric scanner, an electronic beep, and the lid clicked open. She grabbed the Glock and its small-of-back holster, then handed them both to Draker.

He holstered the pistol.

"You'll really be back for the tournament tomorrow?" Sullivan said.

Draker nodded. "Yeah, I swear it. I told you—I'm not quitting. Just done training with that jackass." He gestured back at the gym.

Sullivan chewed the inside of her cheek. "I... I don't know

about this, Draker. This isn't safe. If Alden really is the Watchdog, tracking down this Cavanaugh guy could bring…" she trailed off. "I mean, at least at the Pit there's some structure, and—"

Draker cut her off gently. "I'll be safe." He raised the holstered Glock for effect, then shoved it under his shirt. He grinned. It was good to see a smile on that face again, if even for a moment. Frowning didn't suit Draker.

… but then he frowned again as he glanced at his phone and muttered, "Damn."

"What is it?"

"Eight missed video calls from Milo."

"You gonna call him back?"

Draker shook his head. "I'll text him. He prefers video calls—*much* prefers them—but texting's gonna have to do this time."

Sullivan watched him type, then her eyes shifted to his face. There was real concern there. She remembered the first time Draker had mentioned Milo—his "Pal," the term Beau had given the young man—and how endearing it had been.

Now, even with Draker's frustration at a boiling point, even in the middle of the night, the guy still cared.

So damn cute… no matter how badly he was pissing her off.

Draker finished the text, locked the phone's screen, put it in his pocket, and turned to her. "I need a ride back to my truck."

Sullivan's instincts were still screaming at her—this was a bad idea. She was the one in the driver's seat. She could tell this fool to piss off, to find his own damn way.

But she nodded.

"Fine," she said. She pressed the button, and the Mercedes purred to life. About to put it into gear, she paused, turned to Draker. "Back in the gym, Larkin said Beau gave him some of the details about you. He said Beau told him you were pining for a life you'll never get back. What does that mean? If I'm gonna put so much trust in you, I want some of the details too."

Draker just looked back at her, blinked. For a moment, Sullivan thought he wasn't going to respond. Then, "For fifteen years, I lived a lie. A mission I thought I completed in Afghanistan for the CIA was actually a military contractor's dirty work. Now they're hunting me down. The woman I was married to, Alyssa, was never even my wife. She was one of theirs, an operative, monitoring me for years. Cassandra Wynne."

Sullivan couldn't respond. The serious-yet-pained look in Draker's eyes made her wished she hadn't pressed him. She swallowed. "Thank you. For sharing." A pause. And she felt compelled to add something. "While we're sharing, you remember those phobias I mentioned before? From when I was ten, when Linda locked me in that basement for days?"

Draker nodded.

"I've been dealing with them ever since," she said, looking down at her hands. "Claustrophobia and nyctophobia—that's the fear of the dark. Both hit me hard. Even now. Nearly kept me out of the FBI Academy."

Draker said nothing, just looked back at her.

Sullivan continued, "Yeah, the Academy has these intense physical tests, and I almost failed because of the phobias. Every time I step into a confined space or lose sight in the darkness, it's like I'm right back in that basement. Stupid, right? A grown woman scared of the dark... but I still freeze up sometimes."

Draker shrugged. "It's not stupid. It's human. And you're still here. Still doing the job. That's strong."

Sullivan gave him a faint smile. "Thanks. That means a lot."

She looked at him for a moment longer, then put the car into drive.

As she crept through the parking lot—dodging copious potholes—she gave one more glance to the gym in her rearview mirror and thought of Draker's plan of investigating this Andrew Cavanaugh lead.

She exhaled and said quietly, "I hope you know what you're doing, Draker."

Draker didn't respond.

CHAPTER
THIRTY

Cassandra Wynne awoke in pain.

It had been a few days, but the wounds might as well have been brand-new. They hurt *that* bad, even with the painkillers coursing through her veins.

Her eyes snapped open, body tensing before she even registered why. The dim light filtering through the drawn curtains was amber-colored—from the streetlights outside the crummy apartment—telling her it was nighttime. She must have passed out on the sofa again, but she had no idea how long she'd slept.

Pain meds will do that to you—they'll numb not only the pain but your entire life.

Time had become a blur since... her punishment.

She hissed as she tried to sit up. Pain fissured across her back.

The flogging. A few days ago. When she and her Windbrook associate, Sean Hunsinger, had failed to bring in Ty Draker, Wynne had been whipped across her bare back.

And since Hunsinger had died during the failed operation—eliminated by Draker—Wynne had received her lashes *and* Hunsinger's.

It had been inconceivable agony.

She was still haunted by it. And always would be, even after the nagging pain finally subsided—because her back would be scarred forever.

Some of the lashes had torn all the way through her skin.

The punishment had been decreed by the Captain, her boss at Windbrook—a man shrouded in power and enigma. He expected perfection. To fail him meant facing severe repercussions.

The Captain was a throwback, his mindset old-school, his methods harsh. It was rumored he was ex-Navy, a stickler for long-outdated naval discipline.

Like flogging.

She remembered what the Captain had said to her—via a phone call; she'd never seen him in person—after the whip had finally stopped. *You know why that happened, don't you?*

That voice of his...

Gentle as always, but laced with menace.

Wynne had always been unsettled by how soft the Captain's voice was. He sounded... kind. Warm and inviting. There was a rich mellowness to his voice befitting a sitcom grandfather.

But he was the cruelest person Wynne had ever encountered.

... and that was saying a lot, coming from a Windbrook operative.

For years, she'd managed to avoid the Captain's wrath, even with her occasional flubs during her time undercover as a ridiculous Ventura, California, housewife.

But then she'd screwed up.

She'd let Draker slip through her grasp.

Draker.

The name alone was enough to send a fresh wave of hatred coursing through Wynne. She could see his face so clearly—that infuriatingly handsome face she'd had to wake up to for five long years. Playing the doting wife, Alyssa Draker née Helmond.

What a joke.

A cruel fucking joke.

Gritting her teeth, Wynne forced herself up from the sofa, pain screaming through her body. The apartment sharpened into view—old furniture, thin curtains, and a stifling quiet all around her.

It was drab and plain, equipped with only the bare essentials—a Windbrook safe house somewhere near Great Falls, in the general vicinity of Windbrook's northern Montana facility. This facility's exact location was a mystery, even to someone at Wynne's level. She'd been there multiple times but had always been flown in from Great Falls by helicopter, blindfolded. An honest-to-God blindfold.

The facility was where she'd received her punishment last week. Since then, the Captain had stashed her away in this shithole apartment, keeping an eye on her while she recovered. Until the time came for her to get the second chance he had "generously" offered.

For days, this had been Wynne's life—ordering delivery-service meals and delivery-service groceries. Popping pills. Watching Netflix on her phone. Popping pills. Hobbling painfully around the tiny, one-bedroom floorplan, trying to walk some life into herself. Popping pills. Popping more pills.

She stumbled into the bathroom, caught her reflection in the mirror. The woman staring back was nothing like the polished "Alyssa" character she'd played for the last five years in California. Dark bags under her eyes. Hair a wild mess. And a hollow look that told the story of the past agonizing days.

Wynne leaned in closer, examined. How much of this was from the constant pain, and how much from the sheer weight of her hatred, the toll of vengeful thoughts?

She turned on the tap, splashed water on her face, then fumbled in the medicine cabinet, fingers closing around the bottle of painkillers. Codeine. Good ol' codeine. It had become her friend. Her best friend. She dry-swallowed two pills, grimacing.

As she made her way back to the living room, past the kitchenette, a memory pounced upon her.

Draker, standing in their kitchen in Santa Clarita, tilting his head thoughtfully as his wife returned from a rough shift at the daycare where she worked part-time. *You okay, babe? You seem a little off today.*

Not so much a true, individual memory as an amalgamation. He'd always cared. For years. He'd bought the lie of "Alyssa Draker" hook, line, and sinker.

Alyssa... the little wife.

Ugh.

Wynne's hand clenched into a fist.

Draker had been pathetic. Clueless. Utterly oblivious to the truth.

She sank onto the sofa.

And screamed.

She'd dropped too hard, too fast. Her best friend codeine hadn't worked her magic yet.

The pain was a constant reminder of Wynne's failure, of how spectacularly she'd underestimated Ty Draker. She, who had lived with him for five years, who'd been his "wife," who should have known his every move, every thought.

But Draker was a survivor.

That's what Hunsinger had called Draker. A survivor.

… this was shortly before Draker shot him in the face.

Hunsinger had underestimated Draker.

And so had Wynne.

She'd never been Draker's wife. She'd been his handler, his Windbrook overseer, keeping an eye on the loose asset for five years.

Five years.

How the fuck had she underestimated him so badly?

She could see him so clearly—sitting on the edge of their bed, excitedly explaining the cinematography of some black-and-white film she couldn't care less about. Or demonstrating one of his ridiculous pen tricks. Like an overgrown child, a boy.

The memory shifted, and suddenly she was back in that underground room, not far from here, somewhere in Montana, bent over the table, shirtless, entirely exposed. The crack of the whip. The searing pain. Her back on fire.

The Captain's incongruously gentle voice: *You know why that happened, don't you?*

Her phone buzzed on the end table. She jumped, gasped. A shot of pain across her back.

She looked.

It was the Captain.

A text message. Thank God it wasn't a call. She couldn't bear that voice, not right now.

But after her moment of quasi-relief, Wynne's stomach dropped as she read the message. *I'll be calling soon. There's been a development. Be prepared.*

The phone shook in Wynne's hand.

With trembling fingers, she responded. *Yes, sir.*

CHAPTER
THIRTY-ONE

After so much time in squalor, the shift to a chic urban city center was jarring.

Draker had become so accustomed to the Pit, Larkin's crappy gym, and similar areas that he'd almost lost track of the fact that Louisville was a major city with not only bad areas but good ones too.

He sat in his rented Ford Maverick—engine idling, window rolled down—inside a parking structure that belonged to a sleek downtown hotel, one of Louisville's newest skyscrapers. This was where Sullivan was staying and where they'd decided to stash his truck while he was in the Pit.

Across the way, Sullivan stepped out of her Mercedes. Behind her, the opening of the parking garage's wall served as a picture frame, giving her a background of the Louisville skyline with the Ohio River glittering in the distance.

She glanced his way. Anxious. She'd stopped being angry at him about halfway through the fifteen-minute drive between the Pit and downtown. Now she was just fretful.

Draker responded with a nod, something to reassure her. She turned and walked off. Her footsteps echoed. She pushed through the door to the stairwell and was gone.

Draker pulled out his phone, opened BeauChat. Milo's conversation was pulled up. Back at the gym, the kid had texted a response only a few minutes after Draker sent him a message.

During the ride in Sullivan's Mercedes, Draker had used BeauSearch Lite to research Andrew Cavanaugh and hadn't answered Milo's text. Now he stared at their two-message exchange:

Draker: *Hey Milo. Can't talk now. Going off-grid again for a while.*

Milo: *Oh OK. Be safe mr Ty.*

Originally, Draker had planned on leaving the conversation as it was; he hadn't wanted a full chat mid-mission, knowing he'd have to give up his phone again soon.

But leaving Milo hanging didn't sit right with him.

He checked the time: 1:30 am. It would be 11:30 pm in Phoenix. Milo would still be up; the kid was a night owl, a habit Draker had been trying to break.

Draker began by typing, *Wanted to let you know I got some info on agoraphobia.*

Then, drawing from what he'd learned earlier at the Pit—when he'd read the magazine article "Overcoming Agoraphobia: One Woman's Journey" by Sarah Thompson—he continued with, *There's a technique called exposure therapy. Might help. Start small—try standing in your doorway for 30 seconds a day. Work up to short walks to your mailbox. Breathing exercises & positive self-talk can help too. Remember that recovery isn't a straight line; every little step forward is progress.*

He hit send.

Almost immediately, Milo replied. *Wow thank you mr Ty!!!*

Draker: *You're welcome, bud. Get some rest.*

Milo: *OK.*

Draker put the phone away. And smiled. For what felt like the first time in weeks.

He put the Maverick into gear and backed out. After circling down two floors, he exited the garage onto a well-lit downtown street, deserted in the middle of the night.

Back on track, his mind went to the mission, racing with possibilities. Nina's ex-lover, Cavanaugh, was his next lead. The way Nina had said the man's name nagged at Draker, a gut feeling of incongruity he couldn't quite place. And after his searches on BeauSearch Lite a few minutes earlier, Draker had an address for the guy.

The city blurred past. Empty sidewalks and empty windows and blazing lights. Moments like this—utterly alone in an area that was normally teeming with life—always left Draker with an unsettling feeling. There was something eerie about it.

At a red light, he entered Cavanaugh's address into the truck's navigation system. A moment later, it spoke to him.

In one mile, turn right.

His phone rang. Draker glanced at the screen. It was Beau.

"Shit," Draker said.

Draker had no idea where Beau lived, but assuming he was somewhere in the continental United States, the earliest it would be for him was 10:30 p.m. on the West Coast. Draker had hoped his middle-of-the-night escapade in Louisville would go unnoticed—at least until the following morning—but Beau was always one step ahead, monitoring Draker's movements through the GPS in his iPhone and the rental cars he used.

He swiped to answer, braced himself.

"What're you up to, Draker?" Beau's voice lacked its usual Texan joviality. "Why aren't you at the Pit?"

"I've got a lead. It's important."

"Leon Alden."

Turn right, then turn left.

"Yes, but more specifically, a person tied to Alden: Andrew Cavanaugh. A former Pit fighter and one of Nina's ex-lovers. She was in a polyamorous relationship with him and Alden after the battle, after her boyfriend was killed, and—"

Beau cut him off. "You said you were certain Alden is the Watchdog."

"That's right."

In three-point-one miles, merge onto I-264 East.

"Alden is at the Pit," Beau said. "So again, I must ask, why are you leaving the Pit against my strict orders? You should be at either the Pit or Larkin's gym—nowhere else."

"I told you; I have a damn lead to chase down. I've had enough training."

Beau grunted. "Larkin tells me you've been a handful."

Draker said nothing.

Beau's tone shifted. "Listen, Draker. I have news on the other front. I've got an address for Daniel Harper. The best way for you to address this will be to confront him, face to face."

Draker felt a grim satisfaction. "Gladly."

"After you verify that Harper's our man, that he's Agent Simpson from Afghanistan, get what you can out of him."

"And then?"

"Eliminate him."

"Gladly," Draker said again.

"But I'm not sure why I'm being so generous," Beau said, "with you defying me at every turn. Either way, I'm not giving you the Harper address until after you complete the Watchdog mission. Can't have you chasing vendettas and leaving a Soul behind."

Draker tightened his grip on the wheel. "Fine."

"Whatever the hell you're doing with this Cavanaugh fella, you wrap it up as fast as you can and get your ass back to the Pit." Beau paused, then continued in a more even tone. "Listen, Draker, there's something else. I've been chasing down some intel of my own, and I'm starting to agree with Agent Sullivan's SAC at the Des Moines Field Office. Sullivan might be wrong about the Watchdog attack at the Pit."

Draker frowned. "What do you mean?"

"From what I've been digging up, I think the Watchdog has a partner. It's this partner, not the Watchdog himself, who's within the Pit. This might be how Sullivan got confused in her investigation and thought that the Watchdog was planning to attack the Pit."

"A partner…"

"Yeah, and there's more. I've got a solid lead on a man of interest who seems to be plotting an attack in Cincinnati. I'll hold off on getting you the guy's name until I have confirmation, but his target seems to be a high-profile event at the Worldview Convention Center. It's called 'InfluencerCon'—a major gathering for social media influencers, including more lurid platforms like OnlyFans."

Draker let out a low murmur. "It does sound like a perfect Watchdog target."

"Exactly. The convention attracts thousands of attendees—fans, industry professionals, media. All there to meet their favorite influencers and learn about the latest trends in social media. Clearly, this is more in line with the Watchdog's M.O. than the Pit."

Draker had to agree. While the Pit was a… well, a pit of depravity, it had originally begun as a sort of men's retreat. It lacked the complete marks of societal decay characteristic of the Watchdog's usual targets. This InfluencerCon seemed a more likely target.

Stay in the right lane, then merge onto I-264 East.

"So what's the plan?" Draker said.

"For now, stay in Louisville and chase down leads in the Pit. There's still the partner angle to work on. But be ready to leave for Cincinnati at a moment's notice if I confirm all this. It's about an hour-and-a-half drive."

"Understood," Draker said.

A beep in Draker's ear and the call ended.

After pondering the new intel for a moment, an unrelated realization struck Draker—Beau had barely resisted Draker's decision to independently investigate Andrew Cavanaugh. Now, Draker was en route to the Cavanaugh's house, and Beau hadn't admonished him, hadn't screamed at him to return to the Pit.

That was a victory of sorts.

Draker grinned.

He pressed the accelerator, speeding onto the interstate.

CHAPTER
THIRTY-TWO

The Watchdog should have been relaxed, at ease. But he wasn't. The van was parked in a secluded corner of an abandoned strip mall's parking lot. Devices were spread on the workbench before him. He checked and rechecked each component. This was usually an activity that soothed him, but a nagging sense of unease wouldn't leave him alone.

Something was off. There was a detail he'd missed. He felt it, sensed it.

And it was making his paranoia flare. His eyes flashed to the rearview mirror. Empty parking lot. Just a flickering neon sign of a 24-hour laundromat, a stray cat near a set of dumpsters.

He picked up a modified smartphone. One of the detonators. He felt its edges, searched for any imperfections. It was perfect, of course. He'd checked it a dozen times already.

It was ready for its deadly purpose.

With this simple phone, he'd kill more of them. The worthless scum of this modern society—they were all part of a system that had to be torn down. His mission was just and necessary.

So why did he feel this creeping dread?

The more he considered it, the more obvious the answer became.

His associate—that had to be the weak link.

He'd messaged his associate earlier. Hours earlier. He knew that tech connectivity was often spotty in the Pit, but it had never taken *this* long to receive a response.

Yes, something was off.

The Watchdog set down the phone and pulled out a laptop, whose Wi-Fi was tethered to another phone on the other side of the van—a legitimate phone. He opened the messaged, scrolled through past conversations with his associate.

Had there been any red flags he'd missed? Any inconsistencies in their story?

He read the conversations. Analyzed words, timestamps. Nothing stood out.

Yet...

A memory surfaced. During one of their early planning sessions, his associate had hesitated when they discussed their target: the Pit fighting tournament. This hesitation had been brief, barely noticeable at the time. But now it stood out, glaring.

The Watchdog's fingers hovered over the keyboard. Should he confront his associate? Demand answers?

No, that could spook his associate, and if the individual really was the missing weak link, there was no telling what might happen.

The Watchdog closed the laptop, leaned back, took some deep breaths. Needed to focus.

A moment of this, then he reached under the passenger seat, pulled out a small case, and unlocked it. Inside was a custom-made 3D-printed pistol. It wasn't part of the main plan.

But one must always have a contingency plan.

The weapon was a commissioned job handled by an associate the Watchdog met on the dark web, someone who specialized in untraceable firearms. The result: a marvel of illicit engineering, entirely plastic save for the firing pin and a few other small metal components, designed to slip past metal detectors unnoticed.

There it was, resting on a bed of foam. The Watchdog lifted it up. The plastic was an off-white, bone color, making it look almost organic—unsettling. The gun was terribly light, yet the build quality was undeniable, the fit and finish of the thing.

He inserted the magazine. It gave a satisfying click as it seated.

He raised the pistol, aiming it across the empty parking lot. His finger rested lightly on the trigger as he swept across imaginary targets. The weapon felt natural in his hand, as if it were an extension of his arm.

Click. A duplicitous CEO, carelessly poisoning the world to earn a few more bucks. *Click.* A corrupt politician. *Click.* A tech mogul spreading misinformation.

Dead, dead, and dead.

Each imaginary shot released tension. But it wasn't enough. Not until the mission was complete.

He disassembled the rifle, returned it to its case.

With the rifle stowed away, his thoughts returned to his associate at the Pit. Damn it all. Trust was a difficult thing. He'd believed he and his associate shared a purpose. Now, uncertainty clouded his mind.

He drummed his fingers on the workbench. Debated. And grabbed the laptop, flipped it open. The messaging app was still on the screen where he'd left it. He tapped an index finger.

Should he, or shouldn't he?

No. Radio silence was crucial. The Watchdog couldn't let his doubts show—not yet, anyway.

He moved to the front of the van, to the driver's seat, and surveyed the lot. It was past one in the morning. The world was sleeping, unaware of what was coming.

A turn of the key, and the engine fired up.

He pulled out of the parking lot.

CHAPTER
THIRTY-THREE

A sharp metallic clang jolted Draker awake. He jumped, blinked—disoriented and squinting as the bright orange-red light of dawn filtered through the Maverick's windshield. The scene before him came into focus—a dilapidated mobile home squatting on a junk-strewn lawn.

It took him only a split second to remember where he was: parked outside Andrew Cavanaugh's house. He'd followed the GPS and arrived just after two in the morning. Before settling in for a few hours of sleep, he'd noted the rough neighborhood surrounding him, removed his holstered Glock from its position under his shirt, and shoved it beneath his thigh.

The trailer door banged open and a guy stepped out. Big, six-two, built solid. Broad shoulders under a grease-streaked jacket. Dark hair sticking out from under a beat-up trucker cap, jaw rough with stubble.

Draker watched him. The guy looked like so many of the Pit fighters. Wiry, tough, mean. This had to be Andrew Cavanaugh.

After slipping the Glock back under his shirt and clipping the holster to his jeans, Draker stepped out of the Maverick and crossed the street, moving toward the man. "Andrew Cavanaugh?"

The other guy froze, fixed Draker with a dark glare. "Who the hell are you?"

Draker stopped at the edge of the property, not going any farther. "I want to talk to you about Nina Hollis and Leon Alden."

Cavanaugh sneered. "Unbelievable. All these years later, and I still get this shit. Which side are you on—McGarry's or Burrows's?"

"I'm not on either side."

"You a cop or something?"

"No. Just looking for answers."

Cavanaugh looked Draker up and down, then spat on the ground. "You're a fighter, ain't ya? Got the bruises to prove it. You were at the tournament, huh?" He pulled out his phone, tapped the screen, looked back at Draker. "Tournament doesn't end until tonight. What, did you get kicked out?"

Draker didn't immediately respond. This guy was building up a perfect cover for Draker, all on his own. As long as Draker didn't interfere and mess anything up, Cavanaugh would continue with his assumptions.

Finally, Draker said, "Yeah. I mouthed off one too many times and Nina kicked me out."

Cavanaugh laughed. "Sounds about right. Did she fuck you first?"

Draker shook his head.

"That's too bad. Look, man, I don't know what you and her talked about, but my time at the Pit is over. Nina told me I could be out entirely, no one would ever contact me again. I want everything about the Pit behind me, and she promised me that."

"She told me you left her."

Another laugh from Cavanaugh, louder. "Yeah, she *would* say that."

Draker processed that. "I understand you had a relationship with Nina."

Cavanaugh laughed harshly. "I mean, I had my time with her. Who didn't? But... a *relationship*? She said that?"

Draker frowned. "Yeah. She said you, she, and Leon Alden were a 'little family.' Her words."

Cavanaugh roared at the idea, his whole body shaking with mirth. "A 'little family'? Oh, that's rich!"

"What's so funny?"

Wiping a tear from his eye, Cavanaugh said, "Look, for a while after the Pit's big fallout—you know, when Nina's boyfriend Ryan Hayes got killed—yeah, Alden and I were Nina's top two guys. But you gotta understand, Nina was already playing around with both of us before Ryan bit it. I stuck around her because I felt... you know, bad for her, losing Ryan. She loved that guy. And he was a good dude. But I didn't stay around long. I left the Pit altogether."

"Why's that?" Draker said.

Cavanaugh's expression darkened. "Because she started acting weird."

"Weird?"

Cavanaugh nodded. "Controlling. And not in a dominatrix sort of way, if you catch my drift."

Thoughts were starting to churn for Draker, and he debated his next words carefully. "The other guy. Leon Alden, Nina's bodyguard. I think he—"

"Wait! She's got him working as *her bodyguard* now?" This seemed to amuse Cavanaugh somehow.

"Yes. And I think he might be up to something. Something big. And I think he's manipulating Nina. Could he—"

Before Draker could finish, Cavanaugh cut him off again, laughing even more heartily, slapping a hand on his oil-stained jeans and bending over. "Alden? You haven't talked to the guy much, have you?"

Draker shook his head.

"Alden isn't exactly the sharpest knife in the drawer," Cavanaugh continued, wiping his eyes. "He plays it all cool and mysterious, borderline spiritual with those weird polished stones he's always playing with. But the guy's a complete follower.

Lacking a few brain cells. Got punched in the face one too many times, know what I mean?"

Panic washed over Draker. The pieces were starting to fall into place.

He thought of what Beau had told him...

... that the Watchdog had an associate within the Pit.

... that the Watchdog's next target wasn't the Pit but a convention in Cincinnati.

He said, "So you don't think a guy like Alden could be the person behind a series of coordinated attacks around the country?"

This time Cavanaugh didn't so much laugh as he did snort. "Shit, no, man! You kiddin' me? He's a muscly idiot... and that's coming from me, a guy with a ninth-grade education. Alden's a follower. Nina's puppy dog. He'll do anything for her, always has, even when Ryan was still alive."

In that moment, everything clicked for Draker. The real threat, the true person behind it all—it had been right in front of him the entire time.

He'd been so focused on Alden, he'd completely missed the obvious.

"Thanks for your time," Draker said, already turning away.

He sprinted back to his truck.

CHAPTER
THIRTY-FOUR

"**N**ina Hollis?!*"* Sullivan said, phone pressed to her ear.
She couldn't believe what Draker had just said.
Dawn broke through the floor-to-ceiling windows of the luxury suite. Outside, the morning light gave Louisvile's skyline a palette of pink, read, and oranges, glinting off all that glass. Sullivan wore a hotel robe, and as she paced, her shadow fell long and sharp, slashing across the bed and the plush carpet.

"That's right," Draker said. There was road noise in the background. "It was never Leon Alden. It's Nina. And she's not the Watchdog; she's the Watchdog's partner."

"But… all the leads I tracked on the dark web," Sullivan said. "The Watchdog ran multiple searches—*lots* of them—related to the Pit. And it's such a perfect Watchdog target."

Draker said, "Beau has solid intel suggesting an even more perfect Watchdog target: InfluencerCon in Cincinnati."

Sullivan considered this. She was familiar with InfluencerCon. It only took her half a moment to reply, "Yeah. Yeah, that *is* an even more likely target."

Her words had come out quietly. Almost hesitantly. She wanted to catch the Watchdog, to stop the bastard—of course—

but some foolish, vain part of her simply wanted to be right. For once.

She'd been so damn *certain* the attack would be at the Pit.

She pulled the phone from her ear, put the call on speakerphone, and began a web search. "And InfluencerCon is..." she said, waiting a moment for the results to populate. "Wrapping up tonight, the same night the Pit tournament is wrapping up."

Damn.

She really had been wrong. Which meant SAC Jameson—that smug bastard—had been right to snicker at her.

Draker must have sensed the deflation in Sullivan's tone, because when he spoke again, his tone was gentle. "Beau still hasn't confirmed that his Cincy lead is legit. And we know there's a connection to Nina Hollis and the Pit no matter what. So your Louisville investigation isn't in vain."

There was something about the simple truths Draker had offered up—no frills, no fluff—that was more comforting than any platitude could have been. She found herself smiling.

"But if Nina is the Watchdog's partner and they're not targeting the Pit," Sullivan said, "then what's the connection between the two of them? Nina will be completely preoccupied tonight with the final round of the tournament. How can she possibly help with a Watchdog attack in a different state an hour and a half away?"

"That's what I need you to look into," Draker said. "With our new intel, dig deeper into your initial dark web searches and see what you can find."

"I'm on it."

"Good. Talk soon."

Beep. The call ended.

Sullivan immediately went to the desk, pulled her laptop from her bag, and fell into the overstuffed chair. The leather gave a soft wheeze. The chair was as opulent as everything else in the suite.

She remembered Jameson's dismissive attitude back at the field office in Des Moines. His careless disregard had led to an open spending account for this assignment—his way of shutting her up.

She'd taken full advantage of his quasi-generosity. The luxury suite wasn't the only splurge she'd taken in Louisville.

Bastard.

She opened up a piece of propriety Bureau software—a one-off, fully encrypted web browser that gave her access to even the most soul-wrenching depths of the dark web. This was where she'd initially decoded the Watchdog's online identity and tracked down his searches related to the Pit.

She entered the Watchdog's screen name—*cerberus211212*—into the search field. Unlike her initial searches, she now had additional information with which to search. She typed *nina hollis* into the search field as well, then went to the filter settings and narrowed the list of sites to those from which she'd originally found so much damning information.

She pressed the enter key…

… and immediately gasped at what she saw.

CHAPTER
THIRTY-FIVE

Wynne had made another visit to her new best friend, codeine.

And now she was up and moving—slowly—around the confines of the shitty apartment, waiting for the Captain to call back. She didn't want to risk falling asleep again; she had to be alert when he rang.

She felt it in her bones—this impending call was her chance at redemption. She was sure the Captain would ask her to complete the task she'd begun when Sean Hunsinger called her for assistance in Ventura: bringing in Ty Draker.

As she turned past the kitchenette, she remembered the earlier vision she'd had, the flash of an amalgamated set of memories: Draker, in their kitchen back in Santa Clarita, looking at her, concerned, asking if she was okay.

Her fingers twitched, remembering the feel of a warm, solid body next to her. On their sofa. In their bed. Draker. Always Draker. Even now, she couldn't escape him. The memory of his touch—once a necessary evil of her cover, now some sort of strange specter.

… five years was a long time to play a role without some part of it becoming real.

Wynne shook her head. She couldn't afford such weakness. Not now. Not ever again.

The smartphone on the end table was mockingly silent. The Captain had said he would call "soon"—a purposefully vague word choice.

Prophetically, the phone rang. Wynne jumped, a Pavlovian response to that particular ringtone. A shot of pain flared across her back.

A moment of hesitation.

Then she snatched up the device, took a breath, and answered.

"Sir," she said, hand shaking.

"Cassandra," the Captain said, warm and kind, smooth as honey. "I trust you're ready to prove yourself?"

"Yes, sir."

"Good. I'm pleased to hear that. You've always been one of our most... adaptable operatives."

Wynne swallowed hard, knowing the double edge to that praise. *Adaptable.* Like how she'd adapted to life as Alyssa Draker, housewife extraordinaire. Like how she was now adapting to a life of a prisoner living with constant pain and the bitter taste of failure.

"Thank you, sir," she managed.

"Now, about Ty Draker," the Captain said. "We have some promising leads. It seems our friend has been developing quite the technical aptitude."

Wynne's brow furrowed. "Technical aptitude? Draker? *My* Draker?"

Referring to Draker so possessively caught her by surprise. Just moments before, she'd considered that after five years with him, some real connection must have formed. Maybe a hint of that was showing now.

Or maybe she'd meant to say "Ty Draker," not "My Draker." It certainly came out as the latter. No denying that. It gave her pause.

It gave the Captain pause too.

There was a long moment of no response from her phone.

Slip of the tongue. That's all it was.

Finally, a soft chuckle came through the line. "Indeed. Quite the surprise, isn't it? The man who avoided smartphones and couldn't be bothered to open a Facebook account is now delving into some incredibly sophisticated computer systems."

The revelation hit Wynne hard. Draker, a guy who wore his lack of screen time like a badge of honor, was now navigating complex computer systems. It was even more shocking than it was impressive.

The idea that she might not have known Draker as well as she thought sent a fresh wave of anger coursing through her.

At least, it seemed like anger at first. Then something else—something like betrayal.

"What exactly is Draker up to?" she said.

"He's been using his newfound skills to hack into databases at the CIA, of all places," the Captain said.

The words were so shocking, Wynne had to reach a hand out to the wall to steady herself.

CIA databases?

Draker?

"He was damn smart about it too," the Captain continued. "Covered his tracks expertly. Nearly got away with it. His only issue was he underestimated Windbrook's capabilities."

Wynne was still so stunned she could hardly respond. "What was he looking for?"

"He was digging into his past. Specifically, he was looking for Agent Simpson."

It was a good thing Wynne's hand was still plastered against the wall...

"Agent Simpson"—the alias used by one of the trio of supposed CIA agents Draker met in Afghanistan. The mission that had kicked off this whole twisted nightmare. Fifteen years ago.

"Sir, if Draker manages to uncover the truth—"

"Exactly," the Captain cut her off. "Which is why your mission is more critical than ever. And, being the nice guy that I am, I've set up everything for you. I was able to catch on to Draker's hacking early enough to set a few things in motion." He paused. "We had a lock on him, but he disappeared from the map. But we know where he'll be going next. That's where you come in."

"I understand, sir. I won't fail you again."

"See that you don't," the Captain said. "I'd hate to have to... re-educate you further."

The phantom pain across Wynne's back flared, as if responding to the thinly veiled threat. "That won't be necessary, sir."

"Excellent. With your back the way it is, you're in no condition for fieldwork. You'll be running the show from right there in that apartment. What's it called these days?" A slight pause. "Ah, yes. 'Remote work.' That's the buzzword. You're going to be a remote worker for this job, Cassandra." He chuckled.

"Yes, sir."

"You have unique insight into Draker's mind. Use it, 'Alyssa Draker.' Anticipate his moves. Bring him in."

The line went dead before Wynne could respond. She lowered the phone, mind reeling from the conversation.

The Captain was right. Though she hated to admit it. She *did* know Draker like no one else could. They'd lived together, laughed together, shared a bed.

He'd loved her.

If anyone could predict Draker's next move, it was Wynne.

CHAPTER
THIRTY-SIX

As the Maverick rocketed west on I-264, Draker's phone rang a second time. A few minutes earlier, Sullivan had called with news that had rocked Draker to his core. This second call could have been Sullivan calling back with follow-up information, sure—a detail she'd forgotten to share or something new she'd uncovered in the last few minutes.

But Draker somehow knew it wasn't her before he checked the screen. He knew who it must be.

He looked.

Sure enough...

"Yes, Beau?" he said.

Draker switched the call to speakerphone, then put both hands on the wheel, giving the Maverick some more gas. The interstate stretched ahead. Louisville's skyline faded in the mirror along with last pinkish traces of the sunrise.

"Braxton Reece," Beau said.

"Come again?"

"That's the Watchdog. Braxton Reece. And I was right. He's in Cincinnati. Attack's happening there at InfluencerCon."

"What do we know about Reece?"

"Early thirties. Grew up in suburban Chicago. Bright kid,

excelled in school, especially in critical thinking. Graduated from the University of Illinois with a degree in Business Administration. But he's always felt disconnected, superior to his peers. Sees himself as some kind of intellectual crusader against what he perceives as society's moral decay."

"How are you so sure about Cincinnati?"

"I've tracked Reece's van. It's an older model, no GPS, but I had plenty to piece together from traffic cameras and security footage. He was in the area of the Watchdog's first attacks. Beyond coincidental. It's him.

"Now, Reece has been casing the Worldview Convention Center for days. This InfluencerCon is exactly the kind of target the Watchdog would go for—a symbol of everything he despises about modern society."

Draker took a deep breath. "Beau, I think you're wrong on this one."

"Excuse me?"

"Sullivan just called. She's been doing her own digging on the dark web using Bureau software. She found evidence that the Watchdog and Nina Hollis have been in communication for almost a year. Before they went dark with their own encryption, it was clear they were planning an attack on this year's Pit tournament. There's going to be a bomb at the Pit tonight."

Silence hung on the line for a moment before Beau's incredulous voice cut through. "First off, my intel is never wrong. Second, why the hell would Nina Hollis want to blow up the Pit? The tournament she's led for years?"

"I don't know," Draker admitted. "Sullivan's doing more digging."

"Listen to me, Draker. I am certain there's going to be a major attack in Cincinnati. That's where we need to focus."

Draker's grip on the steering wheel tightened. "I've been on the ground in Louisville. I've met Nina Hollis and Leon Alden. I know something bad is going to go down here. Just give me a bit more time to figure this out."

"Only a few hours ago, you were bitching and moaning about the Louisville assignment," Beau shot back.

"There's this kid here, Ricky. I can't leave him behind to die," Draker said. "And I can't give up on Sullivan's investigation. She's onto something here."

The line crackled with Beau's exasperated sigh. "You've been defying me over and over with this mission. Our partnership is supposed to be about trust. I help you figure out Windbrook, help you get your life back, and you complete my missions... according to *my* rules." A pause. "If you stay in Louisville, then you're not getting the address for Daniel Harper."

Draker felt like he'd been punched in the gut. Daniel Harper, the man he'd known as Agent Simpson. One of the three men from that shadowy meeting in Afghanistan that had led Draker to murder a man for Windbrook, the beginning of the end of his reality.

But then Ricky's face flashed in his mind. And Sullivan's determined gaze. Draker took a deep breath, his decision crystallizing.

"Fine," he said.

Without waiting for a response, Draker ended the call.

CHAPTER
THIRTY-SEVEN

The secure meeting room felt like a pressure cooker. No windows. One door. Conference table. FBI-blue carpeting.

SAC Jameson settled into his chair at the head of the table. He ran a hand over his mustache. He'd been doing that a lot lately.

"All right, Weaver," he said to his trusted agent sitting across the table from him. "Let's hear what you've got."

Weaver, a lean man with sharp cheekbones and a neatly pressed suit, leaned forward. "It's big, sir. Bigger than anything we've seen before."

"Let's hear it. I don't have all day."

"The Pit isn't just some backwater brawl," Weaver said. "We're looking at a sophisticated operation drawing fighters and spectators from across the country. It's an illegal no-holds-barred tournament, savagery at its greediest and most lethal."

"Why was Sullivan so sure the Watchdog would be interested?"

"Her intel suggests the Pit began as a fight club and turned into some sort of brutal tournament—guys beating themselves into brain damage for the chance at winning a few thousand bucks. The perfect target for the Watchdog."

"If this thing's so big, why have we never heard about it?"

"There's a code of absolute secrecy. The only online networking takes place through the dark web."

"Shit..." Jameson muttered. He stood abruptly, pacing the length of the room. Five steps, turn. Five steps, turn. All his idle habits were coming out in full force "You're sure about this?" he said, stopping to face Weaver. "One hundred percent?"

Weaver nodded. "Yes, sir. Our girl's onto something big. And dangerous."

Jameson bent over his laptop, used the trackpad, then the large screen dominating the wall behind him glowed to life, displaying a map of Louisville, Kentucky. He stepped up to it, crossed his arms, studied.

As he stared at the map, the enormity of the situation began to sink in.

He'd sent Sullivan into this mess. Alone. Unsupported. All because he'd been too stubborn, too set in his ways to see what was right in front of him.

Weaver cleared his throat. "What's the plan, boss?"

Jameson turned. "I need everything we've got on the Pit in Louisville. And I mean everything. Official reports, unofficial chatter, all that dark web shit. I don't care if it's written on a damn cocktail napkin. I want it on my desk in an hour."

"Yes, sir."

Weaver stood, gathered his notepad and laptop, and left.

Alone now, Jameson turned back to the map of Louisville. Somewhere in that city—several states away—was an invisible den of underground savagery.

A Pit.

And he'd sent one of his own right into the heart of it.

Hold on, Sullivan, he thought. *Cavalry's coming. Just... hold on.*

CHAPTER
THIRTY-EIGHT

Back at Larkin's gym.

And this time, willingly.

The Maverick's tires crunched on the gravel as Draker pulled into the parking lot. There was the all-too-familiar shabby building before him with Louisville's downtown skyline just visible in a gap in the surrounding trees, its towers tiny and distant.

Among the scattered pickup trucks and multi-colored beaters populating the lot, Sullivan's late-model Mercedes stood out, parked well to the side, waiting for Draker.

Draker hadn't even killed the engine when the Mercedes door swung open. Sullivan stepped out, approached, looked concerned. She hurried in his direction, and as soon as Draker stepped out of the truck—before he could make sense of it—she was hugging him. Tight.

Draker hesitated—just for a moment—then his arms wrapped around her, returning the gesture. They parted. Sullivan's expression was troubled. "Why are we meeting here?"

She motioned with her head toward the building behind them.

Draker glanced at the gym's bland facade. "There's something I gotta do here in a minute." He left it deliberately vague.

Sullivan's eyes narrowed, but she didn't press further. Instead she said, "I found out more. I dug deeper into the initial conversations between the Watchdog and Nina Hollis on the dark web. I broke through the second level of encryption and got to their DM messages—after they met in the open forums but before they took their communication off the grid to a proprietary and unhackable messaging software."

"What'd they chat about?"

"Oh, you know, the usual banter between new friends. 'Hey, I love how much you hate modern society. We should be buddies. By the way, I'm the infamous Watchdog terrorist. Want to coordinate with me on a pair of concurrent attacks?'"

"A *pair* of attacks? At the same time?"

Sullivan nodded.

"That doesn't fit the pattern," Draker said. "The Watchdog has always worked alone, and he's only ever committed one attack at a time, spread out over months."

Sullivan took a deep breath, steadying herself. "It's complicated. Vengeance usually is."

The word made Draker straighten up—*vengeance*.

"What?"

"Nina has wanted revenge on the Pit," Sullivan said, "ever since her boyfriend Ryan Hayes was murdered during the fallout between two factions that split during the schism."

Draker recalled the bits of information he'd gleaned about the Pit's tumultuous history. But from everything Draker had gathered, it was Nina who put the pieces of the Pit back together, brought it to heights it had never seen, monetized it.

Sullivan continued, "Nina pretended to be a mediating figure who wanted to bring the Pit's two factions back together, to heal the wounds, but she was actually orchestrating their slaughter. Plotting, calculating. Years in the making. Revenge-is-a-dish-best-served-cold sort of shit. She didn't have the know-how to execute her plan alone, so she turned to the dark web, looking for a partner. That's where she met the Watchdog."

Draker's mind raced, piecing together the implications. "So they bonded over a shared hatred for the modern world?"

Sullivan nodded. "That's right. And they formed a mutually beneficial arrangement. Nina saw the Pit's savagery as the reason Ryan Hayes was killed. And the Watchdog... well, you know his views on modern society. Nina wanted revenge but needed assistance. The Watchdog agreed to help with her attack on the Pit. He organized it, created the technical plans, and provided her with the explosives and other necessary materials."

"And what did he get in return?" Draker asked.

"In exchange, Nina agreed to stage her bombing to look like the next Watchdog attack. She had to leave enough clues to draw in law enforcement because the Pit—with its savagery and illegal nature—was seemingly a perfect Watchdog target."

"The Watchdog was creating a diversion."

"Exactly," Sullivan said. "With Nina's attack about to take place and law enforcement believing that Louisville was the Watchdog's next target, the heat would be pulled off the Watchdog so that he could organize his *real* next attack."

"InfluencerCon in Cincinnati."

"Right. How'd you—"

"Beau."

"Ah. Yes. Beau." Sullivan grinned, continued. "To the Watchdog, InfluencerCon represents the epitome of everything he despises about modern society—what he sees as the ultimate symbol of societal decay."

"So Nina gets her revenge against the Pit, and the Watchdog gets cover for his true plan. Two attacks at once." Draker paused a beat. "And did the Watchdog ever give Nina his real name?"

Sullivan nodded. "Yeah, it was Br—"

"Braxton Reece."

Sullivan nodded again, looking slightly puzzled before she said, "Beau?"

"Beau." Draker sighed. "Shit! Beau was right. I hate it when he's right. The Watchdog is Braxton Reece, and he's going to attack InfluencerCon; just like Beau said." Then, looking at Sullivan, he smiled. "But you were right too. All along. There *is* an impending attack at the Pit in Louisville. Screw SAC Jameson."

This made Sullivan chuckle.

Draker reached for his phone. Sighed again. "I guess I need to call Beau."

"Ha! I was right!" Beau's smug excitement registered loud and clear through Draker's enhanced iPhone.

Not that the guy was trying to hide it…

Draker rolled his eyes. "We were both right."

He stood a few feet from the Mercedes and the Maverick, beside the trees at the parking lot's edge. Sullivan remained at the vehicles. She sat with her legs out the back of the Mercedes' open rear door, her laptop resting on her thighs—internet connection tethered to her phone—doing some last-minute research.

"Give me a little more time here in Louisville," Draker said. "I can stop both attacks—the Pit and InfluenceCon."

There was a pause on the other end of the line. Finally, Beau replied, his tone cautious, "I'm sure the Watchdog will attack the closing ceremony gala at InfluencerCon at 10 p.m. tonight. That buys you a little time, but not much."

Draker checked his watch. "And there's a few more hours before the final night of the Pit tournament begins."

"Which give you a little while to get your head together," Beau said.

Draker's gaze drifted to the gym. He smirked. "I've got a different idea of how to fill those hours."

"Ah, you slippery son of a bitch. Always mysterious," Beau chuckled. It was good to hear the friendly tone in Beau's voice again. It was good to be partners again. "Good luck, Draker."

"Thanks, Beau," Draker said and ended the call.

He walked back over to Sullivan, who snapped her laptop shut and stood up.

"I'm headed in to see Larkin," Draker said, motioning toward the gym.

Sullivan squinted at him. "I thought you hated the guy."

Draker shook his head. "No. Never hated him. I just hated being forced to get my ass kicked." He looked at the gym again. "But I know what I gotta do."

Sullivan stepped closer. "Nina is gonna open the doors like she did last night—for the wives and girlfriends, friends and family. I could go in with you tonight, as a spectator. You could use an extra pair of eyes."

Draker thought this through. "Too risky. She's onto us now, so if you showed up the second night after not showing up the first, that would be a bad idea."

Sullivan nodded reluctantly. Looked away. Then, her eyes met his. "I want you to know..." she began. Paused. Continued, "These past few days, working with you... it's been... real. Whatever happens tonight, I'm glad to have met you, Ty Draker."

Before Draker could respond, Sullivan closed the distance between them. Her lips met his in a passionate kiss, catching him even more off guard than her hug had minutes earlier. But this response was only momentary. Because then Draker returned Sullivan's kiss with equal fervor.

And for a moment, he forgot about the mission.

He forgot, even, about Kylie Payton in Ventura.

He was alive only there, only in that moment.

As they broke apart, Draker's hand lingered on Sullivan's face—smooth, achingly soft—his thumb tracing the curve of her cheek. Their eyes locked.

Another kiss. Briefer. Gentler.

"Be back in a few minutes," Draker said.

Without another word, he turned and strode toward the gym. Broken asphalt crunched under his boots.

As he reached for the door handle, he cast one last glance over his shoulder at Sullivan. Yards away now, at the opposite end of the parking lot, standing by their vehicles, watching him.

Draker pulled open the door and entered the gym.

CHAPTER
THIRTY-NINE

Jameson was back in the secure conference room, and even though he was solo this time, the space felt even tenser than when he'd been there earlier in the day with Weaver.

At least he wasn't in his office with that damn ticking clock...

Jameson sat at the head of the table once more. And while he was technically the only person in the room, he wasn't alone. Across from him, showing on the screen that dominated the wall, were two senior agents from the Louisville field office, sitting together at a similar conference table with the FBI Seal on the wall behind them, waiting expectantly, faces grim.

"Gentlemen," Jameson began, "we've got a situation."

He tapped a button on his laptop, and a shared image showed in the corner of the screen. It was a map of Louisville with the Pit's probable location highlighted in red—an abandoned warehouse on the southwest corner of the city limits. Weaver had found it by sifting through Sullivan's material, crunching her data.

"Three days ago, I thought this was nothing more than a wild goose chase," Jameson admitted. He stroked his mustache with discomfort at the confession. "Now, I'm convinced we're looking at a potential terrorist attack." He paused. "The Watchdog."

The Louisville agents exchanged glances. Jameson could read their skepticism, their unspoken questions.

He took a deep breath, pushing down his pride. "Special Agent Jenna Sullivan was right. Her investigation has uncovered evidence that the Watchdog is targeting the Pit. We've tried to contact Sullivan, but she's either out of reception, or she's gone dark." He looked squarely at the camera. "I need your full cooperation. Whatever resources you've got, whatever manpower you can spare. We're going in."

The older of the two Louisville agents—a weathered man named Sears—leaned forward. "With all due respect, Jameson, this is our jurisdiction. Why the sudden interest from Des Moines?"

Jameson felt a flare of his old defensiveness. He pushed it aside. "Because I sent Agent Sullivan in there. Because I dismissed her concerns, and now she might be in over her head. And because if she's right about this, we're looking at a tragedy that'll make the Watchdog's previous attacks look like firecrackers."

The conference room fell silent. Jameson watched as the two Louisville agents faced each other, leaned in, said things to each other their microphone didn't pick up.

They turned back to face him.

"Shit," the younger agent said. "If this is true—"

"It is," Jameson cut in. "I've seen the evidence. I've connected the dots. And now we need to move."

He tapped on his laptop again. More items appeared in the shared space of the screen, pieces of Sullivan's research—photos of a decrepit warehouse structure, snippets of intercepted communications from the dark web, and Sullivan's meticulous notes.

Looking at the images, Jameson felt a surge of pride in his agent's work...

... mixed with a deep shame at how he'd initially treated her theory.

Sears nodded slowly, his own skepticism fading. "What's the play, then?"

"We go in hard and fast," Jameson said. "Full tactical team, coordinated with local law enforcement. We need eyes on every entrance and exit of that building before we make our move."

"And Sullivan?" the younger Louisville agent said.

Jameson's jaw tightened. "Finding her is the priority. She's not just a good agent; she's the key to unraveling this mess. We get her, we get the Watchdog."

CHAPTER
FORTY

Only a few more hours to wait. Braxton Reece, the man who for a year had been calling himself the Watchdog, was at his workbench in his van, hunched over a detailed diagram of the Worldview Convention Center. Outside, downtown Cincinnati hummed, oblivious to the danger hidden behind the doors of the bland-looking panel van parked on the side of the street.

Reece traced his finger along the map, double-checking each bomb placement. Main entrance, check. Conference halls A and B, check. VIP lounge, check.

Perfect.

Every location had been strategically chosen for maximum impact.

Looking up from the convention center's diagram, he saw the building itself, through his windshield, standing in the distance. Worldview was an effusive display of modern architecture. And it was a monument to the excess Reece despised. Tomorrow it would host "InfluencerCon," a gathering of social media personalities and their adoring fans. A disgusting thought.

No matter. They were all going to get blown up tomorrow.

Reece's plan was flawless. While his associate, Nina Hollis, created chaos at the Pit fight tournament, drawing law enforcement's attention, Reece would strike at the heart of society's *true* cancer.

These "influencers"—with their vapid content and mindless followers—represented everything wrong with the modern world. They peddled unrealistic lifestyles, promoted consumerism, and contributed nothing of value. These days, the depravity had reached such levels that platforms like OnlyFans had become household names.

The world was living in the epitome of moral decay.

He'd spent hours trudging through social media, witnessing the degeneracy firsthand. It had been necessary research, but it left him feeling unclean. All those perfectly curated images, the constant clamor for attention, the near nudity and full-on nudity, the shameless self-promotion.

He pulled out his phone, checked for updates from Nina. Nothing yet. He wasn't worried; she knew the plan. Her attack on the Pit would serve as the perfect smokescreen, allowing him to carry out his true mission undetected.

Returning to the diagram, Reece ran through the plan one more time. He'd infiltrate the convention center posing as an event attendee, getting his detonator in range of the C4 he'd planted throughout the building months earlier.

He thought of the initial, small-scale test he'd conducted in the trees. There'd been that satisfying crater that had been left in the earth—smoking, surrounded by debris and clods of dirt.

Tomorrow's explosion was going to leave a much bigger mark...

Reece closed his eyes, visualized the scene. The convention center. Packed with people—vile, vapid people—all of them blissfully unaware. Influencers on stage, preening for their audience.

And then... chaos. Panic. A reckoning.

Months. *Months* of planning had led to this moment. Countless hours spent researching, preparing, refining. Reece had sacrificed everything—his job, his home, his connections to the "normal" world. And it would all be worth it.

He turned back to the diagram, made a few final notations. Timing would be crucial tomorrow. He needed to coordinate his attack with Nina's distraction at the Pit in Louisville. Too early, and Reece risked detection; too late, and he might miss his window of opportunity.

His phone chimed. A text message. His associate. Nina.

All is in place at my facility. G2G for tonight.

Reece replied. *Perfect.*

Everything was falling into place.

He deleted the text conversation, began packing up. The bombs themselves were already prepared, waiting in a hidden compartment beneath the workbench. To any casual observer, the interior of his van would seem utterly mundane.

He checked the clock on his phone. It was time to move, to find a place to lay low for the next several hours. A city park. Or maybe a Walmart parking lot. Wouldn't that be ironic?

He would mentally prepare himself, take a nap, and be prepared to act once nighttime came.

Then, in a few hours, he would transform the paradigm. He was going to demonstrate to the influencers the *true* power of influence.

CHAPTER
FORTY-ONE

With the phone call from the Captain in her rearview, Wynne could now afford to sit down again.

Her back thanked her.

Though even with all the codeine, there was still a dull and constant ache, pulsing with sharper flashes of pain.

On the heavily scratched coffee table in front of her, a pair of faces stared back at her from her laptop screen. Muscly guys. Chiseled faces. Former spec-ops types. Windbrook operatives.

Campiglio. White. Deep acne scars on his cheeks, just below his eyes.

Warren. Black. Thick neck. An unusually sharp widow's peak.

Despite their blank, professional faces, Wynne thought she sensed something there, something in both sets of eyes—like hidden doubts or questions they might harbor about their team leader's recent setbacks.

Surely everyone at Windbrook had heard about what happened in Ventura, California. Two operatives—Sean Hunsinger and Cassandra Wynne—had failed to bring in their target: Ty Draker, a seemingly ordinary Windbrook asset who had suddenly become the company's biggest problem. Draker had murdered Hunsinger and spared Wynne only because he couldn't bring himself to kill her too.

Yes, all of Windbrook was surely in the know. These two guys on Wynne's laptop screen were probably laughing at her behind their stony facades.

Wynne pushed aside the thought. She couldn't afford to dwell on her failures now. Not when she was so close to redeeming herself.

She straightened up—eliciting a jolt of pain from her back—and refocused.

"All right, fellas," she began. "The target is Ty Draker."

She clicked a button on her laptop, and Draker's face appeared on the shared area of the screen. It was an old photo, maybe five years ago. Wynne had taken it. There was that feeling again, a reaction to the sight of Draker—hatred mingled with that other sensation that had been toying with her.

"You may be familiar with Draker's background," she continued. "Former Air Force, ex-cop, and until recently, an inactive Windbrook asset. What you might not know is that he's become a significant threat to our organization."

The two men's faces remained blank. But she could see it in their eyes—recognition.

Yes, these fucks knew all about Ty Draker.

Which meant they knew all about Wynne too.

And her failures.

"Latest intel suggests that Draker has developed some surprising technical skills," Wynne said. "But this has given us an unexpected lead on him."

She paused and studied the two hard faces, looking for any sort of reaction. Still none.

So she continued. "Be ready to move."

CHAPTER
FORTY-TWO

Draker hoped this wasn't a mistake. Because swallowing one's pride was a hard thing to do.

He stepped into the gym. The familiar scent was there—sweat, chalk, old leather.

He had texted Larkin earlier that morning—using his iPhone's dictation while he barreled across the city on I-264. The lack of response was concerning.

The door swung shut behind him with a solid thud. Midday sun struggled through grimy windows. A few fighters were already at it, paying him no mind. He scanned the room. Couldn't find Larkin.

Larkin had been right all along—just like Beau had been right all along about the mission. But Larkin had been right in a completely different way.

Draker kept scanning the gym for his trainer.

For two days, Draker had resisted Larkin's teachings, clinging to his rigid, by-the-book approach, to his years-earlier police training. But now, after facing the chaotic reality of the Pit and this twisting, turning mission, he saw the truth in Larkin's words.

Adaptability *was* key to survival.

All the fight maneuvers Larkin had taught Draker, all of the ass-beatings he'd given—none of it was as important as the fundamental notion of adaptability. This realization itself was the most important lesson Larkin could have taught him.

Draker just hoped he'd have the chance to show his trainer that the message had finally, truly sunk in.

He turned past a behemoth pummeling a speed bag and found Larkin standing at the far wall, wiping down medicine balls. Draker approached.

Larkin glanced over, stopped what he was doing. He wore a tank top, shorts, Converse. His eyes stared back at Draker—one brown, one white—offering nothing. He stood up, relaxed but authoritative.

"Hey," Draker said, fighting against foolish pride. "I want to apologize. I need to learn to adapt. And fast. I only have a few hours."

Larkin's face was unreadable. Something was off.

Draker hesitated, then added, "And... I'm also sorry about what I said before. About Octavius. That was callous of me. I didn't understand."

Larkin nodded. "I owe you an apology too. All those personal jabs... that wasn't right. I pushed too hard, cut too deep. That's on me."

But his expression was still off.

They stood in silence for a moment. Draker pointed to the ring behind them.

"Can we begin?"

Larkin shook his head, cleared his throat. "Beau called me. Early this morning. Said our training is over."

Draker waved it off. "No, no, no! I just talked to him. Beau was pissed at me earlier, but we ironed things out." He pulled out his phone. "Here, I'll call him, and—"

Larkin shook his head. "It doesn't matter. We're done either way. You've learned. You're ready."

"But I'm going back to the Pit tonight! I need—"

Larkin cut him off again. "Do you honestly think there's anything I can teach you in the next few hours that's gonna change tonight's outcome?"

Draker didn't respond, couldn't.

"Do you think you *really* learned anything from me during our short training sessions that could get you prepared for a place like the Pit overnight?"

"Yes! Lots! You taught me to pull my leg back when—"

"Stop." Larkin let the word sit for a moment, then, "You always *were* adaptable, Draker. Just stubborn. You had it all along."

Draker blinked, caught off guard by the unexpected praise. "Wait a minute. Earlier, you said you'd met another of Beau's Rangers. What's that about?"

Larkin sighed, leaned against the wall. "It's a long story, kid. But I guess we've got time."

"Hours."

Larkin nodded. "When Octavius died, something felt off to me. Like he'd tapped out, but the ref ignored it."

"Why would the ref do that?"

"Money, I thought. But I had no proof," Larkin said. "For decades, no one believed me. I mean, who'd believe a tale like that from an underground fighting club, right? I'd pretty much given up on ever figuring out the truth."

"So what changed?"

Larkin smiled, the purest smile Draker had seen from the man. "Years later, out of the blue, I get this call from a guy named Beau. Said he could help me uncover the truth. Offered to send someone to sort things out—a field agent, a person he called a 'Ranger.'"

"And I take it the Ranger figured things out."

"That he did. The guy came to town and immediately started digging. Turns out, the fighter and the ref both had a grudge against Octavius over a betting dispute. They... they orchestrated his murder."

"Shit. How did the Ranger handle it?"

Larkin's eyes narrowed, and he grinned again. But this time the smile wasn't pure—it was dark. "He killed them both."

Silence for a few moments. Then Draker said, "And that's how you met Beau?"

"Yeah," Larkin said, straightening up. "The beginning of a long friendship." He stepped closer. "Look, I'm not gonna run you through any more drills. But I *will* show you one last thing. Call it a parting gift."

Suddenly, Larkin's hand shot out and pressed a spot on Draker's neck. Precise. Strong. But nowhere near full-strength.

"Feel that?" Larkin said. "That's a pressure point. Hit it right, and you're gonna knock the other guy out cold. Squeeze with all you got."

Draker nodded, memorized the spot.

"It's not foolproof," Larkin continued. "But in a pinch, it could save your ass."

When Larkin took a step back, Draker sensed a change. The usual tension was now replaced by something akin to mutual respect.

"You're ready," Larkin said.

CHAPTER
FORTY-THREE

A few hours later, night

Nina Hollis was about to blow up a whole a lot of people. Revenge was less than two hours away. She should have been ecstatic. Years of planning, years of patience. All of it was about to pay off.

So why the hell was she so anxious?

She knew the answer: Ty Draker.

FBI Agent Sullivan's inside man was getting closer and closer. He'd gotten close enough to suspect Nina's goon, Leon Alden. Nothing indicated that Draker had figured out that there was indeed an impending attack on the Pit, nor that it was Nina, not the Watchdog, who was orchestrating this bombing.

But...

She hadn't spoken to Draker since their meeting in her office the previous night. And word had come from Cell 3 that Draker hadn't been seen around the Pit all day or all night since.

Worrisome.

Incredibly worrisome.

Nina stood at the edge of the octagon, fingers absently tracing the fencing. The warehouse floor buzzed with anticipation—a low rumble of voices and creaking metal as the bleachers filled. Fighters filed in alongside a few wives, girlfriends, and a motley assortment of hangers-on. The place reeked of men—body odor, sweat, and machismo.

She scanned the crowd, looking for Draker. He wasn't there yet. She catalogued faces she'd known for years. Some had been here since the beginning, when the Pit was nothing more than a handful of laid-off factory workers with too much anger and too little hope. Back when Jay McGarry and Tommy Burrows ran the show, before it all went to hell.

Before Ryan was killed.

The familiar ache bloomed in her chest at the thought of him. Ryan Hayes, with his easy smile and gentle hands. Well... gentle when he wanted to be. Nina liked the rough stuff. And Ryan had been happy to oblige.

But there was more to it than that. A lot more. Ryan was the man who'd loved her, trusted her, even as she explored her desires with other fighters. She'd reciprocated, allowing him whatever outside pleasures he wanted to hunt down.

Most importantly, Ryan had understood her in ways no man ever had.

And they'd taken him from her.

Nina's hands shook as the memory flashed across her mind. Ryan's broken body, twisted on the floor. His face a mess of blood and torn tissue. Battered, contused, nearly unrecognizable. She'd held him—not knowing whether he was still alive or had just died—right there in that godforsaken parking lot. All because McGarry and Burrows couldn't see eye to eye, couldn't control the monster they'd created.

Well, she'd shown them, hadn't she? Taken their precious fight club and turned it into something bigger, more profitable than they could have ever imagined. And now...

Now it was time for the grand finale.

Her hand drifted to her pocket, found her phone. She caressed it. Later, the phone would be the key component of her revenge. The Watchdog had come through, just as she'd known he would.

Braxton Reece—a kindred spirit if ever there was one. He understood the rot at the heart of society, the need to burn it all down and start anew. He had been more than happy to help Nina destroy another pocket of humanity's rot.

For a moment, guilt tugged at Nina, coming at her in a flash. There were good people here, people who had nothing to do with Ryan's death. But, just as quickly, she pushed the feeling aside. They were *all* complicit, all part of the system that had taken everything from her. Just like Reece told her.

"Nina?"

She turned. Leon Alden was at her side. Under the harsh fluorescent light of the octagon, he was looking particularly of-his-age that night, every one of his fifty-something-year-old wrinkles showing in high contrast.

But his pecs and shoulders were alight too, all out on display in that black tank he was wearing. Leon was a good fuck. Always had been. And since Ryan passed, he'd been loyal, always by her side, her protective watchdog.

He sure was a dumb shit though. Loyalty and stupidity usually go hand in hand.

Those three smooth stones clicked softly in his palm—black, white, and gray. An old habit that used to set Nina's teeth on edge. Everyone around the Pit thought there was some great meaning to the stones—maybe Alden was some sort of zen master practicing a rare technique he'd learned from a Tibetan monk on the side of a mountain halfway around the world; maybe the stones were from a voodoo mistress in New Orleans.

Nina knew better. Leon's stone-twirling was just a simple calming technique he'd picked up from a YouTube video. *YouTube.* As for the stones themselves, their black, white, and gray colors... he'd plucked the trio out of the landscaping of a dentist office.

Leon wasn't bright enough for anything more profound than that.

"Everything okay?" Leon said. He'd clearly picked up on her trepidation. That wouldn't do, not with the bleachers filling up. Nina needed to compose herself.

She nodded, forced a smile. "Just pre-tournament jitters. You know how it gets."

Leon's eyes softened. There was a certain kindness beneath the dolt's rough exterior. He'd been there for her after Ryan, had been one of the few things that held her together when she thought she might shatter. For a moment, she considered telling him everything—about the bomb, about Reece, the Watchdog, about the inferno that was about to consume them all.

But...

Nah.

Leon could die with the rest of them.

"It's filling up," Leon said, gesturing to the growing crowd. "Looks like we might break some records. Hope those old bleachers can hold 'em all."

"They'll hold," Nina said. "And I'm gonna give those people a show they'll never forget."

As Leon moved away to check on the fighters, Nina's gaze drifted upward. Somewhere in the rafters, nestled among the steel beams and shadows, was a small device. One of several throughout the building. A simple-looking thing, just a tangle of wires and gray putty, no bigger than a mason jar.

There! Glancing down from the rafters, she spotted Draker in the crowd. Finally. She could keep an eye on him now.

Draker was just taking his seat in the bleachers, the same spot he'd occupied yesterday—next to Ricky Braddock. Ricky was a young, scrawny thing that didn't belong here among these titans. His fighter name was "Tank," a perfectly over-the-top moniker befitting the little twerp. It was no wonder Draker had befriended him; Draker was the do-gooder Boy Scout type.

Draker's eyes came in her direction. Their gazes locked on each other. And held. There was something there in Draker's eyes, a slight variation from what Nina had seen yesterday when he'd told her he was suspicious of Leon Alden...

Yes, Nina's intuition was on point. Her apprehension was warranted. Draker was onto her, figuring it out. She could sense it, could feel the Pit's decrepit walls closing in on her.

But no worries. Draker didn't have time to finish this thing. Hell, he was even scheduled to fight here shortly. Then, in a couple of short hours, he'd be nothing but ash and memory, along with the rest of them.

Nina looked away from him and stepped to the front of the cage. A hush fell over the crowd. All eyes turned to her, hungry for violence, for spectacle. She'd give them what they wanted...

... one last time.

"Welcome," she said, "to the fight of your lives."

As the crowd roared its approval, Nina felt an electric thrill surge through her. This was it. The beginning of the end.

She thought of Ryan again. Twisted body. Bloody face. Cradled in her arms. She'd screamed. *And screamed.* She thought of the years of pain and loneliness that followed. Of the endless nights spent plotting, scheming, building toward this moment.

"Let's get this shit stared!" she shouted.

The Pit erupted in chaos.

Nina retreated to the octagon, threw open the screeching door, and waved an arm toward the bottom row of the bleachers, where the first two fighters were waiting—bare-chest, pumped-up, glistening, dead fucking sexy. They bounded toward her, and as they rushed past, their smell wafted over her, intoxicating.

She slammed the door. It screeched on its hinges, banged shut. Bending over, she grabbed the chain from the floor and sealed the fighters inside the octagon.

Leon rattled the bell.

The crowd roared.

The fighters smashed into each other with a heavy, wet thud.

And Nina reached into her pocket and caressed her phone again.

CHAPTER
FORTY-FOUR

Sullivan felt helpless, impotent.

She was back at the Pit, outside, leaning against her Mercedes, watching people file into the old warehouse through the single open door at the front. Their excited chatter carried across the parking lot, which was filling up rapidly, a motley assortment of vehicles pulling in. The sky above held onto the final remnants oranges and purples, night taking over. Streetlights flickered, giving the area an amber-colored glow.

Draker was in there, in the warehouse, scheduled for another fight and trying to stop a bombing.

And Sullivan was out here. In the damn parking lot. Helpless and impotent.

She'd told him earlier that she could go in as a spectator, provide support and an extra set of eyes. But Draker had shut her down, warning her that Nina was onto them. It was too risky, he'd said.

And yet when *she* had told *him* it was risky for him to leave the Pit and investigate Andrew Cavanaugh, the fool had ignored her warning and did what he damned well pleased.

Sullivan tapped her foot on the ground. This had been her investigation from the start. Louisville was hers. She'd connected the dots when no one else had—not Jameson, not Draker. And now here she was, sidelined, watching from the shadows while Draker took center stage.

She looked at the doors and saw the line of people finally coming to a close. By the body language of the fighter standing guard, it was clear he was about to shut the doors, locking down the Pit for the rest of the night.

Still, Sullivan remained frozen where she was, locked in place by her dual phobias—claustrophobia and fear of the dark.

She knew the inside of the Pit was dark, close, and labyrinthine; Draker had told her as much, and she could see glimpses of the dimly lit interior past the line of people filing in—a black tunnel vanishing into nothingness.

She tried to work up the nerve, tried to will her feet to move…

… but her body wouldn't cooperate.

After the last person entered, the fighter closed the door. It gave a resounding clang that echoed across the parking lot.

Sullivan's heart sank. She'd missed her chance. Again.

Frustration boiled, threatened to spill over. Dammit! She'd locked up. She'd succumbed to her fears. The thought of pushing through that crowd, of being trapped among all those bodies in that dark, confined space…

She swallowed. Suddenly, the wide-open parking lot felt cramped too. The shadows stretched, grew, coming at her like grasping fingers. Her heart hammered, palms moistened. She could almost feel the warehouse walls closing in, even out here in the open.

Get it together, she told herself. She took a pair of deep breaths. But it was no use. The fear had her now, images of dark, cramped spaces flashing through her mind.

She remembered the basement. The four days of isolation. The terror of not knowing if she'd ever see the light again.

Sullivan shut her eyes, willing the memories away. When she opened them again, she looked at the warehouse.

And remembered something.

The transom window on the side. Draker's secret entrance and exit.

For a long moment, she was frozen in place once more, mind at work. The thought of squeezing through that tiny opening made her lose her breath again. But the alternative—standing out here, helpless and impotent—was suddenly unbearable.

She could do this.

Before she could talk herself out of it, Sullivan was moving. She skirted the edge of the parking lot, keeping to the deepening shadows. Her heart pounded harder as she approached the side of the building. She avoided the security cameras, sticking to the wooded area, her shoes crunching on sticks and urban refuse.

And then she saw it.

The transom window. A rectangle of deeper darkness against the weathered brick. She cut through the shadows and stepped up to the wall. Her hands shook as she reached for the particle board covering. It came away easily, its two nails popping right off; Draker had loosened it up considerably with his frequent comings and goings.

She set the board to the side, jumped up to grab the edge of the window, pushed it open, and, grunting, pulled her body up. Through the opening, she saw a narrow, nearly pitch-black hallway beyond.

She nearly lost her grip, nearly fell to the ground.

No. No, you got this.

She took a deep breath, steeling herself. Then, with a grunt of effort, she hauled herself up and began to squeeze through.

Immediately, panic set in. The opening was tight, much tighter than she'd anticipated. Her shoulders scraped against the sides. For one terrifying moment, she thought she might be stuck. Her breath came in ragged gasps. She almost cried out. She wriggled and pushed, the darkness pressing in around her.

Come on, come on! she told herself.

With a final, desperate heave, she tumbled through the window and onto the floor beyond.

Pain in her side. Her head too; she'd hit it against the inside wall.

She groaned and lay there for a moment, heart thundering, lungs burning. She gulped in air. Shook.

But she'd made it. She was inside.

As her eyes adjusted, however, a new fear announced itself. She may have cleared the tiny window, but the hallway stretched out before her—a tunnel of utter darkness.

Every childhood nightmare, every adult phobia came rushing back. She could almost hear Linda's voice, taste the dry bite of the basement air.

No, Sullivan told herself. She hadn't come this far to be defeated by Linda. Her trembling hands reached down, palms flattening against rough concrete.

And she pushed herself to her feet.

She fought for every step forward. Her skin prickled. Shadows came at her, stretching and growing. But she pushed on. One step at a time. She was FBI Special Agent Jenna Sullivan, damn it. She'd faced down criminals and terrorists. She could handle a dark hallway.

An exhale of relief as she exited into a different hallway. But only slight relief. Because this hallway was only slightly wider, slightly brighter.

But the deeper she ventured into the Pit, the steadier her steps became. And quicker too. The distant clamor of the crowd grew louder, and it reminded her of why she was there. Somewhere in that chaos was Draker, possibly at risk. Bomb or no bomb, Sullivan wasn't about to let him tackle this task alone.

She pushed on.

CHAPTER
FORTY-FIVE

People screamed with delight all around Draker as he watched the limp body of the losing fighter get dragged from the octagon.

Alden had the guy by the ankles, walking backward, struggling with the guy's mass—a beast of a man, easily 250 pounds. A trail of blood followed the behemoth, leaking primarily from his head, smearing across the scattered cardboard on the floor.

Next to Draker, Ricky winced. "Shit, that was rough. Glad it wasn't me in there."

Draker was about to offer only a grunt for a response, but then he remembered Ricky's imposter syndrome hang-up. He looked at the kid. "You'd have been fine. All you would have needed was that flying knee strike you were telling me about."

Ricky grinned back at him, beaming, almost bashful.

Draker turned his attention to the corner of the cage. There stood Nina Hollis. She watched with cold indifference as a couple of fighters serving as a clean-up crew mopped up the excess blood. Typically, the blood was left as it was. But this last fight had been so brutal that mops and fresh cardboard were called in.

Nina looked up from the cleaning job, eyes turning to the crowd. She immediately zoned in on Draker. Even from this distance, Draker felt the weight of her gaze. There was something in her eyes, a glint of malice.

It would seem she was putting together the pieces in the same way Draker was.

It would seem that she knew he was onto her.

She mouthed, *Your next*, then finally broke their stare and walked to the front of the octagon.

Nina's voice cut through the din of the crowd. "Next up: Mav versus Blitz!"

The announcement was met with a mix of cheers and jeers. Draker felt Ricky's hand slap his back, urging him to stand.

"You got this, man!" Ricky said.

Draker nodded and stood.

As he made his way through the crowd, he was acutely aware of the varied reactions his presence elicited. A few of them offered encouragement, some slapping an encouraging hand on the shoulder of the fighter they knew as Mav—much like Ricky had just done.

But most weren't so supportive. Quite the opposite. They drew back, hissing and booing as he passed. Some of them shoved him.

Go back to where you came from, Mav!

You don't belong here, pretty boy!

The hostility was thick and heavy, pushing against Draker as he pushed back, shoving his way through the sea of bodies. He looked forward, found Nina's figure by the cage door. She stared back at him, her gaze never wavering as he approached. He matched her stare.

As Draker reached the cage door, he brushed past Nina, close enough to catch the faint scent of her perfume. She smiled.

"Good luck, Mav," she said, voice dripping with false sweetness. "You're gonna need it."

Draker said nothing, stepping into the cage with a final glance at Nina. The metal door clanged shut behind him. Then the rattle of the chain.

Then he was locked in.

Across the octagon, past a field of concrete covered in overlapped cardboard—some fresh, some stained—was Blitz. His frame was taut, coiled, ready to explode. And his gaze was every bit as coiled. The atmosphere was electric with their mutual disdain, an escalation of the tension that had been brewing since Draker first stepped into the Cell 3 room.

"Well, well," Blitz sneered, his voice carrying over the noise of the crowd. "If it isn't the cop who thinks he can play fighter."

Draker did his best to keep his expression neutral, but he could feel his jaw tighten. He'd known this was coming, had prepared for it.

The bell rang, and Blitz was on him instantly, coming forward in a blur. Draker ducked a wild haymaker and counter with a swift jab to Blitz's ribs.

The crowd roared, hungry for blood.

The blow fazed Blitz but didn't stop him. A split second for recovery, then the guy was on Draker again. Draker caught him, wrapped him up.

As they grappled, Blitz kept up a steady stream of taunts. "I know you were gone all last night, cop. You snuck out. Had to have. What were you up to, huh?"

Draker ignored him, focusing on the fight. He landed a solid knee to Blitz's midsection, earning a grunt of pain.

But his opponent was relentless. Blitz lowered his torso, slipping out of Draker's hold. He lowered his shoulder and drove Draker back against the cage, rattling the fence.

The metal dug into Draker's back, painful through his t-shirt.

More cheers from the crowd. The bloodthirsty mob. As Draker stole a glance at them through the diamond pattern of the chainlink, he nearly dropped his guard entirely against Blitz...

... because there was a familiar face among the roaring, growling, sneering mass.

It was *Sullivan*.

Momentary panic threatened to overtake Draker, but he

quickly reaffirmed his grip on Blitz's sweaty back, spinning the guy to the side and wiggling away from the fence.

What the hell was Sullivan doing inside? They'd discussed this, and he'd said she should stay away, warned her of the danger.

The moment of distraction cost him. Blitz's fist connected with Draker's jaw, sending him staggering. The taste of blood filled his mouth. He fought to regain his footing.

"Getting sloppy, copper," Blitz said. "Maybe you should stick to writing tickets."

Draker shook his head, trying to clear the fog. Had to focus, had to push thoughts of Sullivan and the mission aside.

Had to survive.

This fight was a legitimate threat—especially with someone so motivated against him—and if he didn't get his head in the game, he might not walk out of the octagon.

For a moment, there was separation. As they circled each other, Draker stole a glance to the side and caught sight of Nina leaving her post by the cage door.

What?

She *never* left during a fight. Something was off.

This second momentary lapse in concentration gave Blitz another opportunity. A devastating roundhouse kick caught Draker in the side—right in the two ribs Larkin had horribly bruised—sending him crashing to the cardboard floor.

Pain erupted from Draker's side and coursed through his entire body. The impact made him cough out air and saliva and blood. He found himself staring up at the harsh lights overhead, gasping.

Blitz was on him in an instant, raining down blows. Draker felt the grimy floor cardboard him, soaked with sweat and blood, slipping around on the concrete.

As Blitz's fists pummeled him, Draker raised his arms protectively. But his mind raced to places it shouldn't be, places other than the fight.

Sullivan... in the crowd.

Nina... leaving the warehouse floor.

Draker couldn't lose, not now. Not when he was so close to uncovering the truth, to stopping Nina's plan.

Then, like a lifeline in a storm, Larkin's gift came back to him, that final lesson he'd offered—the pressure point.

With the last of his strength, Draker reached up, his fingers seeking the spot on Blitz's neck that Larkin had shown him.

Time stretched on, going taut, thin, as Draker increased the pressure. For a suspended moment, nothing. Then, Blitz twitched, gasped. His eyes rolled back. He collapsed, his mass landing on top of Draker, pinning him against the bloodied cardboard.

The crowd fell silent. A moment of shocked disbelief. And then an eruption—a dichotomous mix of cheers and boos. Draker heaved Blitz's unconscious form off him. He climbed unsteadily to his feet just as Alden clanged the bell.

Draker had won.

Twice, now.

Thanks, Larkin.

Draker quickly brushed the notion aside and looked for Nina. But she was gone. Alden was in the place where she usually stood. His gaze was fixed on Draker, expression unreadable as he unwound the chain from the door.

The crowd continued to roar in a mix of cheers and jeers. Fists swung. Fists pumped. There were a few obscene gestures.

Draker ignored both the crowd and Alden's stare. His focus was on the hallway where he'd last seen Nina heading. Whatever she was up to, he needed to find out. Now.

He sprinted for the cage door, which Alden had opened. As he eyed the hallway ahead, his run came to a sudden halt.

Pain on his arm.

He looked down and spun around, ready for a fight, only to find himself face to face with Leon Alden.

One of Alden's beefy hands was clamped around the back of Draker's arm. Mechanical strength. Unyielding.

"Where do you think you're going, Mav?" Alden said.

CHAPTER
FORTY-SIX

Nina was alone in the Pit.

This wasn't part of the plan. It wasn't supposed to happen this early.

But she'd known all along that there could be complications.

She slipped away from the roaring crowd, down one of the side hallways. The strung-up lights along the ceiling flickered. Her footsteps echoed.

Sullivan! Agent Sullivan was inside the Pit. The image of Sullivan's face in the bleachers burned in Nina's mind. The moment she'd seen the bitch, alarms had gone off in Nina's head, threatening to drown out all rational thought.

Since Agent Sullivan hadn't shown up for the previous night's round—and since Sullivan had insinuated, even before Draker arrived on the scene, that she would not enter the Pit, being cryptic with her reasoning—her sudden arrival on the second night had served as the final confirmation of Nina's suspicions.

Draker and Sullivan were onto her.

That's why she'd left the tournament early.

Her plan needed to be implemented earlier than she'd thought.

She turned a corner and hurried down the next deserted corridor. The distant roar of the crowd faded with each step, replaced by the hollow echo of her footfalls against concrete.

Another deep breath. She couldn't afford to panic now. Not when she was so close.

She reached into her pocket and touched it again—her smartphone. Its calmed her rattled nerves. Because on it was the app Reece had installed. One tap of Nina's finger, and it would all be over.

But first, she had work to do.

She reached the first hiding spot—a loose brick in the wall near one of the warehouse's many abandoned storage rooms. Nina reached her fingernail into the crack and pried the brick free. There it was—the small block of C4 nestled within the hole just past the brick.

She moved swiftly to connect the wire to the miniature detonator. A small LED blinked to life, confirming the connection to her phone.

Moving on. She rushed down the hallway, going for the corner that would lead her to the next location. Her mind drifted to that terrible night. She thought about it a lot, but tonight, of course, she was thinking about it constantly.

Ryan dead. Broken body. Torn face.

The way his hand had grown cold in hers.

For years, she'd played the role of the Pit's peacemaker. For years, she'd smiled and nodded, building the Pit into something bigger and more profitable than McGarry or Burrows could have ever imagined. For years, the rage had simmered just beneath the surface, waiting for this moment.

The ventilation duct above the makeshift medical station— that's where the next block of C4 awaited her. As Nina connected the detonator, she smiled. Reece had set her up so well. She hoped to meet him in person someday, to *thank* him.

A noise. Something from farther down the hall. Nina froze, heart pounding.

Footsteps. Growing closer.

Draker... Sullivan...

Nina took in a shuddering breath and quickly secured the vent cover, praying she hadn't left any evidence of her work.

A fighter rounded the corner, his eyes widening in surprise at the sight of her. "Ms. Hollis? I was just looking for the—"

"What the fuck are you doing back here?" Nina snarled. "Get your ass to the octagon where you belong!"

The man nodded a rapid-fire apology, retreating quickly. Nina's heart still raced as she watched him go.

She'd been careless. Let her guard down.

It couldn't happen again.

She exhaled. Then she moved on. She made her way to the electrical panel near the main generator. Another block of C4. Another connection made. Her fingers trembled slightly as she worked.

The final hiding spot was the trickiest—a hollow space in the concrete at the base of a steel pillar. She had to be careful with this one. She crouched down and slowly, sloooowly removed the false panel. There it was—the largest block of C4 yet.

This was it. The lynchpin of her entire plan.

As she connected the last detonator, Nina's phone buzzed. A message from Reece: *Everything set on my end. InfluencerCon won't know what hit it.*

She smiled. She was happy for him. Truly happy for him. He'd been amazing to her—the best a man had treated her since Ryan died, better than Leon Alden had been and a hell of a lot better than Andrew Cavanaugh.

She texted, *All set here too. getting close now.*

Getting close....

A thrill ran through her. Yes, it was really happening. Years of planning, of smiling and playing nice while rage boiled just beneath the surface.

It was getting close now.

CHAPTER
FORTY-SEVEN

Sullivan pushed through a mass a burly arms and screaming faces, cutting down the bleachers center aisle, going for the fighting cage below in the center of the warehouse floor.

Earlier, she'd been frozen with fear—outside the building, then at the transom window, then in the dark hallways.

Now, there was no time for fear. All she could do was act.

Sullivan had blown her cover, and now Nina Hollis knew she was here. Minutes earlier, Nina had looked into the crowd, spotted Nina, made eye contact. Even from a distance, Sullivan had seen Nina's eyes widen fractionally, unable to mask her alarm. Then, minutes into Draker's fight, she'd left abruptly.

There was no saying exactly what Nina was up to, of course, but Sullivan knew it was no good.

Sullivan had waited on Draker's fight to finish. Though she was certain he was going to win—knew it in her gut—she couldn't abandon him either way. For several tense minutes, her faith had wavered as Draker's opponent—a lean man with long reach and a cold stare who had kept yelling taunts at Draker—had gotten in several good shots, including a devastating roundhouse kick.

Finally, though, Draker had won.

But when he ran toward the octagon's door, a burly man had grabbed him by the arm. Based on the description Draker had given her, she knew this man must be Leon Alden.

That's why Sullivan was moving as fast as she could down the bleachers' aisle, going for the cage—because Alden still had his hand gripped firmly on the back of Draker's arm. The two men were locked in a tense standoff, their bodies rigid with barely contained aggression.

People in the crowd were beginning to notice the standoff as well— heads turning and voices rising in confusion and excitement, some of them pointing at Draker and Alden.

Without allowing herself time to overthink, Sullivan pushed through the last few rows of spectators. She stumbled slightly on the final step. In that moment, the final details of her plan—reckless and impulsive—crystallized.

She sprinted to Draker.

"Oh, baby!" she cried out, loud enough for the nearby crowd members to hear. Before Draker could react, she threw her arms around his neck and kissed him passionately, deeply, in a way that she thought befitted some of the other women she'd spotted in the crowd—rough-looking gals.

She clamped her hands on the side of his head, fingers in his hair, and shoved her tongue in his mouth. Didn't break away. For several long moments.

Draker stiffened in surprise—and in more ways than one—but to his credit, he didn't pull away.

Finally breaking the kiss, Sullivan grinned up at him. "You did so good with your fight, baby," she said, affecting a bit of twang. "So fuckin' proud of you. Come on." She grabbed his hand and tugged him away from a bewildered Alden.

In that half moment of confusion, Sullivan could see the debate written all over Alden's face. He couldn't make a scene, not after so many people had witnessed Sullivan's theatrics. But, with Nina gone, he also couldn't abandon the octagon.

So he just stood there, dumbstruck, as Nina led Draker, hand in hand, away from the cage.

As they moved through the crowd, Sullivan took another glance back. Alden was frozen where they'd left him, his expression finally losing its confusion and reddening with anger.

Draker leaned over. "Thanks."

"No problem. Bet you're surprised to see me, huh?"

Draker's grip on her hand tightened. "You bet your ass I am," he said through clenched teeth. But then he grinned.

Sullivan laughed.

They pushed through the heavy double doors to the side and into the hallway beyond. A moment of instant dread flashed over Sullivan—the tight walls, the darkness, the flickering lights strung up on the ceiling—but she pushed it down.

To refocus her mind, she retrieved Draker's items. His Glock 19 was in its concealed-carry holster clipped to her pants, and his phone was in her pocket. She handed them to him.

"I saw Nina take off," she said. "And I think—"

She broke off as Draker suddenly reached a finger to his ear and tapped twice. He looked away from her, tilted his head to the side slightly. The in-ear communication device, Sullivan realized. Beau must be talking to him.

"Okay," Draker said as he clipped his holster to his pants and pocketed his phone. He listened. "Okay." Another pause. "Understood."

Draker tapped the inside of his ear again.

"What is it?" Sullivan said.

"That was Beau. He has fresh intel on the Watchdog. He's not attacking the gala at the end of InfluencerCon like we'd thought. He's attacking sooner."

Sullivan felt her stomach drop. "What? But that means—"

"What time is it?" Draker cut her off.

Sullivan glanced at her watch. "It's 6:34."

"Shit," Draker said. He ran a hand through his hair. "It's going to take me an hour and a half to get to Cincinnati. And I don't know where the hell to even find Nina first."

Sullivan placed a hand on Draker's arm. She could feel the tension in his muscles. "Hey. I got this here," she said, surprising herself with the confidence in her voice. "I'll take care of Nina."

Draker's brow furrowed. "But look at these hallways," he said, gesturing to the dim corridors stretching out around them. "Your fear of darkness, your fear of tight spaces."

Sullivan swallowed hard, crushing the panic that surged up her throat. He was right—every instinct was shouting at her to bolt, to break free from this choking maze. But she couldn't. Not now.

"I got this," she said, as much to herself as to Draker. "I started this here in Louisville; I'll finish it. You go take care of the Watchdog."

For a moment, Draker hesitated. Then he nodded, his eyes meeting hers. "Be careful," he said softly.

She nodded.

As Draker turned, she called out to him. "Draker!"

He stopped, pivoted to face her.

"Get the bastard," Sullivan said.

"Yes, ma'am."

Draker spun back and bolted down the hallway. He turned a corner and vanished.

Sullivan was alone.

She took a deep breath. The shadows pressed in around her. The air grew thick and heavy. And dry.

But she pushed the fear aside.

And focused on the task at hand.

One step forward into the darkness. And another.

Then she was moving.

CHAPTER
FORTY-EIGHT

Reece sat in the driver's seat of his van, eyes fixed on the spectacle unfolding before him.

The Worldview Convention Center towered over the sprawling parking lot, its sea-green glass panels and globe-like structures gleaming under the glare of spotlights. A sea of vehicles filled the massive lot, all there for InfluencerCon.

From his vantage point at the end of the lot, Reece had a clear view of the red carpet rolled out before the all-glass main entrance. A steady stream of guests made their way inside, each vying for their moment in front of a line of photographers on the opposite side of a velvet rode held up by brass stanchions. Reece sneered as he recognized faces from Instagram, YouTube, and some from more unsavory corners of the internet like OnlyFans.

Degenerates, all of them.

Reece adjusted his tie, glanced down. His suit might have looked jarringly out of place in the van's musty driver's seat, but it was immaculate and wrinkle-free. Reece had taken it to a dry cleaner earlier in the day; there had been no other way of making it look passable for the later event, not in the hands of someone who'd lived in his vehicle for a year.

On the center console, next to his thigh, was the oversized invitation—printed on thick card stock with gold metallic print. It said, *InfluencerCon General Admission*. He'd hoped for a "guest of honor" ticket but hadn't been able to manage one; the irony would have been just *too* delicious. Oh well.

Three months ago, he'd walked the halls of that massive building in front of him as a maintenance worker, a temp job he'd acquired for one purpose only. He'd carefully placed C4 explosives throughout—nestled in ventilation ducts, tucked behind panels, and hidden into the very electrical systems that would power tonight's event. It had been meticulous work. But worth it.

He grinned, remembering Nina Hollis's part in all this. The fool had actually believed they were partners in this, that she was helping him as much as he was helping her. The truth was decidedly different, of rouse. Her little sideshow in Louisville had provided the perfect cover, drawing the FBI's attention and paving the way for his true masterpiece. Nina had served her purpose beautifully. But her silly revenge-based vendetta paled in comparison to what Reece was about to do here in Cincinnati.

He checked his watch. Still an hour before the staff began to let in the audience members. He watched as another group of influencers strutted down the red carpet, their faces aglow with self-importance. His lip curled in disgust. Very soon, he'd give them the fame they were so desperate for. Infamy, rather. He'd be sure they "went viral."

The convention center's unique architecture suddenly struck Reece as fitting. Those globe-like structures, meant to represent a "worldview," would soon bear witness to a truly world-shaking event when Reece showed them all just how fragile their carefully curated reality truly was.

Reece's fingers itched for his smartphone—the detonator—but he held back. Patience had gotten him this far; he could wait a little longer…

… and then the chaos that would unfold. The screams. The

panic. The mass realization that their vapid little world was crumbling around them, from a false and comfortable reality to an awful new truth full of pain.

A cleansing fire.

CHAPTER
FORTY-NINE

Sullivan could hardly stand it.
She truly thought she might pass out; her heart was pounding *that* hard. Vision oscillating. Fingers tingling.

The light bulbs strung along the ceiling flickered, barely lighting the space. Long stretches weren't working, entirely dark.

She stumbled forward, caught her balance, and gripped her gun tighter. It was a Glock 19M, standard FBI sidearm, nearly identical to Draker's Glock 19, minus a few changes made to the Bureau's liking. The weapon's weight provided a small comfort—safety, familiarity.

Her legs shook. Each step forward was a battle of wills against her own internals. The walls inched closer. Her lips quivered.

She couldn't let her phobias win. Not now. Not when she was so close to stopping Nina.

Focus, damn you, she told herself.

The roar of the crowd was growing more muffled the farther she ventured into the depths of the building. Now it sounded like it was coming from another world entirely, one less anchor to something stable and real.

Untethered. Alone…

… save for Nina somewhere out there.

But Sullivan still had her Glock.

As she rounded a corner, the hallway narrowed even more. Her chest felt tight. Sweat broke out across her forehead.

Somewhere in the back of her mind, she heard Linda's taunting voice. And for a moment, she was small again, back in the suffocating darkness of that basement.

Her fingers felt clammy on the gun's grip; she could sense the diamond texture slipping beneath perspiration. The entire gun shook.

She could always turn back.

No! She couldn't. Draker was counting on her. The entire operation in Louisville hinged on her pushing through this fear.

This was *her* case. She'd been on her own until Draker arrived. Jameson had laughed at her, shipped her away on what he felt was a fool's errand.

And now her only friend in this entire mess, Draker, was gone.

Louisville was all Sullivan's. She had to finish it.

A faint sound. From somewhere ahead. Echoing out of the darkness. The soft scuff of a shoe against concrete.

Sullivan froze, straining her ears.

There it was again. And… something else. Breathing.

Nina.

Sullivan swallowed. Her feet wouldn't move. The shadows were darker. The walls were upon her.

Her knees gave. She nearly tumbled over.

But then…

… she was moving again.

She surged forward, Glock at the ready. Cleared the corner. Looked.

The hallway split into two even narrower passages. The one on the left was pitch black—a void. The right was marginally brighter, but so tight she'd have to turn sideways to squeeze through.

Another sound. Yes, definitely footsteps. They drifted from the left passage.

Sullivan's mouth was bone dry. She swallowed hard.

No other choice. Taking a deep breath, she plunged into the darkness.

The walls pressed in on either side. Rough concrete scraping against her skin. Sullivan's breath came faster.

Keep moving. Keep moving!

She progressed step by step, one hand holding the Glock, the other trailing along the wall for guidance.

Just when she thought her mind couldn't force her legs to take another step, the corridor widened slightly. A faint light spilled from around a corner up ahead. Sullivan inched closer, both hands on her gun.

She cleared the corner, peered around it, and there, bathed in the green glow of a smartphone, was Nina Hollis. Her back was to Sullivan, hands working frantically at something Sullivan couldn't see.

"FBI!" Sullivan said. "Hands where I can see them, Nina!"

Nina spun around, eyes wide. Shock, rage. A smartphone glowed in her hand, the screen bright green with a circle in the center.

The phone must be the detonator...

"You bitch," Nina hissed. "You were never supposed to find out. You were supposed to think it was someone else, not Nina Hollis, the Pit's savior, the frightened little face of the tournament. They killed my Ryan. Don't you understand?"

Her finger went toward the phone.

And Sullivan fired.

Crack!

The roar of the Glock was deafening in the tight space—making Sullivan's ears instantly start ringing—and though she couldn't see it, she sensed the bullet ricocheting once, twice against the concrete walls.

Both Sullivan and Nina ducked instinctively. Blood poured from Nina's shoulder.

Nina had dropped the phone in the chaos, and it now lay glowing by the wall—closer to Sullivan than Nina.

But before Sullivan could go for it...

... Nina lunged.

The two women collided in a tangle of limbs, grappling furiously in the dim light. Sullivan's grip on the Glock was already shaky, loose, and wet with perspiration, so the impact sent the gun flying, skittering across the floor and disappearing into the shadows.

Nina fought like a woman possessed. Even with her shoulder wound. Feral. All nails and teeth and raw desperation.

Sullivan tried to match her ferocity, knowing what was at stake, but Nina was strong. Damn strong! Sullivan wondered if Nina had ever joined in the Pit's fighting in some capacity, because she certainly had skills.

They crashed into the wall. Sullivan's head slammed against concrete. Instant pain. Stars exploded across her vision.

Nina let out a howl of rage and swiped her hands at Sullivan's face, trying to break free from Sullivan's grip, reaching for the phone which was now a yard away from them.

Sullivan's lungs burned. The walls pulsed and shrank in her peripheral vision, threatening to close in and swallow her up.

With a burst of strength, Sullivan managed to flip their positions. She was on top of Nina now, and she pinned the other woman against the wall.

Nina's hand shot out, fingers clawing desperately for the phone. Her fingers brushed the edge.

In that split second, training took over. Sullivan released her hold on the other woman and rolled for her gun. Her hand closed around the grip just as Nina snatched up the phone.

Crack! Crack!

Two more deafening shots rang out.

Nina jerked. The phone slipped from her hand, hit the concrete with a crack. She collapsed, face frozen in a look of shock. A dark stain spread over her chest.

Sullivan lay there, half propped up with her back against the wall, Glock heavy in her hands. Her entire body shook. There was the smell of gunpowder and blood.

She stared at Nina's motionless form.

It was over. She'd stopped Nina. Prevented the bombing. Completed the Louisville mission.

Noises. Sudden and loud, making Sullivan jump. Bangs and shouts so piercing that they carried all the way down the hallways to this distant part of the warehouse.

Something big was happening. Chaotic. Even more chaotic than the fighting and the roaring crowd had been.

Then Sullivan heard something, a three-letter acronym barely audible. Someone in the distance had shouted, *FBI!*

Someone else: *Federal agents!*

And another, echoey and distant, over the sounds of yelling and chaos: *FBI!*

Sullivan immediately realized what had happened.

SAC Jameson...

For a moment, there was pride—Jameson had come around, must have figured out that Sullivan had been right all along.

But then... anger.

As the adrenaline began to fade though, the reality of her surroundings came crashing back. The walls pressed in. So did the darkness.

She had to get out.

With trembling hands, she retrieved Nina's phone, careful not to accidentally trigger anything.

As she stood up, Sullivan realized the panic wasn't as strong as it had been when she arrived. She gotten herself this far, stopped a bombing, averted a mass murder.

She could get herself back out.

CHAPTER
FIFTY

Draker had asked a lot of this small rental pickup truck. Now he was asking a bit more.

The Maverick barreled northeast along Interstate 71. The Kentucky landscape blurred past in a monotonous stream of moonlit fields and trees. Draker's attention kept flashing to the clock on the dashboard screen. Barely half an hour until InfluencerCon's main event started, and he was still several miles from Cincinnati.

"Shit," he said.

He pressed down harder on the accelerator. The Maverick surged forward, engine growling.

But then he checked the speedometer...

Draker was walking a razor's edge—every second counted, but a police pullover would derail everything.

He thought about Sullivan back in Louisville. He'd left her there, alone in that labyrinth of dark corridors... with her phobias. What if something had gone wrong? What if Nina had—

Draker shook his head, pushed the images away. He couldn't afford to dwell on maybes right now.

As if helping to refocus him, a soft chime played in his ear. He double-tapped the device.

"Beau," Draker said. "I'm in route to Cincinnati."

"I see that."

"But I don't know what happened with Sullivan back there. She's not picking up my calls. Straight to voicemail."

Straight to voicemail—meaning Sullivan's phone was either dead or had no reception. Draker pictured the long, tight hallways of the Pit's warehouse home. He imagined Sullivan in there, scared shitless, looking at a phone whose reception was blocked by the very walls she was trying to escape.

Beau's voice crackled in his ear. "If she reaches out, I can patch her through here." A pause. "But I haven't heard anything yet, Draker."

Draker exhaled, squeezed the steering wheel.

"If this Watchdog attack is anything like the others," Beau continued, switching gears to the mission at hand, "it'll be devastating. New Orleans, Menlo Park—the Watchdog doesn't do anything small scale. And…"

"And what?"

"From what I've pieced together, this should be even bigger than those attacks. Of all society's perceived ills, the topic of the convention seems to be particularly irksome to Braxton Reece."

"How many people will be in attendance?"

"Thousands."

"Okay."

The implications were clear.

"The best thing to do," Beau said, "would be to stop the guy before he even has a *chance* to detonate that C4. The previous bombs were set off via WiFi connected to his phone. But Worldview isn't opening the doors to general admissions until the main event starts."

Draker checked the time again.

Now he had *less* than half an hour.

"Okay," Draker said again.

He would have to move fast once he reached the convention

center. Find Reece in the crowd. Neutralize him before he could trigger the explosives. All while staying under the radar himself.

And when it was over…?

Then, not only would Draker stop the attack, but he'd get his reward—the address of Daniel Harper, the man who'd gone by the name of Simpson years ago in Afghanistan. Windbrook operative. And presumably one of the higher-ups hunting Draker down.

And even if Harper wasn't a higher-up, the man had been there. In Afghanistan. In that tiny building. He was one of the men who'd sent Draker to kill Frederick Al-Khattab.

Whoever the hell *that* guy was.

Lies upon lies.

No matter the outcome, Draker's confrontation with Harper would bring him one step closer to unraveling the mystery that had upended his life.

But first—and more importantly, less selfishly—he had to stop a terrorist who had been fooling the entire world for a year.

"You still with me, Draker?" Beau's said.

Draker hadn't realized he'd been lost in his thoughts for a moment.

"Yeah, I'm here." Draker checked the clock again. "Just trying to figure out how the hell I'm going to pull this off."

"Do me proud, boy. Remember your training with Larkin." A slight, purposeful pause. "Stay adaptable."

There'd been a certain emphasis on the word *adaptable*.

Larkin must've told Beau about Draker's struggles with the concept of adaptability.

That old bastard.

Draker grinned.

Larkin had hammered the lesson home. Finally. And Draker would need every ounce of his new-found adaptability tonight.

The sky darkened as dusk settled in, the first stars peeking out above the horizon. A green highway sign flashed past in the Maverick's headlights: *Cincinnati, 15 miles.*

"I'm getting close."

"Be safe, Draker. And get the bastard."

Get the bastard—Sullivan had offered the same encouragement.

"Will do," Draker said.

CHAPTER
FIFTY-ONE

Nearly there.

Reece stood outside in a long line stretching out of the Worldview Convention Center main entrance—a pompous affair of lights and glass and an oversized, wannabe-Bellagio fountain. The nighttime air was cool, crisp, comfortable. His invitation was in his hand.

The line ahead of him teemed with excited people in what passed for evening-wear in the 21st century—some of them were in fucking sweatpants. Their chatter was a constant, grating buzz in Reece's ears.

Ignoring them, he craned his neck to take in the convention center, which towered over everyone. The distinctive sea-green glass panels and globe-like structures gleamed in the spotlights, the moonlight. As Reece understood it, the building had been designed by a renowned architect, but to his eye, it was ostentatious, gaudy—a perfect representation of both InfluencerCon and everything Reece despised about the world he was forced to live in.

He watched as a group of giggling young women walked past —faces caked with makeup, phones held high as they snapped selfies. "Oh my god, did you see what TrashyQueen69 posted? Slay! She's totally here tonight! I know, right?"

Reece's lip curled in disgust. This was what society had devolved to—vapid conversations about "influencers" who contributed nothing of value to the world. He felt even better about his decision—if that was possible. Tonight, he would cleanse this rot from the face of the earth.

The line began to move. Shuffled forward a yard. And stopped.

Reece heard more of them. Surrounding him. Closing in.

I heard PornPrincess is doing a meet-and-greet at the after party!

Dude, I'm gonna get so many followers tonight.

Did you see the merch? I low-key like it. A total vibe. I'm buying everything.

Each word, each asinine phrase, felt like a nail being driven into Reece's skull.

False idols. Fleeting fame. Lowered standards.

Reece slipped his hand into his pocket, pulled out his phone, and tapped open an app. A very special app. One he'd crafted himself. The screen glowed red. A large button labeled *BANG* dominated the center. At the top, it read *OUT OF PROXIMITY* in smaller letters.

Months of planning, of meticulous preparation, had led to this moment. The explosives were in place, hidden throughout the building. All he needed to do now was get inside—past the signal-blocking thickness of Worldview's walls—and press that button: *BANG*.

One touch, and he would wipe these cretins off the face of the earth.

He thought of Nina Hollis. By now, she should have executed her own plan, gotten her revenge.

Good for her.

As the line inched forward again, Reece scanned the crowd, mentally rehearsing his next steps. Get inside, find a quiet corner out of the blast zones, detonate the bombs. Then watch as chaos engulfed these vapid, self-obsessed morons who—

Reece froze. Something was wrong.

A man way at the back of the crowd caught his eye—six-foot-one, athletic build, light-brown hair. He wasn't lining up like the others. Instead, his gaze swept methodically over the attendees, as if searching for someone.

Panic flared in Reece's chest. He knew that look, that stance. This wasn't some overeager fan or event security. This man moved like law enforcement—like someone hunting a specific target.

"Shit."

How had they found him? Reece's mind cycled through several possibilities before quickly landing on the most likely culprit: Nina. The bitch must have talked, must have given him up somehow.

The man's gaze was getting closer, his sightline working its way through the crowd toward Reece.

Reece pulled to the side, tugged up on the collar of his suit jacket.

But it didn't work.

The man saw him.

They locked gazes.

Recognition flashed across the stranger's eyes, so clear that Reece could see it even across the distance. Whoever this guy was, he knew Braxton Reece's face and he knew Braxton Reece would be waiting in line to get inside Worldview Convention Center.

Which meant the man knew Reece was the Watchdog, knew the target was InfluencerCon.

The plan had been compromised.

For a split second, panic.

Then, just as quickly, an alternative idea formed. Reece was skilled at thinking on his toes.

There was a back entrance to Worldview, way around the

massive bend of the structure. A spot with loading docks and copious trash units. Reece had seen the location both in Worldview's schematics and during his in-person reconnaissance of the convention center several months back.

Reece moved out of the line, shouldering his way through the throng. He took off running. Shouts of protest came from behind as he shoved people out of his way, but Reece didn't slow down.

He sprinted toward the edge of the building, thighs burning instantly. Of all the preparations he'd made, he wished he'd stayed in better shape. He would make a note of that.

Worldview stretched on and on before him. Its southern curve was seemingly endless; it taunted him as he ran. He stole a glance over his shoulder.

The big guy was still there, gaining on him.

Reece pushed harder. The building's facade blurred as he ran, an endless expanse of steel and sea-green glass. For a moment, he thought the curve had ended, that the loading dock was just ahead…

… only to find more of the same stretching before him.

Another look back. The guy was closer now. Reece could see the dead-cold determined look on his face.

Shit.

Reece's lungs burned. He pushed on. Ahead was a stretch of temporary fencing weighted down with sandbags. Without breaking stride, he vaulted over it, one shoe catching, nearly falling over.

"Stop right there!" a voice bellowed from his left.

Reece turned, half-expecting to see the big guy. Instead, he locked eyes with a security guard—a fatass in an all-blue jumpsuit, red-faced and puffing, trying to keep up.

Reece almost laughed. This guy would never catch him.

But the big man behind him was another story…

Finally, Reece rounded the curve.

And then he saw it—a loading bay, an idling tractor trailer, workers milling about. Some wore catering uniforms; others were in custodial gear.

This was it—Reece's way in to InfluencerCon.

CHAPTER
FIFTY-TWO

After all the beatings he'd received the last few days, Draker wouldn't have thought he could move this fast. Yet he was running. Sprinting. Legs pumping furiously. Gaining on Reece.

The Watchdog still had a good lead on him, however, and Draker could do nothing but watch Reece round the edge of the Worldview Convention Center and disappear.

Draker's heart pounded harder, and for a few moments, he thought he'd lost Reece for good. But as he rounded the curve himself, he spotted Reece ahead—a sprinting silhouette in the exterior lighting—heading straight for a utility entrance. A loading dock with rubber bumpers. An idling semi. Workers milling about, several of them on a smoke break.

Shit.

Draker realized Reece's intent. This back entrance would give the man access to the building and, once inside, he'd have the proximity he needed to detonate the bombs.

Reece plowed through the crowd, shoving aside custodians and caterers. Screams. A few people tried to block him, but Reece didn't slow. He sent one of them flying off the concrete ledge.

Draker sprinted full-speed, cutting through the panicked

workers. His eyes locked on Reece's hand, catching a flash of the cell phone's screen glowing red. He had to assume it would turn green when Reece was in range.

A detonator.

Time was running out.

Reece made it to the back, slammed through the double doors. The metal detector screamed. A pair of security guards in blue uniforms rushed to stop him, but he was already moving down the well-lit hallway at a sprint.

Suddenly, Reece whipped around, pulling a strange-looking, all-white gun that Draker didn't recognize. In a flash, he fired twice.

Crack! Crack!

The guards crumpled to the floor.

Workers screamed and scattered as Draker processed what he'd just witnessed. Instantly, he put it all together—the metal detector had gone off for Reece's phone, not the gun. This had clearly been the plan all along: get the detonator past security disguised as an everyday smartphone while smuggling in a plastic gun undetected, which must have been some sort of 3D-printed .22. The small-caliber rounds were likely chosen to evade the metal detectors, a detail Reece would have meticulously researched, including the specific make and model of the detectors used at Worldview.

Draker had left his own gun in the Maverick, knowing he'd have to pass security.

He navigated the panicked crowd, through the doors, past the blaring metal detector, leaping over the wounded, moaning guards. He barreled down the hallway—a plain, utilitarian affair with linoleum flooring and fluorescent overhead lighting. It was cluttered with catering supplies, creating an obstacle course of carts and containers.

As he had a moment earlier, Reece suddenly turned and took aim with his weapon.

This time, it was pointed at Draker.

Without hesitation, Draker lunged. He tackled Reece mid-aim. The gun went flying from Reece's hand, skittering across the floor.

They crashed through another set of double doors, tumbling into yet another service hallway.

As they grappled on the floor, Draker caught sight of Reece's phone. The screen glowed green, an ominous circular *BANG* button just a press away from disaster.

Reece's finger inched closer to the screen.

"No!" Draker roared, grabbing Reece's wrist. He slammed the man's hand into the floor, sending the phone racing across the linoleum. Reece squirmed free and crawled desperately, hands-and-knees, toward the device.

Draker lunged, snatching the phone just as Reece's fingers brushed its edge. With all his might, he hurled it down the hallway. It disappeared into the shadows.

But Reece wasn't done.

The plastic gun was inches away, and Reece snatched it up, scrambled to his feet, and aimed the weapon at Draker.

Draker didn't give him a chance to get the shot off. He bolted forward—his hands wrapping over Reece's on the gun's handle—and smashed the smaller man into the wall, cracking the sheetrock. They struggled, muscles straining as they each fought for control.

Draker twisted hard, trying to wrench the weapon away. But Reece countered with surprising strength, slamming Draker's wrist against the metal doorframe. The impact sent a jolt of pain up Draker's arm, loosening his grip for a moment. But he held on, refusing to let go.

They spun, grappling for dominance. Reece's finger quivered over the trigger, but Draker held it back. Draker gritted his teeth. The gun wavered between them, barrel jerking left, right, dancing dangerously close to each man's face.

With a sudden burst of energy, Draker forced the gun upward. He pivoted, using Reece's weight against him, rocking him over his hip. Using this new advantage, he brought the gun's barrel under Reece's chin.

And clamped his hand down on Reece's finger.

His *trigger* finger.

Crack!

The shot tore through Reece's head. Blood and pieces of Reece sprayed the wall. He collapsed, instantly lifeless.

Draker stood there, panting heavily.

Lines of blood—mixed with bone and flesh—streaked down the wall, chasing Reece's body as it slid to the floor. He came to rest in a motionless heap, eyes open.

After a moment to catch his breath, Draker pried the gun from Reece's lifeless hand. It was feather-light. He examined it briefly, figured out its workings, then released the magazine. Empty. It had only held three rounds.

Yes, Reece must have carefully calculated the amount of lead and casings that would pass undetected through Windbrook's metal detectors, down to the exact number of .22 rounds he could safely carry.

Three rounds. All used.

Footsteps echoed from the other hallway. Approaching rapidly.

Draker put the gun back in Reece's hand, then took off running.

CHAPTER
FIFTY-THREE

Three hours later

After the chaos at the Worldview Convention Center, Draker sat in his latest rental car, now three states away from Cincinnati—almost four, as he was only miles from the Missouri-Kansas state line—staring at a dilapidated house on the outskirts of Kansas City.

The surrounding neighborhood was pure decay. Crumbling sidewalks, overgrown lawns, houses with peeling paint, all buckling beneath the weight of years of neglect.

This address—a rundown, single-story house with the flicker of a TV glowing through grimy windows—was supposedly Daniel Harper's place. Agent Simpson from Afghanistan. One of the men who'd been in that so-called CIA meeting, one of the men who'd set Draker on this path, a life of lies that led to him being hunted by Windbrook a decade and a half later.

Beau had told Draker to eliminate Harper after getting any intel he could.

And Draker was looking forward to doing so.

Only two weeks earlier, Draker had been hesitant with one of the roles he now held within his new position as Beau's Ranger: that of an assassin.

Now, after killing so many people in such a short amount of time, the jitters were gone. And he couldn't wait to eliminate those who'd destroyed his former life.

Draker had gotten to Harper's place fast after escaping Worldview—Beau had set him up with a plane flight. Usually, his handler had insisted on ground transportation, paranoid—rightfully so—about leaving a digital trail. But as a reward for eliminating the Watchdog—and more importantly because of the time constraint—Beau had pulled strings and arranged a flight to Kansas City that very night.

For ten minutes, Draker had sat there in the rented Accord. Watching. Surveilling. Scanning for security cameras. Working the sightlines.

Now he was satisfied.

Now he was ready to go.

Draker stepped out of the car. The night air was cool, damp. The street was silent, save for the low hum of Harper's television. As he moved closer, more details came into focus—siding peeling away, a sagging porch that creaked under his weight, weeds crawling up the walls.

He reached to the small of his back, pulled out his Glock.

Something felt off. Why would a Windbrook operative—who had at one point likely been a legitimate CIA agent—be holed up in this dump? The only answer Draker could formulate was a carefully maintained cover of suburban normalcy.

But as he looked at his surroundings, that seemed like an awfully big price to pay for a little security.

The front door wasn't even locked.

Draker slipped inside. The interior matched the exterior's decay—faded furniture, strewn garbage. The place stank. In the dim light of the TV—the only light source—he made out a figure slumped in an armchair.

"Daniel Harper," Draker said.

The man jerked awake, spun in his chair, eyes wide as they locked onto Draker's drawn weapon.

Harper was older than Draker expected, easily in his sixties, with a frail build. Though he was still half-hidden in the shadows —with the pulsing television glow showing the contours of only part of his face—Draker saw that he was considerably thinner than the photo Beau had provided, the one from which Draker had made a positive ID.

"Who the hell are you?" Harper said. His voice shook. A bag of Doritos was on his lap, spilled onto his legs.

"You were in Afghanistan," Draker said, slowly continuing forward, gun aimed.

Harper nodded quickly. "Yes. National Guard."

Draker considered this. "The Guard? Army or Air?"

"Army."

Draker came to a stop. "And Windbrook."

"What's Windbrook?"

Draker felt the hairs on his arms begin to stand up. "How about the CIA?"

Harper's mouth fell open. Said nothing.

"The CIA!" Draker repeated, shouting.

Harper nodded again, even faster. "Yeah. Yeah, they... they approached me. I did a... a mission for them. That's all I can say!"

Draker took another step forward. "And they told you they'd hold onto you as a sleeper agent?"

Harper did his rapid nodding again.

Another step forward. More of Harper was revealed in the television's glow...

... including a prominent mole on his right cheek.

Back in Afghanistan, Simpson had had no mole.

Draker would have remembered a mole. He had a great attention to detail and a photographic memory for such things.

In fact, the freckle on the iris of Simpson's associate—Agent Burleson—had been the way Draker had IDed the man last week in California, a decade and a half after first meeting the man.

As Draker moved closer, he kept the Glock aimed at Harper while he pulled out his phone with the other hand. He unlocked the phone, opened BeauChat, swiped through the photos Beau had sent, the possible Daniel Harpers.

The image that Draker had told Beau belonged to Simpson looked nothing like the man shaking in his armchair in his smelly house with Doritos spilled across his lap.

Daniel Harper—*this* Daniel Harper, at least—was not the same man as Agent Simpson.

Draker lowered the Glock.

"The CIA told you you'd be a sleeper agent," Draker repeated. "They said they might call you up again, even years down the line, but likely never would. They told you that your country thanked you for your service. And you've never heard from them since."

Harper nodded.

"They told me the same thing," Draker said. His shoulders slumped. The Glock weighted down his arm, threatening to topple him over. He swallowed, refocused, looked at Harper. "You were never with the CIA. The people you associated with in Afghanistan were a military contractor. Windbrook. And they used you."

"What?"

Flashing on what he just told Harper—*They used you*—a new thought dawned on Draker.

This is a trap.

"We gotta get out of here!"

"*What?*" Harper said.

"This place isn't safe. I need to get you out. *Now!*"

This got a rise out of Harper. Struggling, he freed himself from his armchair. Doritos rained onto the matted carpet. He came at Draker, stabbing a finger.

"Listen, man! You broke into my house. In the middle of the night. Aiming a fucking gun at me! And now you're—"

Draker leveled his Beretta at Harper again. "I'm not asking. I'm telling you. We. Are. *Leaving!*"

"But I—"

Crack! Crack!

Draker's instincts kicked in before his mind could process. He lunged at Harper, shoulder crashing into the man's soft midsection, tackling him to the carpet. Bullets tore through the space where they'd just stood, punched holes in the wall.

"Stay low!" Draker hissed, grabbing Harper's shirt and dragging him toward the front door.

But before they could reach it, the door exploded inward, wood splintering. A figure burst through.

Draker caught a split-second glimpse of the intruder—Caucasian, a strip of deep acne scars on his cheeks, black tactical gear, Heckler & Koch MP5 submachine gun—before rolling to the side.

Instantly, more shots rang out.

Crack! Crack! Crack!

The floor where Draker had just been erupted in splinters and torn carpet.

Draker launched himself at the operator. They collided in a tangle of limbs, smacking into the wall, denting it, falling.

His hand found the hilt of a tactical blade on the other man's thigh. He yanked it free from its sheath, drove it into the man's neck, just above the body armor.

Hot blood squirted on Draker's face, blinding him.

A gurgle. A spasm. The operator went limp.

Draker crouched, wiped the blood free from his eyes, and glanced to the side. Found Harper.

He'd been hit.

Hands on his side. Legs kicking at the floor, spinning, going nowhere. Blood pooling out of his side.

No time to help him. Not yet.

Another shot rang out from the back of the house.

Crack!

Drywall exploded next to Draker's head, showering him with dust and debris, which stuck to the blood. He wiped his face again, squinted, fighting to clear his vision as he dove for cover behind a mildewed couch.

He saw a flash of another silhouette. For a split second. Then it was gone.

Harper's house was a maze of neglect—trails of garbage, mounded clothing. Draker used it all to his advantage, slipping from shadow to shadow as he stalked the other man…

… who was somewhere up there, near the short hallway that must lead to the house's single bedroom.

A floorboard creaked. Draker froze. Listened.

The sound came again. Closer.

He inched backward. His hand closed around a beer bottle discarded on an end table. He crouched behind the table's edge.

As the second operator—black, muscle-bound, sharp widow's peak—rounded the corner, Draker hurled the bottle. It shattered against the man's face.

Blood. Beer. Shards of glass.

The impact stunned the man just long enough for Draker to close the distance.

He grabbed the operator's gun arm, twisted. A pair of shots from the MP5 went wide, punching through the ceiling. Chunks of plaster rained down.

The man was strong. Damn strong. Of course he was. He worked for Windbrook.

But Draker knew a thing or two now about using a man's strength against him—hard-learned lessons from one Grady Larkin.

Draker maneuvered behind the operator and yanked his arm into a hold. He pressed his Glock against the man's back, fired.

The man emitted a primordial gasp a second before the body slumped to the floor.

Draker aimed the Glock down and fired twice more into the skull, making sure.

Sirens wailed in the distance.

Draker sprinted back to the front of the house. There was the first operator, lying where Draker had left him.

Two more shots to the head for this guy as well. Insurance.

Harper hadn't moved. Draker went to a knee beside him, pressed a pair of fingers to the man's carotid. Nothing.

Harper was gone.

The sirens were louder now. No time left.

Draker cleared the house, Glock in front of him, not letting his guard down for any hidden traps, any more operators.

He reached the front door, cracked it open, paused to survey the scene outside.

Trees to his left. More decrepit houses to the right. The Accord waited at the curb.

The sirens were even louder, not far away.

Too many possibilities to cover them all. He just had to go for it.

With a deep breath, Draker sprinted for the car.

Waited for gunfire.

Waited for pain.

None came.

He reached the Accord, yanked the door open, threw himself inside.

The engine roared to life. Tires screeched, spun, grabbed hold.

Draker peeled off.

CHAPTER
FIFTY-FOUR

I t was the start of a new day.
Well, technically the day had started several hours earlier. Sullivan had slept in considerably after the previous night's events at the Pit, followed by the requisite office work with local law enforcement and a debriefing at the Louisville Field Office.

She'd been up till 1 am.

The local cops—who'd worked in cooperation with the FBI—had asked if Sullivan had any help with her investigation. She told them the only one who'd assisted her was a rogue Pit fighter, someone who'd figured out Nina Hollis's plan and wanted to stop it.

Her helper, she told them, had only given her his fighter name, Mav, and he vanished at the end of the night. When the cops asked for a description, Sullivan said Mav was short, dark-haired, rough-looking, and covered in tattoos. Didn't ring any bells with the cops, didn't match any of the fighters they knew were connected to the Pit. But they said they'd be on the lookout.

The cops also mentioned that they'd arrested Leon Alden. Sullivan had been pleased it was the local guys and not the feds who caught him. She didn't want Jameson feeling like a hero back in Des Moines, not after how he'd treated her. Jameson had come around, accepted that he'd made a mistake, and tried to do the right thing.

But he was still a pompous ass.

After all that, when Sullivan's head hit the pillow inside her luxury suite at 1 in the morning, she'd fallen asleep immediately.

Now it was almost noon. She stood outside her hotel skyscraper in downtown, waiting for the valet to bring her car. Fidgeting. Because Draker hadn't shown up yet.

The sun was warm on her face. She wore sunglasses, jeans, and a loose top. The Ohio River shimmered in the distance. Around her, Louisville pulsed with life—the hum of traffic, the chatter of passersby, and the occasional beep of an Uber or taxi arriving at the porte-cochère.

Footsteps approaching. She turned. Draker strolled in her direction. Just in time. She didn't want to miss seeing him before she left.

He looked different somehow in the daylight—no longer the chiseled fighter, the elite operator working for the mysterious Beau. He looked like... an everyday guy. A handsome one at that.

His white v-neck t-shirt clung to his athletic frame. Dark jeans. Boots. Covered with bruises, nicks, and scrapes. He looked like he'd gotten his ass beat. Which he had. Multiple times. Despite coming out on top in the end.

Still, despite the wounds, Sullivan couldn't help but admire how the casual outfit accentuated everything he had going on physique-wise.

Which was a lot.

"I can't believe you made it all the way to Kansas City and back," Sullivan said as Draker stepped up to her.

Last night, when she and Draker had finally linked up on the phone, Draker had told her he was going to Kansas City that very night, that'd he'd be back in Louisville to wrap up a few things and with time to tell her goodbye.

Draker shrugged. "Beau knows how to work miracles."

"Congratulations are in order," Draker said as he stepped up to her. "You got the job done here in Louisville."

Sullivan smiled. "Thanks, Draker."

"SAC Jameson's sure to give you the respect you deserve now."

Sullivan scoffed. "Screw Jameson."

They both chuckled.

She thought back to those first tense meetings, the skepticism from Jameson and her other superiors, the desperate race against time. It all seemed so distant now, a half-remembered dream.

As she looked at Draker, who was still smiling, she realized she liked this—the easy familiarity they'd slipped into. But now it was about to end. Quick to form, even quicker to fade.

Sunlight bounced off the skyscrapers, throwing bright reflections across the busy street. Sullivan watched a group of teenagers pass, their excited chatter at odds with the businesspeople marching with purpose, clutching attaché cases.

"I still can't believe it's over," Sullivan said, more to herself than to Draker. "I worked for weeks on this case—all alone until Beau called and sent you over."

She thought about Nina Hollis, about the dark corridors of the Pit—the tight walls, the shadows. She remembered the fear she'd faced... and conquered. Pride swelled up inside her, but also a bittersweet realization that this transitory phase of her life was coming to an end.

And with its closure, Draker too was exiting her life.

Draker nodded. "You faced your demons head-on. Not many people can say they've done that."

Sullivan felt something inside, and without overthinking, she leaned in to Draker, put her hands on his shoulder, kissed him. A soft kiss.

It was the third time they'd kissed, she realized. But unlike the frantic, adrenaline-fueled moments before, this one felt tender and sincere.

Draker's hands encircled her—one going to the middle of her

back, the other lower, at the curve. And he kissed her back just as gently as she was kissing him.

As she pulled away, Sullivan looked up at him. "What I said before still stands. When I said that no matter what happens, it's been good to have met you—I mean that."

Draker didn't respond. Only looked down at her, one hand still on her, the one on the curve of her back. Sullivan's words hung between them.

Finally, Draker smiled.

The moment was broken by the arrival of her Mercedes pulling up to the curb. The valet—white shirt, black pants, shiny name tag—stepped out and approached with her keys, grinning.

"Your car, ma'am."

Sullivan nodded her thanks, took the keys, and slipped the valet a generous tip. She turned back to Draker.

"Well, bye, Draker," she said softly.

"Bye."

She looked at him. He looked back.

Hesitation.

Sullivan opened the door, slid into the driver's seat. A few moments to get everything situated, and then she eased the car forward.

She glanced in the rearview mirror and took in one last image of Draker standing by the hotel steps, his figure against the backdrop of the city. A mental snapshot.

She pulled away from the curb, merged into the flow of traffic.

Another glance at the rearview mirror.

The spot on the hotel steps where Draker had stood was now empty. He was gone.

CHAPTER
FIFTY-FIVE

An old tube-style television in the corner was playing *The Good, the Bad and the Ugly*. The image was flickering. The colors were faded.

For many people, this would have been considered a poor—even dismissible—viewing experience. But Draker loved old movies, and something about watching Clint on a broken-down fossil of a TV added to the experience.

No sound, though. Only captions. It would have been nice to hear the film, especially Ennio Morricone's celebrated and hauntingly gorgeous soundtrack. Those first few notes were the most famous part of the movie, after all. But even if the TV's sound had been on, Draker would have had a hard time hearing it over the dull rumble of the crowd surrounding him.

Besides, Draker had his own soundtrack going. He had one earbud in, and playing via YouTube on his phone was "Ventura Highway" by the band America.

A song that held a special meaning for him after the Ventura mission.

Watching a stone-cold classic like *The Good, the Bad and the Ugly* in *any* format—even with subtitles and the wrong soundtrack—was a good way to pass the time while he waited for his companion to arrive.

Draker was seated at the bar area of the Riverview, a local favorite bar and grill just outside downtown Louisville. The place buzzed with activity—a constant flow of people, the sound of clinking glasses, laughter. There was the smell of grilled meat. Through the large picture windows on the opposite side was the Ohio River, shimmering in the midday sun, only a few yards away—hence the establishment's name.

The bartender had obliged Draker's request for a pen, so as he watched Blondie abandon Tuco in the middle of the desert, Draker absent-mindedly guided the pen from the vertical plane into a horizontal rotation around his pinky.

Over and over. Not thinking, not looking, just watching the movie.

He'd mastered the third step of the Tri-Phase Cascade. Soon he'd begin mastering a new pen-spinning trick.

He took another swig of his Corona and shifted in his barstool. A second Corona was on a paper coaster in front of him.

His mind went to Sullivan, to the very recent memory of their goodbye kiss outside the hotel. Bittersweet. Charged with unspoken possibilities. She was tough, sharp as a tack, and didn't take shit from anyone. In another life, maybe...

But...

No. If Draker truly had the luxury of another life, he wouldn't choose to be with Sullivan, as great as she was.

Because there was Kylie.

Kylie Payton.

And because "Ventura Highway" was playing in his ear, transporting him back to the sunny California side street where he'd last seen Kylie.

Last week in Ventura, he'd shared a bittersweet goodbye with Kylie that was quite similar to the one he'd just had with Sullivan. Hell, not just similar; nearly identical. They'd looked at each other, just like Draker and Sullivan had. They'd kissed. They'd parted.

Draker twisted the beer bottle in his fingers.

Two women, two cities, two versions of a life he couldn't have.

He shook his head, forced the thoughts away. There was no room for that kind of distraction, not with Windbrook still out there.

Windbrook... and their operative, Cassandra Wynne. Hunting Draker.

His phone buzzed. He looked. Milo's name was on the screen. A video call, of course.

Draker opened BeauChat, bracing himself for a clingy love bomb.

The kid meant well...

"H-hello, Mr. Ty." There was Milo, his wild red hair as unruly as ever, his wide face filling the screen.

"Hey, Milo. How you holding up?"

"I'm doing f-fine, th-thanks to you. I've been m-making progress with the therapy. What did you c-c-c-call it again?"

"Cognitive-behavioral therapy," Draker said and grinned.

"That's great to hear. I'm glad things are looking up for you."

Draker felt a sharp slap on his back. Turned. There was the guy he'd been waiting for, Ricky, sliding onto the stool next to him, a grin plastered across his boyish face.

Draker turned back to the phone. "I gotta run, buddy. Talk soon."

"Bye, M-Mr. Ty."

Draker ended the call, then slid the second Corona toward Ricky. "I hear congratulations are in order," he said. He'd offered the exact same phrase to Sullivan. It was a good phrase to have to repeat.

Ricky shrugged, trying to play it off, but pride glowed in his eyes. "Yeah, second place ain't bad, huh?" He beamed. "I was hoping for first place, of course, and that fourteen-thousand-dollar prize. That would have been... life-changing. But five thousand bucks of profit is still damn good."

"Hell yeah it is."

"I went with the flying knee, just like you told me I should. Had I not listened to you, I would never have won my last fight. So thank you for that."

"You bet."

Ricky's grin widened, and he snickered. "Ya know, the other fighters all thought you quit, that you ran out, that you were scared or whatever."

Draker shrugged, taking a long pull from his beer.

"Say, I know you can't tell me the whole truth," Ricky continued, switching gears, "but are you like a fed or a cop or something? It's okay if you are! I won't tell nobody."

Draker met Ricky's eyes. Considered things for a moment. "Just know that I'm someone who's able to help you out. And I have."

"With the flying knee. Yeah, I know, and I—"

"That's not the only way."

Ricky stared for a moment. "What do you mean?"

"You were hoping to turn a thirteen-thousand-dollar profit by winning first place, but you only got the second-place prize."

Ricky's brow furrowed. "Right…"

"My… employer got you the rest of the money. And more. Just check your bank account."

Ricky blinked. Then pulled out his smartphone, did a few quick swipes. His eyes widened as he stared at the screen. When he looked back up at Draker, his mouth was open and his face was a shade whiter. He couldn't speak.

Draker filled the silence for him. "Just promise me one thing."

"Sure."

"The feds claimed to have shut down the Pit for good. But it's an *underground* tournament; it's likely to spring up again someday. Even if it doesn't, there are other tournaments like it. Promise me you'll never fight in the Pit or any other illegal tournament again."

Ricky nodded slowly. "Okay. I promise." Another glance at his phone. A disbelieving shake of the head. "Is there anything else I can do?"

"Yeah. You can enjoy this beer with me."

As they clinked bottles, Draker felt a bit of the weight lift from his shoulders.

Milo was doing better. Ricky was out of the Pit.

But Windbrook was still out there. Simpson was still an unknown. And Cassandra Wynne and the other operatives were still hunting Draker.

There was still plenty of weight on Draker's shoulders.

All the same, he could enjoy this moment. At the Riverview. With Ricky. Drinking a beer with a stellar movie playing silently in the background on a shitty television set.

He took another swig.

CHAPTER
FIFTY-SIX

Wynne's back throbbed.
 But she hardly noticed it. Finally, something had distracted her from the pain.

The pain was nothing compared to the storm of emotions raging within her.

Draker had slipped through their fingers. Again.

The confrontation at Daniel Harper's house had been a disaster. Wynne had watched through the laptop screen, connected to her team's body cameras, as Draker killed both of her operatives and escaped.

If only she'd been allowed a larger team! The Captain had refused, citing her failure in Ventura as a reason not to trust her with more people. Windbrook, he'd contended, had always used small teams for stateside operations anyway, one of the many keys to their successes.

But really, he'd set Wynne up to fail. Yes, that had to be it. The Captain, with his unsettling avuncular voice and his fetish for punishment, wanted Wynne to lose Draker again. This must have been his plan all along.

Now, as Wynne waited for the inevitable call, her mind raced.

She replayed every moment, every decision, searching for where it had all gone wrong.

How had Draker done it? Where did this sixth sense of his come from?

Once more, she thought of what Hunsinger had said in Ventura—just before Draker killed him. Hunsinger had called Draker a survivor, someone who always found a way.

How true.

Her phone rang on the coffee table, rattling. Wynne jumped. Pain in her back. She gasped.

And just stared at the phone.

A moment of this, then she steeled herself, took a deep breath, answered. "Sir?"

"Cassandra." The Captain's voice was soft, gentle even. "I'm disappointed."

Wynne's hand shook violently. "Sir, I—"

The line went dead.

Wynne froze. The phone slipped out of her hand, hit her thigh, fell to the floor. She dry heaved.

She just sat there.

Shaking, gasping.

She shot up off the sofa, which sent pain blazing across her back. She screamed.

Two words.

Who would have thought that two benign words could be so impactful?

I'm disappointed.

Wynne understood the implication.

She dry heaved again.

CHAPTER
FIFTY-SEVEN

Draker had been bamboozled.

He remembered Beau's words about the transportation methods he would be using between missions. It would vary, and often the options would be unglamorous. Draker might even have to hitchhike on occasion, though Beau had guaranteed him this would be a rarity.

With that assurance, Draker hadn't imagined he'd be hitchhiking after only his fourth mission.

Or under such miserable conditions.

Draker was walking along the shoulder of the interstate highway, thumb out, rain pouring down. I-75. Northern Georgia. Going south. Four lanes and a grassy median, trees on either side. Somewhere just past Dalton.

The sweatshirt he'd bought in Louisville was soaked through, clinging to his bruised and battered skin.

His new backpack—also purchased back in Louisville, also soaked—was slung over his shoulders. It held a couple changes of clothes and basic toiletries.

And an ink pen.

His hair was plastered to his head. He'd removed his equally drenched baseball cap—another Louisville purchase—to shield his phone from the deluge as he talked to Beau.

Vehicles zoomed past, spraying him. Semis threw gusts of wind and mist, making an already unpleasant task even worse.

His entire body ached, head to toe. He'd gotten his ass beaten more times in his two days in Louisville than he had in his entire life.

Also, Draker felt uneasy hitchhiking on an interstate, as it might attract unwanted police attention. But he was left with no choice after his last ride unexpectedly took him onto I-75 and dumped him unceremoniously at a rest area, nothing but forest all around.

"You wanted some time off, so stop bitching," Beau's voice crackled through the phone.

It was the third time in the last two days Beau had told Draker to "stop bitching." Draker frowned.

Beau continued, "Lord, boy. I'm even setting you up with some time on the Florida beaches before I finish cooking up your next mission down there."

Draker sighed. "Yeah, well, I gotta *get* there first."

"Our security measures are going to be tight for a while," Beau said. "Hitchhiking won't be your only hurdle. It seems Windbrook caught onto my hacking the moment I started digging into Simpson and breached the CIA's backend. They were... perfect. I had no clue they were there. That's how they almost trapped you at Daniel Harper's place." He paused. "I owe you an apology for that, son."

Draker wiped rain from his brow, squinted. "No problem."

"Those pictures you saw of the different Daniel Harpers—they were Windbrook plants. They slipped in a photo of the man you knew as Agent Simpson in Afghanistan, knowing you'd ID him. They linked that photo to an actual Daniel Harper—another poor bastard who got duped by Windbrook in Afghanistan, just like you did. They used Harper to get to you."

Draker gritted his teeth. "And Harper ended up dying for it."

He remembered Harper's body on the floor, putting two fingers to the man's neck. Harper had died in his own home, minutes after a break-in. Confused and scared. And alone.

Now Draker had another reason to bring down Windbrook.

"On the bright side," Beau said, "Windbrook got sloppy toward the end. Their tracing me allowed me to trace them. It's been a real battle of digital attrition, but from the bits and pieces I've been able to decode, it seems Cassandra Wynne was the one in charge of the Harper attack, and since she failed, she's facing some sort of administrative action."

Administrative action—Draker couldn't determine if that was Beau's diplomatic word choice or Windbrook's official terminology. Draker didn't ask. Because it didn't matter. He knew Windbrook. Whatever was going to happen to Cassandra after a second failure, it was going to be awful.

And... it hurt him.

Somehow, knowing Cassandra would suffer made Draker suffer. In the pouring rain. On the side of the highway in the middle of nowhere.

Because Cassandra was Alyssa.

And the fantasy of Alyssa was still alive somewhere inside him—not consciously but buried in the depths.

He couldn't shake her.

Even after Alyssa... no, *Cassandra* had attacked him.

A second time.

"And more good news," Beau said. "In all the hullabaloo, Windbrook has lost your trail again. If we stick to these security protocols, you should have smooth sailing to Florida."

The pouring rain eased off. Suddenly. Draker looked to the sky. The monstrous cloud that had been plaguing him had moved east of the median.

"Even more good news," Draker said. "It's starting to let up here."

"See? Stop bitching. Happy trails."

Draker removed his hat from the phone. "Thanks."

He ended the call and placed the hat on his head. Sopping wet. It only made things worse. He took it off again.

Looking down the highway, Draker saw the clouds breaking, a hint of sunshine peeking through, right where the big dark one had been. He caught the scent of rain on asphalt. Smelled good. A momentary peace.

Slipping off his backpack, he retrieved his earbuds, took one out, stuck it in, opened YouTube, and played "Ventura Highway" by America.

There was that guitar again.

And part of him was back. In Ventura. With someone he'd gotten to know.

Draker shouldered his bag. With the rain suddenly gone and the world smelling so good and the highway receding so far below him from his position atop a gentle slope, he almost felt like he could just walk the entire way to Florida and extend this respite for all it was worth, aching body be damned.

Too late.

A car finally heeded his raised thumb.

A ten-year-old Ford Focus slowed down in front of him, hazard lights flashing.

Draker smirked. "Right when the rain lets up,"

In response, Beau's words echoed in his mind: *Stop bitching.*

Draker approached the car…

… which he noted had a Florida plate.

Nice.

Chances were, he now had a ride all the way to his destination. Hours and hours to sit and recuperate.

The passenger-side window rolled down. A pleasant-looking man with silver hair and a walrus mustache leaned down to make eye contact. He smiled and said, "Need a ride?"

Draker popped the bag off his shoulders. "You bet I do."

Make sure to join our Discord (https://discord.gg/5RccXhNgGb) so you never miss a release!

THANK YOU FOR READING RAW DEAL!

We hope you enjoyed it as much as we enjoyed bringing it to you. We just wanted to take a moment to encourage you to review the book. Follow this link: Raw Deal to be directed to the book's Amazon product page to leave your review.

Every review helps further the author's reach and, ultimately, helps them continue writing fantastic books for us all to enjoy.

Also in Series:
BURN IT DOWN
RAW DEAL

JOIN our non-spam mailing list by visiting www.subscribepage.com/aethonthrillsnewsletter and never miss out on future releases. You'll also receive three full books completely Free as our thanks to you.

Don't forget to follow us on socials to never miss a new release!

Facebook | Instagram | Twitter | Website

Want to discuss our books with other readers and even the authors?
JOIN THE AETHON DISCORD!

Looking for more great Thrillers?

Veronica Walsh's meticulously created 'normal' life was torn apart by the public revelations about her past. She is trying to put the pieces back together when a desperate Mikaela Alonso comes to her asking for help. She claims her husband Tony did not commit suicide–that maybe he isn't even dead. Dealing with domestic strife caused by her resurfaced childhood and happy with a distraction, Veronica jumps right in. When they uncover a connection between Tony and a recently murdered senator, Veronica realizes there is much more at play than she originally believed. As Detective Emilia Brown investigates the Senator's death with her new partner, Veronica and Mikaela dig into Tony's past to try to uncover exactly what happened at a house that locals call World's Edge, and who wants to unearth every last one of its secrets. **The thrilling follow up to RUN, From the mind of debut author Matthew Becker. Find the truth behind a string of murders in a novel perfect for fans of David Baldacci, Alex Finlay, and Isabella Maldonado.**

Get Don't Look Down Now!

From desk agent to unexpected field agent. The safety of the world hangs in the balance. Kate Malone is an intelligence analyst specializing in Russian military and politics. When asked to debrief a Russian defector in Paris, she considers it just another routine assignment. Routine becomes chaos and leads to a desperate chase through the capitals of Europe... With no training as a field operative, Kate must learn the ways of a spy even as Russian agents hunt her down. Failure could lead to another world war, but success depends on survival. And in the world of international espionage, survival is never guaranteed. **Experience a gripping tale of international intrigue and espionage perfect for fans of Tom Clancy, L.T. Ryan, and Saul Herzog. Join Kate as she must leave the safety of her agency office behind and face the dangers of life as a field agent.**

Get Too Soon A Spy Now!

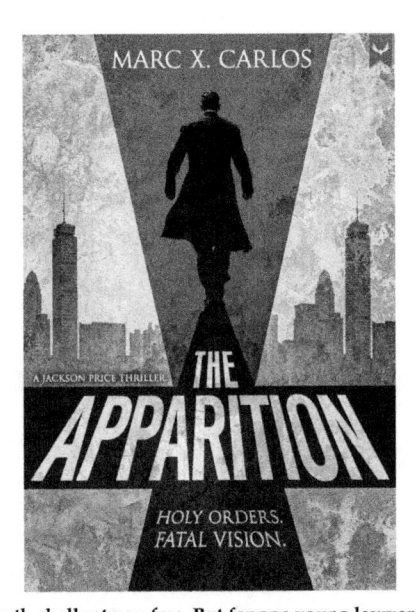

The truth shall set you free. But for one young lawyer, it might just cost him his life... A popular priest is accused of a horrific assault and tied to the murders of two other women. Jackson Price and his mentor race to uncover the motives of his accuser. At the same time, detectives uncover a checkered past of inappropriate behavior with women and mental health issues. The case may hinge on the truth of an apparition and the impact it has on everyone involved. As the case races through the criminal justice system, Jackson finds himself caught between reality and the delusions of a killer. One could end his short career; the other could end his life. Strap in and follow the investigation to the thrilling end! **The Apparition is a gripping psychological legal thriller with high stakes suspense and vivid courtroom drama. From debut author Marc X. Carlos, it's inspired by one of his real cases as a career criminal defense attorney with extensive experience in high profile crimes, courtroom technique and crime scene investigation.**

Get The Apparition Now!

For all our Thrillers, visit our website at www.aethonbooks.com/thriller

ABOUT THE AUTHOR

ERIK CARTER is the author of multiple bestselling action thriller series.
   To find out more, visit www.erikcarterbooks.com.

instagram.com/erikcarterbooks
   facebook.com/erikcarterbooks
   amazon.com/stores/Erik-Carter/author/B01MV30DEB
   bookbub.com/authors/erik-carter
   goodreads.com/author/show/16525766.Erik_Carter

Printed in Great Britain
by Amazon

54080110R00152